W9-BGM-432

THE SPRINGTHORPE AGENDA

A NOVEL

DALE RIPLEY

THE SPRINGTHORPE AGENDA

Copyright © 2018 DALE RIPLEY

This book is a work of fiction. Names, characters, places, and incidents are products of the author's imagination or are used fictitiously. Any resemblance to actual events or locales or persons, living or dead, is entirely coincidental.

All rights reserved. This book or any portion thereof may not be reproduced or used in any manner whatsoever without the express written permission of the author except for the use of brief quotations in a book review.

Cover art by: BZN Studio Covers – covers.bzndesignstudios.com

Printed in the United States of America

First Printing, 2018

ISBN-13: 978-1984984128

ISBN-10: 1984984128

10 9 8 7 6 5 4 3 2 1

www.daleripley.com

In Memory of Richard & Joyce

and

In Memory of Kathy

CHAPTER ONE

He hummed as he walked, swinging the simple black bag from side to side and bobbing up and down with the cheerful tune. He wasn't sure where he'd heard it, but he liked the melody, and it made the others smile.

White halls reflected white coats and white sneakers, golden rays of the fading afternoon sun spilling into the open facility. Patients beamed as he passed by, their eyes glazed over and their toothless smiles too big.

Medicine hour, he thought, pausing to take a moment he didn't have to wink at the brunette handing out the pills as one would hand out candy to children.

The patients who could still move on their own grouped around her while others, stuck in their wheelchairs, inched forward as much as they could. Each held out eager hands or pulled at the woman's blouse like beggars desperate for spare change.

When the woman paid him no attention, the man moved on, resuming his song and winding further down the halls.

The deeper he walked into the enormous building, the quieter and gloomier it became, until the silky darkness swallowed him and made the shadows tangible. He squinted, hoping his eyes would adjust to the darkness. But it wasn't possible.

No matter. The man knew the hall by heart.

He pictured it in his mind, following the sanitary, white tiles around a corner and down a small flight of stairs. When he stopped at the dead end, the man paused and glanced back into the endless black.

When he was sure he was alone, he fished a plastic ID card from his back pocket and grazed it across the empty wall. There was not a rivet out of place on the wall, nor a single bump. However, the walls peeled away from one another and a smaller set of doors appeared in the darkness, lit only by a dim light on the ceiling.

The doors parted further, revealing an elevator large enough for one or two people. The man stepped inside.

He clasped the black bag to his chest, fingers drumming against the soft fabric as the elevator descended into the earth below.

As the lift came to an abrupt halt and the doors glided open once more, there was sudden light, so much so that, though he was expecting the blinding brightness, the man had to blink stars out of his eyes. He nearly dropped the bag as he stumbled outward onto the thick concrete floor.

"Did you bring it?" another man in a white cloak asked, grasping rough hold of the fingers gripping the bag and trying to yank them away.

The humming man shook his head, refusing to stop his song even when a scowl formed on his face. He hugged the bag tighter against his chest.

Irritated, the white-coated man sighed with a shake of his head and pushed him along the hall.

The man sucked in a deep breath, whistling now instead of humming, pressing the air out so hard between his lips that his lungs burned. When he had to stop and inhale again to start his song over, he heard them.

"Help…"

"Please, I want to go back!"

"Where am I?"

The man kept his eyes focused down the hall as he passed by the steel cages, writhing bodies, and crying forms huddled in crumpled heaps.

Weak hands reached out, grasping at him as he passed, but he kept his gaze straight forward until the familiar little room at the end became visible. He ended his song with relief, sagging his shoulders, letting the bag loosen in his hands where he had been clasping it so hard his knuckles blanched.

He stepped into the room. The doors closed and blocked out the dull whines and cries of those he'd passed. He smiled without a word, holding out the bag he had clung to so fiercely.

"Thank you, Graham. You did well," said the redhead in the lab coat as she took the bag.

Another woman caught the corner of his eye. She was bound to an examination table and had shaggy gray hair hanging in her calm, willful stare. She continued staring at the ceiling when the sharp instruments, needles, and serums were withdrawn from the satchel and arranged on the table beside her.

Like the man, she recognized the situation without having to take a single glance at the atrocity. She anticipated what would happen to her, but she wasn't afraid. They'd already taken all they could from her, so she had nothing more to fear.

The man lingered by the door and waited for her to beg or cry. Instead, the woman set her mouth in a stern line. Her brown eyes blazed like wildfire and pierced the ceiling.

When she spoke, her voice was soft, fading as the needle pricked her arm. As stubborn as she was, she was no match for anesthesia. Though she fought against it, her eyelids grew heavy.

"Today," she whispered, straining against the medicine pumping through her veins, "is my best day."

CHAPTER TWO

Mark stared at the text message, took a bite of his pizza, blinked hard once, then stared at the text again.

Dad died. Need you to collect his things.

"What's up, Mark?" the waitress asked, leaning one hand on the table to pick up his finished tray. "You got pale all of a sudden."

"My sister texted me…" Mark said, rubbing his eyes and squinting down at the bright screen of his phone one more time.

"Aw, how sweet," the girl sighed. "My sister never texts me. Never calls me either. I practically have to knock down her door to get her to talk to me." She laughed, brushing dark curls away from her eyes. "Ready for the check?"

Mark nodded, leaning back in his chair and staring down at his greasy plate.

Was this real? Dad really died? He was too stunned to grieve yet.

It wasn't exactly a surprise, especially after how much the anguish of losing his wife last year must've haunted Ralph Hogarth. All the same, it was still shocking.

Ralph had been a mountain of a man even as he approached eighty. He was powerful as an ox, and just as hearty, with an inner warmth that enveloped his loved ones like a soft fleece blanket. Mark would have put money on his father having at least ten more years left. Mark had been sure his father would make it to at least ninety, though he'd thought the same thing about his beautiful mother, Joan, as well.

As the waitress slid the paper receipt across the table, Mark brought up his contacts on his phone to find his sister's number. *Like hell, Liv was going to spring news of our remaining parent's death through a damn text message.* She was forty-two, two years older than Mark, and she was plenty old enough to know when to pick up a phone and call instead of sending a text.

Before he could press the button to call her, the phone buzzed in his palm. Mark recognized the area code. San Francisco. The nursing home was located near there.

"Hello?" he said, pressing his cell phone to one ear while cupping the other so he could hear more clearly in the bustling pizza place.

When he was unable to make out what the person was saying, Mark threw down a wad of cash and rushed out of the little place. He darted down the sidewalk, gray clouds swirling over his head.

It was going to rain later. He enjoyed sitting by the window with a book and listening to the gentle patter while it rained.

"Are you there?" he asked, turning down a quiet alleyway.

He didn't often make it a point to creep down the scattered dark backstreets of New York City, but, since it was still early and this was an emergency, he supposed it would be okay just once.

"Yes, hello, my name is Claire Matthews. I'm the head nurse at Springthorpe Manor. I'm calling for Mark Hogarth?"

"This is he," Mark said, glancing up as an embracing couple stumbled into the alley in front of him.

Though it was just past eleven in the morning, the couple was drunk, falling over each other as they giggled. Mark rolled his eyes and hurried further down the lane.

"Your father is Ralph Hogarth, correct?" The woman spoke with a sweet southern drawl that made Mark crave sausage gravy and sweet iced tea, though he'd never had either before.

"Yes. I got this text from my sister that said-"

"I regret to inform you that he passed three days ago. I do apologize it's taken some time to get in touch with you. There was a mix-up with the contact information. We've already cremated his body as per his wishes." The woman spoke as though she were reading from a script.

How many family members of the deceased elderly patients in the nursing home did she have to call every day?

The place was huge and housed hundreds of patients at a time. It was a fortress, a red brick building overlooking a sprawling cemetery whose headstones rolled across the hills like concrete flowers.

Though the sky had been cloudless and blue the day Mark had seen it, it still seemed gloomy and dreary.

He hadn't liked the place at all, but Liv and his parents had.

When it became clear the aging couple needed living assistance, the four of them had hunted for the best nursing home. It hadn't been an easy decision to place his parents in the facility, but Springthorpe had so many clubs, programs, and events planned out in their oversized calendar that he'd hoped they were making the right decision.

He'd doubted their choice when Joan Hogarth passed away not six months into their stay. After that, Mark had wanted to take in his father, to bring him to New York to stay, but Mark made a meager living as a small town newspaper editor. While Mark was away at work, his father would need a personal caretaker, and Mark didn't have the extra cash to hire one. Ultimately, he and Liv decided that it was best for their father to remain at Springthorpe.

"Oh," Mark mumbled. He had been quiet for some time, but Claire had waited for his response.

"We'll need you to come and collect his things. They're boxed up and ready for you."

No doubt they already had someone to fill his space at the retirement home. Ralph and Joan had been lucky they'd gotten in when they did, as the waiting list had already been growing for some time. It was by pure luck they'd managed to secure their spot.

Running a hand through his hair, Mark paused in the alley to lean against the concrete and press his forehead to the cool brick of the building. He closed his eyes, letting his phone rest between his ear and his shoulder so his weary arms could hang limply at his sides.

Is this a dream? Will I wake up and my father still be alive?

"We'll need you to do this as quickly as possible, sir," Claire continued.

Mark nodded though he knew she couldn't see the action.

"Um, okay. I'll get a flight as soon as I can."

"We'll see you soon. I'm sorry for your loss."

"Thank you. Is there any way I can get a copy of the official paperwork? I just want to have a look."

What had Dad's last words been? How had he spent his last days? Mark wanted to know anything he could.

"Of course, I'll email them to you."

After providing the information and exchanging final pleasantries, Mark hung up the phone and searched for flights. Fortunately, there was one departing to San Francisco in a few hours. If he hurried, he could make it.

Not thinking straight enough to pack anything, Mark hailed a taxi and finalized his plane ticket while on his way to the airport.

Getting through security and aboard the flight was a breeze thanks to Mark having only his phone and wallet–no laptop and no luggage–with him. Soon he was settled into an uncomfortable seat upon the plane. He was stuck right next to the engine, which would blare in his ear and not allow him to sleep, but at least he was by the window. For now, he was grateful they remained on the ground. Flying made Mark nervous.

The child sitting in front of him leaned his seat back as far as he could. It knocked against Mark's knees. Mark rolled his eyes and pulled out his phone.

Opening the email browser on his cell, Mark found the message that Claire had just sent about his father. He clicked on it. The body of the email was blank, containing only the electronic signature for Springthorpe Manor.

Helping you achieve your dreams since 1867. Find your home away from home at Springthorpe. Service is our priority!

Mark rolled his eyes at the tacky motto and opened the attachment.

The file consisted of three pages. Mark was surprised. He knew from the interviews he'd done with nurses and doctors that there were often copious amounts of paperwork involved in the unexpected death of a patient.

He scrolled through the files, his eyes flickering over the cremation orders, last statements, and notes.

None of it was out of the ordinary, but it was heart-wrenching to read.

Why couldn't I have visited my father more often? It was pointless to mull over such a thing now, but Mark couldn't help it. He'd thought he had more time.

He paused when he read the cause of death, Mark's head cocking to the side. Something didn't seem right.

"Sir?" A flight attendant tapped his shoulder, jerking her chin toward his phone. "You'll need to turn that off."

"Oh, I'm sorry," Mark mumbled, rubbing his tired eyes and shaking his head. "I'm a little...my father just died."

"That's terrible news." The flight attendant smiled, but her eyes were firm. "But, as I said, you have to turn your devices to airplane mode now."

Mark gave a faint nod, turning off his phone and sliding it back into his pocket.

He leaned back in his seat, turning his head to the window and the tarmac outside. Workers bustled back and forth across the pavement, loading luggage and directing nearby planes.

His father had loved planes. He'd been an Air Force pilot when he was young. It was during that time Ralph had given up any and all drinking.

"Too many good pilots die too young thanks to booze," he'd always chuckle when turning away a glass of wine or a free beer from a friend.

For a man who hadn't had more than a sip of alcohol for most of his life, how had he managed to consume so much that it interfered with his medicines and led to his death?

CHAPTER THREE

M rs. Keller? Excuse me, ma'am? Mrs. Keller?"
Liv lurched, turning to face the woman holding
out the steaming paper cup of coffee.

Twenty-four years of marriage and she was still unused to being a Keller. The name didn't fit her right. Hearing it felt like she was dragging one of those bulky, wool sweaters over her head, the fit too loose on the arms and too tight around the neck. She had to fiddle with it, trying to force it into being comfortable.

Sometimes she wished she'd never changed her name, so she could still be Liv Hogarth. The night before the wedding, her father had taken her hand in his warm, calloused one and squeezed it. It was that little motion that told young Liv she was going to dislike whatever the man had to say. He was too kind to be blunt.

When Ralph expressed to Liv that she didn't have to marry her fiancé, she'd stuck up her chin like most eighteen-year-olds did and proclaimed she loved him, she was going to walk down that aisle, and she was going to be a damn Keller. It'd been the first and only time she'd ever cursed at her father. She'd regretted it for years.

The wind blew cool and quick, sending Liv's blonde hair into her pale face and the fallen gold leaves skittering across the sidewalk.

Liv disliked fall. She didn't like the way the air could be warm one day and cold the next. She preferred summer and winter when there wasn't a dilemma about whether she'd need flip-flops or a sweater.

Her hair clung to her sticky lip gloss, making her spit it out as she thanked the barista of the small coffee stand by the city park. Turning back to gaze across the lot, she shuffled out of the way, digging her free hand into the pocket of her sweater.

The park contained a rarely used tennis court on one side and a big, busy playground on the other. The grass was mostly untended, and the bushes were out of control. Green vines curled from within the cracks of the sidewalk, stringing their way along the pavement like worms after a rain shower.

Benches were sparse along the browning green of the lot. Liv was forced to find a space at the playground to sit and sip her coffee, as she had done every day for the last six months since starting her new job across the street.

She didn't like to sit in her cubicle and drink coffee while the phones rang and her co-workers chatted about sales techniques, pitches, and new leads. She preferred the carefree giggle of children waiting for their school day to begin.

Actually, she preferred pure silence, but there was no quiet to be found unless Liv wanted to drink her coffee in the women's bathroom. Even that tended to be filled from time to time with chittering gossipers who had nothing better to do than tear each other apart.

So, instead, she'd watch as parents scuttled after their kids and their kids squealed with joy. Liv would lament that she never found the happiness those other joyful mothers and fathers seemed to find in raising a family. That was funny to her, since she and Thomas had raised three children of their own, but Liv had always had a strange sense of humor.

Those three girls were possibly Liv's only contribution to the world. She found it to be a meager contribution at best.

Her daughters weren't notably pretty, nor were they notably smart or talented. They were unremarkable, and they'd inherited their mediocrity from their father—not that Liv was allowed to say such a thing. She wasn't allowed to say that she hadn't enjoyed being a mother either, just like she hadn't been allowed to say no when her husband asked for another child, and then another, after the accidental first was born when Liv was a teenager. She'd been lucky with her last. It had been high-risk and ended with both her and the baby nearly dying. Her husband's requests had stopped then. Otherwise, Liv might've ended up like the nursery rhyme mother who lived in a shoe with all her kids.

Glazed gray eyes settled on the playground, observing the unfocused rainbow blur of bright shirts, skirts, and pants spinning like a carousel over the plastic toys that were molten clay under the children's soft fingertips.

Almost every day, the same cute little girl would play in the park. Liv enjoyed watching her play. This week, however, she had not seen the youngster. Liv recalled how the little girl in hot pink leggings had stood perched atop the slide, her tiny fingers coiled around the upper ridge. She looked around with excited eyes, making sure an adult was watching. Liv had recognized that face, the same expression her eldest daughter had as she walked across the floor of her high school graduation, seeking out her father. It was peculiar, how little that validation-seeking expression changed between four and eighteen. Liv had seen it in photos of herself before as well, as she stood tucked under the arm of her beaming father. She'd never seen it on her younger brother's face, though.

A beaming grin had burst over the young girl's small lips as she tumbled down the slide, blinking sneakers making a cloud of dust spring up around her as she landed.

Many days, the child had played as Liv watched. Each day brought a new pair of bright neon leggings, but her hair was always in neat, twin pigtails atop her little head. The girl often hopped in the mud puddles strewn about the large park, her knobby knees stained brown and her curly hair bouncing.

Liv envied the lightheartedness of the children as they played. Sometimes, she wanted to leap up and down on the playground herself and dangle like a chimp from monkey bars that were much too close to the ground for her. Likewise, slipping down the slide would wrinkle her cardigan and cotton skirt.

She glanced at her watch again. It was time for her shift. With one hand shielding the morning sun off her cheeks, she looked toward the slide once more and found it empty. The little girl was not there. No doubt, she was either scampering across the chalk-drawn hopscotch squares or spinning around on the old metal roundabout until her stomach tossed and turned.

Shrugging, Liv took a long sip of her coffee, which had turned cold. She dumped the nearly full cup into the nearby garbage can before marching a slow path across the road to the large telemarketing building perched on the corner.

It was a tall structure with tinted windows that reflected the sun, though Liv hadn't spent much time studying it or wandering the multiple floors in the last six months. She wouldn't be there much longer. She never made it more than a year at a place of employment. Sometimes, it was because she disliked the position so much that she had to leave, but, more often, it was because she was so apathetic about her job, her co-workers, or her performance that her boss had no other option than to let her go.

They would call her into the office and give her the same gentle spiel then wait for Liv to grow upset or angry, but she would just sigh, ask for her final paycheck, and leave without a word more. She would never contact them again, even for a reference.

As she trudged through the lobby of the building, dodging welcoming smiles and glances from people whose names she would never remember, she snatched hold of a free newspaper and tucked it under her thin arm.

Pressing into the full elevator, Liv watched the numbers soar higher until they flew to a stop on the tenth floor. That was her favorite part of the day, the feeling she would get when the elevator shot upward so fast her stomach would flip toward her feet.

It was the one time of the day she would smile.

Tiredly, despite the full night of sleep she'd gotten, Liv made her way to her desk.

Her cubicle looked like everyone else's. She was proud of that. Liv worked hard to fit in. She'd decorated the smudged wooden desk with little knick-knacks, photos, and scribbled notes from her youngest child.

Her third daughter was nine and excited for her tenth birthday. Liv had promised to bake her a cake though she'd never baked a cake in her life. Agreeing to it had probably been a mistake.

She would have blamed it on one too many glasses of wine, but she no longer drank. Liv lied and told people her doctor had instructed her to change her diet. Perhaps Liv liked denying herself the small joys of life. She didn't drink, and she ate a careful diet of lean meat and raw vegetables. She'd said goodbye to cheese, milk, hot chocolate, and anything that actually tasted delicious. Coffee with cream was her only vice.

Under the glaring fluorescent lights of the grocery store, she and Stella had picked out the cake mix as well as purple sprinkles and edible pearls, appearing to the world as a happy little pair. Then Liv's phone rang. The loud trill had covered her daughter's voice as the girl excitedly gestured toward vibrant candles, candies, and frostings.

Though the office was free of a draft, recalling that phone call made Liv shiver.

Eager to forget the news about her father, she unfurled the newspaper over her keyboard and brushed her fingers over the black and white text.

Her husband didn't understand why she felt compelled to read it every morning. She had little urge to explain it to him. They talked as little as necessary, coexisting the same way a snake and grass coexist in nature. One slithers by and the other crumples to allow it.

"Newspaper is a dying industry. There are barely even real journalists anymore," he claimed every time she brought a paper home. "There's no use in reading such biased articles."

Still, Liv continued her ritual as she had ever since she had started copying her father. While he would sip coffee, young Liv would sip her orange juice and keep one watchful eye on him at all times.

Her gaze swept over the headlines. She turned from page to page until her hands stiffened in place, her entire body falling still.

The little girl from the park beamed up at her, curly pigtails frozen mid bounce on her shoulder, small chin tipped back with laughter Liv could swear she heard aloud. When Liv blinked, she fully expected the child in the picture to move.

Savannah Bennett. Missing, it read in bold red printed letters that screamed at her from the sea of black and white on the page, *last seen one week ago.*

CHAPTER FOUR

Y ou must be Mr. Hogarth." A woman with braided red hair and a faint southern accent Mark recognized from the phone greeted him as he stepped through the doors of Springthorpe Manor.

Though outside it was humid and dark, the inside was bright and so cool that Mark shivered, goosebumps prickling over his forearms.

The foyer was vacant, lined with empty wheelchairs and a muted television playing a black and white movie to a bare couch. Soft classical music played through speakers somewhere overhead.

"You have the same eyes as your mother," she continued with a faint laugh that did not make her green eyes crinkle at the edges.

The woman smiled, if it could be called that, her round face set and firm. Her teeth were pearly and small, organized like polished piano keys between thin lips.

She was pretty in a severe kind of way. When she smiled, Mark couldn't shake the feeling she was patronizing him.

"I hear that a lot," Mark said, hands shoved deep into his pockets.

He wished he'd brought a heavier jacket with him. He'd forgotten how cold it was in the old retirement home. His dad had probably hated that. For a big man, Ralph had poor circulation and was always cold. Half his wardrobe had consisted of thick sweaters.

Mark glanced around as Claire flipped through some papers on her small desk, clicking her tongue.

Not that he had expected much to have changed since he was last at Springthorpe, but he was still surprised by how much it remained the same. The place was impeccably clean, the floors gleaming even in the dark of the fallen night. He thought they must wax them every night. Joan had liked how spotless the facility had been when Mark and Liv brought them here for the original tour. Ralph had waited at her side as she'd checked for dust in the dining area, sniffed at the sheets in a bedroom, peeked under desks, and then deemed it all suitable.

"We don't usually allow guests this late in the evening, but I know you must've had quite an exhausting flight here."

Mark shuddered and nodded in agreement.

The flight had indeed been exhausting, full of turbulence and crying babies. He was already dreading his return home. He pondered renting a car for the cross-country trip home.

"I would take you to his room myself, but I've got to finish this paperwork. You should be able to find it easily enough. Room 36C, just head down this hall and it'll be on the right."

Claire smiled another of her stern, forced smiles and held out a nametag clasped between two rose-painted nails.

Mark Hogarth was printed in large letters on the white sticker. Taking it, he slapped it onto the center of his chest and headed down the hallway.

The rooms were windowless, at least facing the hall, with thick doors that blocked out all sound within. The scent of sanitizer was heavy, stinging Mark's nose as if he'd stuck his whole face into a tub of it.

When he came to room 36C, he had to pause before opening the door.

The last time he'd swung open the heavy wood door, his dad had been sitting in a rocking chair, hands folded over his lap, his favorite book pressed in his weathered fingers.

Now the man had been reduced to ashes in an urn somewhere.

Swallowing the thick lump in his throat, Mark pulled the large door, flipped on the light, and stepped inside.

The door slid to a noiseless close behind him, and Mark leaned against it for strength.

In front of him, in the small room with the crisply made bed and the empty rocking chair, were four boxes that contained the last of his father's belongings. Everything his father did or was or had in this building fit into those barely full cardboard cartons.

Unexpected anger flurried up inside of Mark as he approached the boxes, glancing down at the sheets of paper, books, and folded pants inside. It could have belonged to anyone.

This wasn't his father.

Ralph Hogarth was a laugh so loud the neighbors would hear him at night, a strong body to curl into when one of his children had a nightmare, an occasional raunchy joke, and a tender, sweet gaze at Joan from across the room. He wasn't a pair of mismatched socks and a frazzled hairbrush.

Irritated, Mark sank down onto the bed that creaked under his weight, his feet accidentally kicking out against the nightstand by the bed.

A small but thick book tumbled out from somewhere behind it, resting on the floor before the startled man.

"What?" he murmured aloud. He leaned down to pick up the book and brushed his fingertips across the front.

The leather was furling and faded, well and often used. Curious, Mark laid it on his lap so he could inspect it. It was familiar. His father had carried it everywhere.

With gentle hands, Mark turned the cover. His father's neat, tidy handwriting on the pages within came to life before him.

The first few sheets did not surprise him.

Ralph had always written everything down, ever since the habit was drilled into him while in the Air Force. He loved writing down where he'd gone and what he'd worn and people he'd met. He also loved making little notes about surprises for Joan. He'd mention a flower patch for a picnic spot, gift ideas, and important dates.

In the forty-nine years his parents had been married, they were inseparable. They'd never spent a single night without the other. His father had never forgotten a birthday or anniversary. It didn't shock Mark that Ralph hadn't made it long after his beloved Joan passed. During his childhood, they were never apart.

Mark sighed and continued flipping through until the writing on the pages ended and the remaining ones were blank. He turned back to the last few, frowning as his eyes skimmed the pages.

There was jumbled nonsense that made Mark's heart ache to read. His intelligent, witty father had been reduced to idle ramblings.

He wrote of Joan, visiting her, touching her, and kissing her. He wrote of winding and confusing tunnels.

Clearly, Ralph had been all but delirious in his final days.

Mark had never even known. He felt terrible. With a heavy heart, Mark flipped to the last page full of writing. It was no different than the others, rambling on about seeing Joan again. The date was three days ago–the day he had passed.

It isn't safe anymore, Ralph had written in a quaky, hurried hand that used to be so straight and steady. *But I have to see Joan. No matter what. I promised her.*

Mark lifted the book to his nose, inhaling the scent of old leather and yellowing pages. Ralph had carried this journal around with him for years, so much so it still smelled of his cologne. When Mark was a child that scent used to comfort him. Now it made tears well in his eyes.

With the journal pressed close to Mark's face, he noticed tiny beads of ink leaked through from the other side. He was not on the last page of the journal after all.

He turned the page over. A single sentence was scrawled across the top half of the paper.

The date was two days ago, one day after Mark's father had died.

Among a strange smear of ink blots where a pen had rested in thought, one line was scribed in urgency, though definitely still in Ralph's unique handwriting.

I am with you.

CHAPTER FIVE

Ralph was floating. He was almost sure of it.

Moments before, he had been stumbling along a path. Then he had fallen into something and hit his head.

Struggling, he attempted to stretch his arms out to his sides, but he couldn't sense the ground beneath his body. He couldn't tell if his arms were pinned at his side or extended and he couldn't tell if his legs were broken and maimed or on solid ground. His eyelids strained, too heavy to open, eyeballs rolling into his skull.

His whole body hurt, a deep ache welled inside of him like the spring at the bottom of Lake Jarvis. He closed his eyes, wishing to be taken back there, praying that his floating body might sail away to a more peaceful time.

Lake Jarvis was a sanctuary, the one place where nothing bad could happen. No matter what was going on in the world, no matter how stressed Ralph was over his job or with life, he always knew the beautiful water was waiting for him and Joan.

The water had been crystal clear the first year he'd taken Joan there, reflecting the sun like the diamonds in her new wedding ring. Standing together, they'd watched the tiny minnows darting back and forth. Smooth pebbles had brushed against their toes when they sank into the warm, gentle waves.

He'd wanted to surprise her, instructing her to pack for a skiing trip instead. When they'd arrived, she'd had nothing to swim in. They'd gone swimming anyway.

The thought made him want to chuckle, but his throat burned, and the laughter died before it could gurgle out of his chest.

That first dreamlike anniversary they'd spent at the lake hadn't been meant to turn into a tradition, but Joan had been so struck by the shimmery water and gorgeous deep green of the trees that Ralph had little choice but to indulge her the next year–and the year after that–until neither could imagine doing anything else but spending that beautiful time together every anniversary.

For forty-nine years they had never missed a trip.

When Joan had balked on their eighth anniversary, the year she had gotten pregnant–after they'd tried and failed and tried again for so long they had both lost hope–it was Ralph's turn to beg. He'd taken her hand in his, kissing each fingertip and gazing deep into her honey brown eyes, uniquely flecked with shards of green.

She'd sighed that sweet sigh, and, when she nibbled on her lower lip, Ralph knew he'd won. After pressing a palm against the round girth of her swollen stomach, she relented as Ralph knew she would.

'No' was seldom spoken in their household. Joan and Ralph could rarely refuse one another.

They'd had two marvelous nights at the lake before Joan's water broke and they sped thirty-three miles to the nearest hospital. He'd found that number hilarious–though Joan most definitely had not–because it was the same age as his panting, laboring wife.

Fortunately, the roads had been nearly empty at two in the morning, and they'd reached the hospital quickly, though not quickly enough for an epidural. Joan hadn't let him forget that for years.

He'd been struck by her stony silence during the birth. Her eyes had squeezed shut and her hands had balled into fists as she clasped the sheets tightly. He kept waiting for the screaming or crying, but there was none. The nurses had told him he should leave and wait outside the room, but Ralph had never before left Joan's side for very long. The birth of their child was not a time he would desert her.

Liv, too, was silent when she burst into the world. It was the doctors who became loud, passing her tiny limp body back and forth as they cleared her nose and spanked her and flung her around until the baby gave the smallest gasp of a cry.

That was it for Liv, who gazed up at him with glassy gray eyes as she rested in his arms. There was no loud, long wail. There was no shrill banshee screaming. There was just harmony.

When Ralph had gazed at Joan, she had been smiling.

Joan had practically had to kick him out of the house when it was time for Ralph to return to work after the birth. He and little Liv had bonded fiercely. It was hard to imagine leaving her and sitting in an office all day. Until his second child was born two years later, he'd thought it was impossible to love such a tiny little thing as much as he did.

It was at Lake Jarvis that Ralph had discovered Joan was expecting again.

While Ralph worked, she'd spent two days making day trips with her blonde toddler all the way down to the lake. By the time he'd get off work, Joan would have long been back home, dinner already prepared and their little girl scribbling in a coloring book.

Ralph had never had a clue what she'd been plotting.

He'd been shell-shocked when they'd stepped into their small cabin at the lake that weekend. His mind had been in a simple place, anticipating a day of fishing and canoeing and watching the sun pool on the silky hair of the love of his life as she lounged with her toes dipped in the water. When he had pushed open the door, while carrying at least seventy-five pounds of luggage in both hands, he'd found the little cabin decorated with small posters, prints, and sweet ornaments reused from Liv's baby shower.

A rainbow-stitched Father's Day banner had hung on the wall, and, for a second, Ralph had been bewildered. It wasn't anywhere near Father's Day yet.

When he'd turned to question his wife and saw her wide brown eyes and flushed face, happiness had flooded his body.

Ralph had dropped to his knees, buried his face into his wife's still flat belly, and wept with joy.

That all felt so recent. It was hard to believe so many years had slipped by already. The seventy-eight-year-old had walked many paths in his life.

He'd gone to college; he'd been in the Air Force; he'd dabbled in painting and whittling and even calligraphy. But he had never been sure he was heading in the right direction until the day he'd met Joan.

She'd been dancing, hands twirling over her head as she spun by herself, at a college party. Ralph was unsure why he'd been there or who he'd been with, but he'd never forget the moment his eyes met hers across the room as she laughed breathlessly. She'd been wearing a pink cotton dress that swirled around her knees.

In that second, everything else had vanished. There was nothing else that mattered in the world.

Joan.

A sharp pain in his leg brought his thoughts back to his current state. When he tried to speak, he could make little more than a grunt.

He tried to move again, and this time he could sense the jagged earth beneath him. It dug into his shoulder and snagged at his pants. One of his feet felt cold. Apparently, one of his shoes was missing.

A shiver rolled through him. He tried again to force his crippled body to move. His head fell back to the ground.

Ralph had never been this tired before. Not after a twelve-hour shift as a pilot nor even in the nights and weeks following either of his children's births. This exhaustion was heavy and thick and inescapable, like a fog rolling over him and smothering out his strength. It was the kind of lethargy that clung to one's bones, seeping all the way through to the core with sharp, icy tendrils.

Ralph had never been one to give up on anything, but he could not open his eyes, and he could no longer sense the coldness of his exposed foot. All he wanted to do was sleep. Typically, when he took a nap, Ralph would lay his head on Joan's soft lap and she'd stroke his silvery hair.

This time, there was no gentle touch. There was only the cold.

As his body stilled, just his lips were free to move. They were so dry and cracked that, when they parted to whisper her name, a slow stream of blood slithered down his pale cheek to coil like a crimson snake on the earth beneath him.

His mouth pursed shut, a soft hum warbling through his aching throat, the melody of the only song that brought him comfort any longer.

Softer and softer the tune became until he surrendered to the icy grip of silence.

CHAPTER SIX

Ms. Larissa was on the move again.

Claire followed in skilled silence behind her down the hall, her white Keds quietly traversing the marble tile gliding beneath her slim body.

The head nurse clutched a plastic clipboard to her chest, rounding hall after hall as the elderly woman paced ahead of her. A pen hung from the clipboard's metal chain and swung back and forth with every stealthy step Claire took.

The older woman's gait was stumbling and noisy compared to the petite nurse's, her bare feet slipping along the waxed floor like a beast crawling across the shallow earth.

Claire was reminded of those zombie movies her sister had been obsessed with while growing up. She couldn't count the number of times they'd squished together on the couch to watch *Night of the Living Dead*, red hair a tangled mop on their matching heads. Zombies shuffled this way and that, mutilating people, while her sister cackled, her cheeks stuffed with popcorn like a squirrel's would be with acorns.

"Zombies can do whatever they want." Claire's sister had beamed, still laughing and spewing little half-nibbled chunks of popcorn.

The undead didn't frighten Claire, but, unfortunately for her, Ms. Larissa was just as likely to bite or claw as one of those silver screen creatures.

Claire shuddered, envisioning the poor orderly whose arm had been mauled last week.

Round and round they ambled, making chaotic and lazy loops past the cafeteria, the rec room, the library, and back to the main hall. Claire would have been bored had she disliked the mindless wandering. But, in this case, it was nice to turn off her brain and just follow for a little while, even if it was crazy Ms. Larissa she had to trail.

That morning, the straggly-haired woman had been pretending to be a parrot, asking over and over for a cracker.

When Claire had relented and brought the woman some saltines, Larissa had stuffed them between her pale lips, given a few quick chomps with her sharp teeth, and spewed them back out all over Claire. She was still picking bits of cracker out of her long red locks.

The wandering woman paused at the main hall, gazing up and down the white tile floor before trudging to the glass of the front door. Claire had a moment of panic, praying she'd locked it after Mark Hogarth had stopped by a few hours earlier. She'd been begging to have automatic locking doors installed, but the building had been built so long ago that any updates had an extensive approval process.

Ms. Larissa pushed at the big doors, which did not swing open. Claire pressed a hand against her pounding heart. The last thing she wanted was to go chasing after an old woman in the dark.

Claire cleared her throat, just loud enough to catch the other woman's attention while still keeping a safe distance from her powerful jaws. Ms. Larissa stiffened and cast a slow glance over her shoulder at the nurse.

It was unclear who Ms. Larissa was today. It could have been anyone.

Sometimes Ms. Larissa was a man; sometimes she was a sugary sweet duckling; sometimes she was even Claire; rarely was she Larissa.

"They're coming, you know," she said, her voice gravelly and raw like she wasn't used to speaking out loud. "I saw them again."

"Who is?" Claire asked, walking over to her small desk to lean against it. "Who'd you see?"

She was proud of how tidy and neat her work area was. She'd seen how messy the other nurses could be. She was the head nurse for a reason.

"*They* are." Larissa shrugged, rolling her eyes like it was undeniable and it was Claire who was clearly the confused one. "Didn't you hear them moving around? They call to me. They're noisy. I can't sleep."

"Oh. Of course," Claire responded with a patient and practiced smile. "Are you ready to go back to your room now?"

"Are you ready to go back to your room now?" Larissa squawked back, her eyes going glazed. "Are you ready to go back to your room now?"

"Come on," Claire sighed as Larissa squawked and mimicked her again.

Over and over, the old woman cawed Claire's own words until the forty-year-old nurse was able to guide the woman back into her small room, locking the door as she left. Larissa's room was the only one with three bolts.

Claire paused in the dim hall, leaning her back against Larissa's door as her green-eyed gaze settled across the hall at room 36C.

Behind her, through the sturdy wood door and the concrete walls, she could hear the old woman inside jumping up and down and squawking like a bird. Claire ignored it. She was good at that.

Claire had spent hours of time in many rooms, but 36C hadn't been one of them.

Patients like Larissa were greedy with their desire for attention. They absorbed all available energy and time from Claire and the other nurses and orderlies.

Ralph Hogarth, however, had been something else. He hadn't been one to beg for his medicines, scratch at her arm, or pull at her hair. He'd been a watcher–quiet, kind, and interesting.

She'd liked him, as much as she'd liked any of the patients, anyway. She'd been sad while making his bed with new, crisp sheets and fluffing the pillows where his head used to lie. He'd been a peaceful sleeper. However, the last few weeks had been stressful for him.

The first time Claire had come face to face with tall, robust Ralph Hogarth, she'd been intimidated, though that was not easily done. The redhead stood no higher than five foot two inches, and Ralph was at least six feet before his bones became frail, but Claire was not one to be frightened. She couldn't be in this line of work.

Ralph was all broad shoulders and conveyed a firm sense of severity. But then he spoke, and his voice was tender, warm, and soft. He would be no trouble.

Among Claire's many talents was reading people correctly–especially prospective patients. She could tell when one would be an easy patient and when one would be an issue.

Larissa, for instance, had been one of those Claire knew would be trouble.

Claire glanced up and down the hall to make sure there were no more free-roamers who had managed to escape their rooms for the night. She turned the doorknob and entered Ralph's old room. She didn't close the door behind her but flipped the light switch with a delicate, slender finger. She wasn't sure what she'd expected the flickering bulb to illuminate, but she found the room to be quiet and tidy, much the same as any of the other rooms, as though Mr. Hogarth had never even been there. It was easy to pretend the man had never existed at all.

That was all well and good, she supposed, since another patient was arriving in the morning to take his bed.

It would be foreign enough to the new patient without any reminders of who'd rested in their quarters before them—and what happened to the previous resident.

Death was not a topic of conversation there. No one spoke that word aloud.

Claire eased further into the room, sinking down on the old mattress the facility labeled as a bed, and laid her clipboard at her side. She shifted, wrinkling her small nose at how uncomfortable the stiff mattress was. It creaked under her slender body, and she was glad she had a regular bed to sleep on once she finally returned home. Claire wasn't home often. She liked being there inside the manor with the rest of the staff and patients. Springthorpe felt more like home than anywhere else.

The nurse pressed a curious hand against the pillows, shaking her head at their rough texture, and cocked her head when she saw something peeking out from behind Ralph's nightstand.

She reached over, prodding the strange thing, before tugging it toward her. A small leather pouch pulled free from where it had hung concealed behind the white painted wood. She leaned over to check again behind the nightstand. There was nothing else that remained back there.

Curious now, she inspected the small pouch, unsure of its origin.

It wasn't like anything the patients crafted in the art room. It was made from a careful and skilled hand. Small stitched swirls curled along the edges of the leather clasp. Claire pulled the upper flap open and dug her fingers inside.

The pouch was small, and Claire's hand barely fit within the smooth leather. Her fingertips brushed across something hard and thin inside.

She tugged it free, laying a small plastic ID card on her palm. After flipping over the plastic square once, then twice, she lay both items side by side on the bed, chewing her lower lip for a long second before grasping a radio dangling from the waistband of her scrubs.

Pushing the button, she listened to the static waves hiss and then go silent before holding the black receiver to her lips.

"We have a problem," she stated, scooping the items back into her hand with a grave sigh.

CHAPTER SEVEN

Mark paced in front of the boxes which he had pushed halfway into the tiny coat closet at the front of his hotel room. They'd been nauseatingly easy to haul up to his room. Mark had needed only one trip to carry the relics of his father's life up three flights of stairs.

A corner of the carpet, creased from careless construction, seized Mark's shoe with a shaggy claw, sending him headlong toward the crooked couch he'd been afraid to sit on. He crashed into the side of it, received a minor bump on his head, and then rolled onto the flat cushions. The sturdy couch was about as comfortable as a block of concrete. He stood up again.

Due to the short notice of his reservation, he hadn't been able to swing a luxury reservation–not that Mark could have afforded that anyway. He'd spent most of his free cash on the ticket out there. Mark was stuck in the San Francisco area for almost a week. All the other flights back to New York were already booked up, thanks to some comic convention.

He wasn't sure what he would do for that much time. Tomorrow, when he would receive his father's ashes, he'd be left with nothing but time to kill.

It didn't help he wasn't in a touristy mood. While he was mourning the loss of his father, none of the usual vacation haunts appealed to him in the slightest. Plus, he was out in the country far away from the bright lights of the city. There wasn't much to see unless he wanted to take another tour of Springthorpe. He considered finding a bar and drinking the rest of the week away while his father's urn judged him.

Mark's stomach rumbled but he ignored it.

The only thing within walking distance of the hotel was a small pizza joint. After receiving the news that he had earlier that day while chowing down on pizza, he wasn't sure he'd ever be able to eat a cheesy slice again.

A shame. Pizza had been his favorite food.

Had it really been less than twenty-four hours since I received that text from Liv? It felt like another lifetime ago, like he'd been a whole different person just twelve hours prior.

Kicking off his shoes but leaving his socks on, Mark eased down onto the bed, wiggling until there was some semblance of comfort. He sniffled and swiped at his nose before glancing at the pillows with a frown and chucking them off the bed. Down feathers. Mark was allergic.

The mattress was hard beneath his head as Mark lay atop the scratchy blankets, moonlight peering into his hotel room through the thin curtains. The AC unit heaved and lurched before choking to life. The drapes fluttered and sent moonlight dancing around the room. Unamused, Mark shifted, resting one arm behind his skull as he lifted his phone up in front of his face.

For a few minutes, he wasted time, playing on Facebook and Wikipedia and even a quick solitaire game, trying to forget for a little while the swirling grief growing inside him. There were so many emotions twisting inside, the battle made his stomach knot and his heart hurt.

Regret. Sorrow. Anger. It was endless.

Was I really so busy I couldn't have made more frequent trips out to see Dad? Hadn't I learned anything after Mom had unexpectedly passed?

His phone beeped, the little battery icon in the corner flashing.

Mark ignored it like he ignored his starved stomach and his shattered heart. He pulled up his email browser and navigated to the email from Springthorpe.

He sighed, scrolling through the paperwork one more time as his phone beeped again, the sharp ding making his throbbing head pulse even stronger. He had only minutes left of the charge on his phone.

The forms were no more believable now than they had been before. Every page was stamped with the same bold, black lettering. *Deceased*. He just couldn't grasp it. His father was dead, gone forever from this world. Maybe it was still a fragment of his childhood that made Mark struggle so much with the concept of his dad's death. To Mark, his father was immortal, omnipotent, and strong.

In some ways, Mark was a lot like his father. He wasn't as quick-witted or funny, but Mark was just as intelligent as Ralph was. After growing up watching his dad take meticulous notes on everything around them, Mark had started doing something similar, though he kept his notes organized within his mind instead of on paper. Mark's handwriting was so bad that, days later, he probably wouldn't be able to read his own notes.

Though his sister's handwriting was poor like his, both of his parents had beautiful handwriting. Joan's was small and swirly. Ralph's was big, blocky, and clear.

He still couldn't seem to wrap his mind around the fact both of them were gone now. Their written notes were all he would ever have of them.

When he closed his eyes, he was a child again, blowing out swirling birthday candles while his mom laughed that beautiful, joyous laugh and his dad wrapped a jubilant arm around her as his silvery gray eyes brimmed with pride.

Mark saw his mother and father dancing a slow circle in the kitchen the night before their anniversary, talking in hushed whispers how they would spend their day at Lake Jarvis, where they always went together on that special day.

Ralph lifted a hand, spinning Joan then bringing her back close to his chest, beating hearts pressed together as one. He would lay his cheek against the top of her head, winking at their young son as Mark peered at them from around a corner.

The memories flashed through his mind like an old-fashioned photo reel set to the hiss of the AC unit and the thump of booming bass from one floor down. When his eyes remained closed, Mark soon slipped into a restless sleep.

Faces swirled around him in the shadows of his unconsciousness. Some he knew, and some felt familiar though he couldn't place them.

Ralph leaned into his son's ear, strong and cold fingers cupping Mark's shoulder with a roughness uncharacteristic of the gentle man. He whispered something Mark couldn't understand. When Mark tried to ask what was going on, he found his mouth glued shut, his tongue thick and heavy behind the prison of his lips. Struggling, Mark tried to reach his hands toward his mouth but found his hands heavy as sandbags, his whole body bound to the ground.

Before he could scream, his eyes peeled open, chest heaving with hurried breath, woken by the shrill beeping of his dying phone. Mark sucked in a breath, rolled onto his stomach and dragged the phone back toward him.

For once, he was happy with the infuriating sound. At least it ended his bad dream.

Rubbing a tired eye, he squinted at the electronic images of the papers, a slight frown flickering over his face. He had missed something before. He pulled it closer to his face seconds before his screen fell black.

Ralph and Joan had revised their wills together three times: after their marriage and after the birth of each of their children. Only once had Ralph modified his own will, precisely two days after Joan's death, when the cloud of grief that bound him up like a smothering blanket relented enough for him to visualize more clearly–as clearly as he could in his fading state of mind.

Why would Dad update it again just a month ago?

CHAPTER EIGHT

"Mark...It's four in the morning," Liv groaned in a whispering hiss as Mark leaned against the concierge desk, half turning his back to the suited man.

The dark-haired clerk behind the desk stayed as far from Mark as he could while still within earshot, pretending to be filing papers at the other end of his counter. He'd learned long ago that calls placed in the middle of the night could be quite interesting.

"I can't believe you'd text me that Dad died. Seriously, Liv? A text?"

"I was in a meeting. What was I supposed to do?"

"Oh, I don't know, leave the room and call your brother?"

Liv rolled her eyes, waiting until Mark gave an angry sigh that signaled his rant was over.

"I'm sorry, okay?" she mumbled. "I was as surprised as you were. I wasn't thinking clearly."

Mark quieted, leaning against the counter, his arms folded and his chin propped on the back of his hand. He could understand the numbness that came from the news. He wouldn't have wanted to jump on the phone either. Still, he couldn't shake the lingering waves of ire that swelled in him. Maybe it was part of his grieving process.

"Are you coming? His ashes are being released to me tomorrow. I think he'd want you to be there, too."

Ralph had always adored his daughter. Though he loved both of his children, Liv had been special, his firstborn. Mark thought it was probably how similar the two were, with their matching gazes that seemed to see everything and their quick minds. Mark was much more a mixture of his parents or like neither of them in particular. Had his eyes not been the same shade as his mother's, no one would've guessed he was related to his family at all.

"I've got a flight in the morning. I'll be there before lunch."

Mark gave a slight rumble of approval, twirling the cord of the phone around one finger. The two siblings fell quiet, and Mark could hear the soft meow of Liv's kitten on the other end. She was always getting cats, collecting them like their mother had collected those little turtle figurines. Joan had proudly displayed the unique knick-knacks throughout each room of the house.

"Are you bringing Thomas?"

Forgettable, sleepy-eyed Thomas. Liv had shocked everyone when she'd become pregnant right out of high school and married the unambitious slacker. While she was valedictorian, he wasn't in a single club and had barely maintained his C average. Ralph had never thought Thomas was good enough for his only daughter, but he'd kept the opinion to himself. That didn't stop all of them from seeing it in his disheartened eyes every time he met his dreary son-in-law.

"No. He's working."

Mark wanted to laugh. Thomas didn't work. He played in a garage cover band, pretending he was still eighteen and not forty-three.

Twisting the phone cord around another finger, Mark watched his fingertip turn bright red. The guilt he'd been trying to suppress rose up like that inside his heart.

"When was the last time you visited Dad, Liv?" Mark asked, praying someone at least had visited the old man before he died.

Liv sighed, a small gust of air crackling over the phone. He could hear the creak of her bed as she settled back into it, kicking her feet out from under her heavy blankets. She was like Ralph in more ways than Mark ever was, including being ever chilly.

"Cold hands, warm heart," Joan had loved to say, squeezing her daughter and her husband so tight neither could easily breathe.

Joan was always like that, an overzealous hugger. Mark had perfected dodging those hugs as a teenager, but he would give anything to be all wrapped up in her arms one last time, the subtle scent of her Chanel perfume swallowing him whole.

"I don't know. Over a month ago, maybe? It's a two-hour flight out from Nevada. I couldn't make it out as much as I wanted to."

Mark grunted again, running a hand through his hair.

At least it hadn't been months of loneliness for his father. Mark had called when he could, but no one in his family liked talking on the phone much. They all preferred face-to-face meetings.

"Did you notice anything odd about him? Was he acting strangely?"

"You know Dad. He was always a little weird," she replied, "a real goofball."

"No, like really weird. I found a journal of his. It made no sense at all."

Liv chuckled, padding across the carpet to slip out of the bedroom and down the hall. She crouched at the edge of their stairs, making sure her daughter's light remained out.

"Really, he was still doing that?"

"Yeah, but like I said, those last pages are just complete disarray. His handwriting was a mess and what he wrote, Liv, it was so muddled and confused. I hate to think what he must've been going through."

"Mark, Dad was almost eighty. It makes sense. They told us he could decline quickly. Listen, it's late–"

"I'm sorry for waking you. I can't sleep. I keep imagining him in that room, all by himself."

"We all knew he wouldn't last long after Mom died. They were two sides of the same coin. They couldn't exist without the other." Liv used the same tone she did when adolescent Mark used to complain to his older sister about a bully in school, a failed test, or a scraped knee.

Back when they were younger, Liv had been beautiful. But the strain of life and marriage and children had left her gray eyes dull and her blonde hair limp. She was frail and flaccid, like a deflated balloon left floating too long.

"I'll see you at Springthorpe tomorrow," Mark said as his sister yawned and bade him a quiet goodbye. "Oh, you should bring a sweater."

When the line went dead, he hung up the phone, staring down at the receiver with a quiet sigh.

"You had a family member who was at Springthorpe?" the concierge asked, a polite smile on his face. "Same here with my mom. Nice place. Great family sushi nights on Wednesday."

Mark could not imagine his steadfast father nibbling on raw fish. He only liked fish he caught, filleted, and cooked himself.

"Both my parents were residents, for a little while."

The man nodded with a sympathetic smile that Mark loathed. The flight attendant, the head nurse, even his own reflection in the mirror had all seemed to pity him.

Leaning his elbows on the counter, the man tilted his head. "Say, what floor are you staying on tonight?"

"Third."

His mind a blur of exhaustion and adrenaline and sleep deprivation, Mark could barely concentrate on the simple conversation.

"You know, out the east window, you can see the place when the moon is out. You'll know it when you see it."

All Mark could envision was tomorrow, a day he hoped wouldn't come. Mark didn't care if the stars twinkled or the moon lit up the sky. He only wished the sun didn't have to rise.

In a few hours, he would hold an urn the size of a small vase that contained the remains of his tall, strong father. It was odd, to imagine mighty Ralph Hogarth reduced to nothing but little black specks and charred molars. He'd get placed up above a fireplace or a windowsill like a little china doll. Eventually, he'd be forgotten and grow dusty. Then someday, he'd be knocked off by a great, great grandchild and his ashes would be swept away into the trash like moldy bread by people who didn't know him other than by a faded photo on the wall.

Mark nodded, thanking the man and heading toward the stairwell as the concierge called after him one more time.

"You should tell them you want to see the art room," the middle-aged man said. "You might find some stuff from your father there."

Mark could imagine his father painting a watercolor as much as he could picture him eating sushi. Barely paying him any attention, Mark gave another limp nod and turned the corner.

The elevator was broken, but he liked taking the stairs anyway. He counted every step as he climbed, hoping to clear his exhausted but frantic mind so he could get a bit of sleep.

Unwilling to see the four boxes of his father's belongings, Mark did not turn on the light as he stepped back into his room.

He slipped his thin cotton jacket off his shoulders, letting it fall to the floor. He was a tidy man, but at that moment he didn't care about clutter. The jacket landed with a strange thud, drawing Mark's bloodshot eyes back to the crumpled heap of fabric.

A corner of the brown leather journal peeked out. He'd been carrying it around like his father once did. It was comforting, like Mark had a tiny piece of Ralph with him always.

With a faint sigh, Mark picked it up and held it between his hands before heading toward the window where the light shone in.

He flipped the journal to the last page, the one with the single sentence, and brushed his thumb over the scrawled message.

What had Dad been thinking about that night?

The doctors had warned Liv and Mark when they were signing the contracts and forms at Springthorpe that the late stages of Alzheimer's often brought on paranoia and strange hallucinations.

Mark hugged the journal to his chest, wishing for all the world he could go back in time and visit his father once more. He wasn't sure he would ever be able to forgive himself.

The air conditioning unit once again gave a considerable rumble and shook, blowing the drapes away from the thick glass of the window.

Mark's gaze swept out over the streets and parked cars that appeared smaller from the third floor. There was no one outside tonight, no headlights winding down the highway or zooming around the bend.

The concierge had been right about the Springthorpe building. It rose in the distance, looming stout and large among a canopy of curling trees. Even the headstones were visible from where he stood, reflecting the moonlight so they glowed.

A fog had rolled in, twisting along the road where the streetlights glittered like diamonds, cutting a bright path upward toward the facility.

The manor itself remained enveloped in darkness. Not a single window on the building glowed yellow. The only lights within the gates of the manor were those that shimmered atop tall barbed wire posts, though some of the lights had been long forgotten, no longer working.

As Mark turned to face his bed, he caught a flash of light flickering among the graves, but then it vanished like a candle blown out in the distance. Mark whirled back around in surprise, cupping his hands around his eyes and peering into the blackness, but everything was still. There had been something strange about the way the light had moved and the way it had disappeared that made the hair on the back of his neck stand straight on edge. Watching and waiting for another quiver of light, he stood there until the sun crept across the horizon, lacing the sky with a crimson glare.

CHAPTER NINE

Smoky fog clung with white claws to the cracked gravestones and the browning earth outside while the first noises of the rising patients within Springthorpe echoed down the halls.

The sounds were soft at first, from the creak of the elderly residents creeping out of bed to the gentle slither of nightgowns and fleece pajamas falling to the ground to be replaced by khakis and oversized dresses, at least for those mobile enough to clothe themselves.

Some lay still in their beds, bodies rigid like planks and eyes wide open, as though they hadn't so much as blinked all night, their chests delicately rising and falling. The crisp white blanket lay atop them like a sleeve, swallowing their fragile bodies. Others had spent the long, dark hours thrashing in their beds, their sheets tangled around them like serpents they'd been wrestling.

As the morning sun rose and the dreams from last night faded, each elderly patient woke to the new day, their bare feet sweeping over the cold marble floor.

Hungry and cranky as children, they pounded palms on their heavy wooden doors and waited to be released from the rooms in which they stayed locked during night hours.

In the main hallway where Claire had stood guard all night, a nurse fiddled with the audio settings, glad the uptight head nurse had retired for a few hours so they could turn the music up louder. Claire would return well before lunch, her hair braided and her small hands ready to lay down the law. She had little patience for bent rules.

Frank Sinatra's melodic voice soared through the loudspeakers dotting the ceilings and was punctuated by the sharp tap of upbeat percussion. The nurses and orderlies danced down the hall, their feet moving in time to the tunes, their fingers unlocking the doors and gesturing for the patients to come out from their small quarters and head down to the breakfast hall.

A gray-haired woman stumbled out from where she had been pressed to the door all night, gripping hard at the hand of the young nurse.

"Good morning, Ms. Larissa!" The nurse smiled, scooping an arm around the frail woman's waist to steady her. "Did you sleep well?"

Larissa didn't respond. Even the upbeat music didn't seem capable of reaching the depths of her blank mind.

The patients shuffled, a herd of crippled, sleepy-eyed masses, as they followed the scent of frying bacon and cooked eggs to the large cafeteria. Sunlight pooled on the floor of the broad, white space, warming the tile and the shoulders of the patients as nurses gave them plates of food that were labeled for each of their dietary needs.

Ms. Larissa gazed down at her bran and toast, her beady brown eyes flickering over the faces of those sitting next to her. No one spoke that morning, though that was not unusual. There wasn't much to say anymore. Mostly they talked to themselves, whispering about fragments of memories they could recall.

With a deliberate lift of her eyebrow, the young nurse tapped the corner of Larissa's plate. Larissa glared and took a small nibble from the edge of the unbuttered toast. The nurse smiled, squeezed the old woman's frail shoulder, and moved on.

The nurses were constantly watching. There wasn't a shadowy corner of the facility they didn't see. Larissa could sense them watching her even as she lay stiff in bed, her quilt tucked up under her chin, her toes hanging out from under the other end of the blanket. She could sense their eyes following her up and down the halls, no matter whether she was good and sat with the others at the television or whether she hissed and bit and scratched. It didn't matter. Nothing mattered.

Days bled together there until you weren't sure of anything anymore. The toast, the movies, the music, it was always the same. The only thing that changed was the revolving door of faces that swept through. Tomorrow, those sitting at her table would be different, and the day after that, they would again be replaced.

No one stayed too long. No one except Larissa. She had been at Springthorpe for so long she was no longer sure a time before it existed in her life.

The song changed. Frank Sinatra's voice melted into a soulful woman's. The plates were collected. When she took Larissa's still full plate, the young nurse sighed and made a note on the clipboard in her hand. When Larissa refused to stand, the nurse slid Larissa's frail body into a wheelchair.

As the patients were shuffled down the halls toward the recreational rooms and classes, Larissa tipped her head back and watched the lights of the hallway ceiling flutter. She blinked over and over, watching the light flicker like a movie reel.

When Larissa tilted her head back down, the young nurse from earlier was crouched in front of her chair, holding the same clipboard in her hands.

"What would you like to do today?" she asked with a beaming smile much too perky for the halls of Springthorpe.

To Larissa, the girl's eyes were too big for her face–like an alien. The bright fluorescent lights turned the nurse's cheery face pale and hollow, gaunt as a skeleton. Larissa didn't answer, shuddering and squawking instead. The nurse patted her knee and gave a little nod, her eyes meeting those of another nurse across the hall. Larissa knew that nurse was signing up the others for the myriad of activities designed to keep them as quiet and still as possible.

"Mr. Anderson, what classes would you like?" The young nurse shifted from Larissa's side, addressing a yawning man beside them. "Do you like making crafts?"

The man grunted and shrugged, rubbing his eyes as though he were so tired he could barely keep on his feet.

"Why don't we get you signed up for the art room, hmm?"

When he nodded, the other nurse came round and scribbled his name on her long list of classes.

As the big-eyed nurse left and the other nurse turned, however, Larissa saw what was penned on her clipboard. When she read it, she squawked again, louder this time, puffing up her chest like a parrot she'd seen in a movie on the television last month.

She liked being a parrot, imagining bright red feathers springing from her bony shoulders and frail body. Again and again, she squalled until the young nurse came back, patted her on the back, and whispered gentle words in her ear to soothe her. But Larissa wasn't soothed. She wouldn't be soothed. Not until she was out of there.

CHAPTER TEN

Mark couldn't wait until the 10:00 a.m. visitor check-in time to get to Springthorpe.

The retirement home sat in the distance, mocking him, calling and taunting him until he could no longer stand the monstrous building swathed in a billowy haze.

He hadn't slept at all, unable to tear his eyes away from the cemetery. His back and shoulders were stiff and knotted from standing straight and still all night, and his feet ached. Mark knew what he'd seen. He was sure of it.

Someone had been down there, but, no matter how long he had watched, he never saw another light.

Frustrated, Mark dashed down the stairs of the hotel and past the empty concierge desk. He didn't have time to call and wait for a taxi. Instead, he set his eyes on the building towering over the horizon and stormed toward it.

His feet marched in a straight beeline toward the manor. Mark cut over roads, highways, and lots without following the green guidance of the parks and their paved paths. He even climbed over a fence and tromped over someone's planted petunias.

Though it was morning, fog stretched thick as smoke across the streets. Far in the distance, Mark could see the glowing orbs of headlights traveling across the highway. Springthorpe felt detached from the city, a quiet little stretch of land residing on its own.

Most of his long walk was easy. There were no steep inclines or drops. There was no traffic or other wandering pedestrians to impede his gait.

There was only the manor, rising like a beast and looming over his head from its perch on the hill.

The entire area was so silent Mark could hear the faint beat of his heart behind his ribs. His ears strained for the distant caw of a raven gliding overhead.

When at last Mark stood at the bottom of the large knoll, he had to lift his chin high to gaze up at the glowing red brick of the menacing building. Haloed by dull morning light, the manor seemed even more substantial than it had when he'd visited the previous night. Though that had been mere hours ago, it felt like weeks had passed.

His feet throbbed. Painful blisters formed on the back of his heels where his thick socks had rubbed the skin raw. Sweat gathered at the nape of his neck, dripping down the collar of his shirt.

Before him stood a gate, wide, tall, and gleaming a metallic black. It would be impossible for cars to pass up the path heading toward the facility, but it was less defensive to a tenacious man. It helped not to be as big as his dad. Mark grabbed hold of the gate and managed to force himself through two of the thick bars, as it was impossible to climb over the barbed wire top.

Despite a bruised rib or two, he swallowed, gave a small nod of encouraged resolve, and continued up the road. No cars passed by him one way or the other as he walked, and, by the time he had walked the entire two-and-a-half-mile distance from the door of his hotel to the entrance of Springthorpe

Manor, he was breathless, achy, and tired. His sleepless night was catching up with him, making him disoriented and detached. He was having trouble putting a complete thought together.

Whatever had dragged him from his hotel room at such an early hour was a mystery. All he knew was the cemetery seemed to call for him, begging him to get there as fast as he could.

Like a quilt his mother might have stitched, the graveyard swept outwards, rolling over the hill so far that Mark couldn't see the other end, its wide breadth dotted with small splashes of fading flowers left at the graves. It was beautiful. Each gravestone stood like a sentinel welcoming those who came upon them.

Who had mourned for them—and did they still?

The muggy haze clung to the grass. The higher elevation caused Mark to pull at one of his popping ears as he yawned. The fog seemed alive, swirling around him like a churning storm, scraping at his clothes with icy fingers. It drew him closer and closer to the fence which blocked him from setting foot on the dying grass. This time, the bars were too narrow for Mark to slide through.

The graves made him queasy and nervous, though he supposed that was a reasonable response when surrounded by hundreds of the buried dead.

In the distance, something moved.

He blinked hard, expecting the mysterious thing he saw to vanish among the headstones, brittle trees, and haze. When he rubbed his eye, the figure was still there.

The figure swayed in the distance. The fog wrapped around the ethereal form as it straightened, standing tall and insubstantial, like the faint curl of smoke above an extinguished flame.

Mark squinted his brown eyes and curled his hands around the cool metal of the black fence, pressing his cheeks against the grate as though he could become as transparent and wispy as the figure floating among the headstones and slip right over to it.

When Mark blinked again, it was closer, drifting toward him as if it were a cloud rolling through the sky. It seemed to separate the fog, cutting through the haze like a knife.

His brain screamed at him, telling him to run and hide and get away as fast as he could, but Mark found himself immobile. His feet were heavy as concrete blocks, his entire body bound to the ground by what felt like thick and thorny vines curling around his thighs. His fingers remained frozen against the gate.

It was only when the ghostly figure crept close enough that Mark could reach out and brush a hand through its vapor-like face that his body sprang back into motion. He jerked backward with a shrill cry of terror ripping through his throat, stumbling over his clumsy feet and freefalling until he fell flat on his back.

The rocky lot of Springthorpe Manor welcomed him with a painful embrace, jagged pebbles and concrete biting through his clothes and into his back and shoulder blades.

For a second, incited by pure fear, extreme lack of sleep, and a possible concussion, Mark tried to remember how ghosts killed the unlucky people like him who stumbled across their undead paths. It'd been years since he'd seen a scary movie, and he could not for the life of him recall how exactly he was going to be punished by the afterlife. He groaned, accepting that a ghost was about to eat him alive–or do whatever it was that ghosts did–but, when a twig snapped beside his ear, his eyelids flew back open.

It was not a ghost who stood before him but a woman, a real woman with milky skin and chestnut brown hair that curled into her suspicious eyes.

Mark's earliest, most treasured memory was a morning from his youth when he'd clutched his father's hand as they stood together on the beach of Santa Monica. Liv and Joan had still been asleep back in their hotel room, and it had been so early that there were no others on the shore.

The sand had been warm and soft as microscopic, sugary grains under Mark's little feet, and he'd tipped his head back to grin up at his father. Ralph had been illuminated by the beautiful blue of the cloudless sky. Though Mark could not clearly see his father's rugged features, he could see the gleam of his white teeth as he grinned back and gestured toward the rolling tide before them.

The sun was rising, spilling golden light over the golden sand and deep blue waves. Tiny Mark sucked in a breath, startled even at his young age by the splendor of nature.

That moment and that image had lingered in the back of Mark's mind ever since. At the time, he swore up and down that the peaceful sea that day was the most brilliant blue he would ever experience.

For nearly forty years, that had remained true.

While Mark laid atop crushed violets with rough rocks pinching into his ribs and spine, his confident conviction was proven wrong.

The deep shade of sapphire lighting the eyes of the woman before him was the most stunning shade of blue he would ever see.

CHAPTER ELEVEN

"D id you make it, Livvy?" Thomas asked, with little affection attached to the pet name. "I heard some flights were grounded because of a storm."

"I'm here," Liv responded with equal listlessness.

The forty-two-year-old woman tugged her wool sweater tighter around her as she waited by the baggage claim for her luggage, switching her cell phone from one cheek to the other. Talking on the phone always hurt her ears. She'd have preferred to text, but Thomas refused. He considered texting too impersonal. Instead, they would sit in strained silence while waiting for the other to finally have something worthwhile to share.

"The girls miss you," he added, the uncertainty in his voice painful.

Her oldest girl, Samantha, definitely did not miss her and hadn't missed her in the last six years in which they hadn't spoken. Liv wasn't sure how often Thomas saw the twenty-four-year-old, but he would sometimes come home late from work with takeout from their eldest daughter's favorite restaurant. Their middle child, Stephanie, was a freshly-minted teenager and wouldn't have missed Liv if she died, but at least that one was ambivalent about her father as well. Stella, her youngest, possibly would miss her when Thomas presented her with a can of cold SpaghettiOs for dinner.

Black leather bags and worn backpacks floated by on the grating carousel. Liv's polished black shoe tapped on the ground. She fiddled with her hair, tugging it free of the messy bun atop the crown of her head and pulling it back again.

She'd paid extra for priority handling of her small luggage, and though she could have carried the light suitcase with her onto the plane, she hated the thought of that. Flights were cramped and uncomfortable enough without having to deal with baggage at the same time.

"Tell them I miss them too," she mumbled.

"Okay. Have fun, Livvy."

Liv didn't answer, rolling her eyes as she hung up her phone and shoved it into her back pocket.

Yes, Tom. I'm going to have a blast picking up my father's ashes, she'd wanted to snap.

When they'd gone to therapy a few years ago, Thomas had told her she was too rude. Since then, she'd kept those remarks locked up behind her closed lips.

The same lime green polka-dotted suitcase circled by for the third time. She let out a loud huff and stormed over to the nearby desk where an attendant was speaking to someone on the phone.

Staring at her watch, Liv leaned against the desk and rested her chin on her hand until the dark-haired man turned to face her. A minute ticked by and Liv glanced again at her watch. The tiny hand hadn't budged. Frowning, she tapped the glass with a harsh finger until it lurched and started moving again.

"My bag," Liv sighed when the dark-haired attendant hung up his phone and leaned over the desk toward her. "I haven't seen it."

"Have you been watching closely?" he retorted without a blink, making Liv's jaw go slack in surprise.

Liv's lips pursed and she lay her arms down on the wood, trying to ignore the bristling irritation crawling up the back of her neck.

"Yes," she muttered, "I'm not blind."

"I didn't say you were. Just inattentive, maybe." He laughed as though he was joking, but it didn't dampen the anger that swelled in Liv.

Though her tongue had a few choice words, she didn't answer. Liv clasped her hands. If she'd have had any inclination toward confrontation, she would've asked for his manager, but Liv didn't like making a scene. She didn't enjoy calling attention to herself. When she'd first started dating Thomas, Joan had told her not to become a doormat, but it had already been too late for that. Liv had been born a doormat.

"What's the name?" he continued.

"Hogarth. I mean Keller. Liv Keller."

"Are you sure?" he smirked, shaking his head as his fingers typed with lightning accuracy across the screen.

He paused, a frown crossing his mouth.

"Ah. I'm so sorry about this. Your luggage never made it onto the plane." His fingers moved again, dancing over the keys as they clicked away beneath his fingertips.

"Are you serious right now?" Liv barked, stamping a foot in a way that would make her bad-tempered nine-year-old proud. "That's so ridiculous. There was barely anyone on the flight!"

"Like I said, I'm deeply sorry for this. I've refunded your charges for the baggage. As soon as we track it, we'll have it delivered to you."

"I can't believe this. I don't have any clothes to wear!"

The attendant gave a smile of false sympathy. "I do apologize for the inconvenience. I'll see what else I can do for you."

He typed, clicking his tongue. "So, Mrs. Keller, what brings you to the San Francisco area today?"

"My father died," she replied as the man cleared his throat and glanced at her from the corner of his eye.

"Oh, I can get you a twenty-dollar credit at the airport gift shop."

"Great, so I can go around rocking flip-flops and a sweater emblazoned with a tacky screen print of the Golden Gate Bridge."

"Do you need anything else here, ma'am?" he asked when Liv remained standing there for a few more minutes, her hands clasped around the edge of his desk like it was keeping her upright.

Liv hated many things, though the one that bothered her most was being called 'ma'am.' Her skin prickled, dull eyes narrowing on the attendant.

He winced under her glare, grimacing as though those eyes of hers caused him pain. "I'm sorry, but twenty dollars is all I can do."

She resisted rolling her eyes. Her lips pursed tight on her stern face. She inhaled through her nose and let the air press out from between her lips like the therapist had taught her to do.

Right now, she had to focus. She had to get to the manor and see Mark so they could retrieve the ashes or else he was going to call her griping in the middle of the night again.

"I'd like directions, I guess. Springthorpe Manor. What's the fastest way to get there?"

"I'll call you a cab and have them put the cost on our tab. We have them take pilots to hotels occasionally."

Liv didn't answer except for a simple grunt.

"You know…my mom was a patient there," he continued.

"I'm sorry," Liv sighed.

"For what?"

"You said *was* a patient. Past tense."

He gave a forced chuckle and a slight nod. "Your cab is going to be here in a few minutes, Mrs. Keller. I hope your day gets better from here. If you need anything else, take this card and call me."

He held out a plain white business card imprinted with his contact information in tiny black letters.

When she finally looked him in the eye, Liv noticed that his eyes were different colors, one more dark brown than the other golden one. Unsettled, she left his card on the counter as she hurried toward the doors.

CHAPTER TWELVE

Sarah Kramer had seen many strange sights in her four years as a nurse at Springthorpe Manor.

She'd seen patients run naked down the halls and fling themselves against the waxed floor like they were trying to use a slip and slide. She'd seen blood transfusion bags explode in the hands of attendants, coating them in dark crimson. Hell, Sarah had even seen a nurse chug hot sauce from a bottle in the kitchen on a dare from some of the elderly residents.

Never, though, had Sarah seen a gaunt face staring at her from the gate of the cemetery. His pale fingers had been clasped tightly around the black bars, his face pressed so hard against the metal grate that his eyes practically bulged out of his skull.

The poor guy had been lucky she hadn't decked him, but, then again, he'd managed to hurt himself all on his own by throwing himself on the ground and scraping up his elbows something fierce.

"Who are you?" Sarah asked as she opened and then walked through the gate. Smoothing a long lock of brunette hair back from her face, she wrinkled her brow in mild bewilderment. "What are you doing out here?"

Was this crazy guy just a young patient who'd managed to sneak away? While most residents were older than seventy, there were a small handful of youngsters dealing with early-onset diseases.

His bloodshot eyes rimmed red and his face pale as a sheet, the man looked like he could be one of the patients.

"Ghost-" he stammered as Sarah clicked her tongue in pity.

Yep, they'd gotten another runner.

She reached forward for his arm when he shook his head and cleared his dry throat.

"Mark. Hogarth. Mark Hogarth," he gasped, blinking a few times as though she dazed him.

"Did you hit your head, Mark Hogarth?"

He shook his head. With a wince, Mark pulled himself upright to a sitting position. Brushing dirt from his shoulders and rubbing a sore shoulder, he heaved a quiet sigh.

"No...I didn't bruise anything more than my ego."

Sarah laughed and Mark couldn't help the smile that parted his lips. He watched her, inspecting the white coat draped over her shoulders. A name tag was clipped to the front of it. *Sarah Kramer.*

"What were you doing out there, Mrs. Kramer?" he asked.

Her smile faded, casting a glance back at the gravestones. For a moment she was quiet, and Mark was glad he had the sense of mind to respect that.

"It's Ms. Kramer, but you can call me Sarah," she said, tapping at her chin. "Ms. Kramer makes me feel old. Or like a teacher or something."

Mark gave a quick nod of his head, rubbing a throbbing elbow.

"My Grandpa is out there," she added with an embarrassed shrug and a faint blush, though Mark wasn't sure why she'd be self-conscious. "He raised me. I visit him before my shift when I can."

"I'm sure he appreciates that," Mark replied without thinking.

Sarah raised a sage eyebrow, the corners of her lips curling. "He's dead, Mark. He doesn't appreciate anything anymore."

It was Mark's turn to redden, rubbing a hand over the scruff growing on his jaw. "I meant...you know..."

"I know what you meant," she teased with a grin.

The pair fell quiet, the still stones and wilted flowers underfoot.

"When we found out he was dying, he told me to etch his name on a tree instead of on a concrete slab, so he'd still be alive for me. He was always corny." Sarah chuckled, blue eyes shooting toward Mark. "I made sure he got a tombstone anyway."

"My dad used to say stuff like that sometimes." Mark smiled, his head tossing back and forth with a shake. "He'd always say, 'Never skip a funeral. It isn't for the man in the coffin; it's for his grieving family left behind.'"

"Wise words. Must've been a wise man."

"I like to think I got that from him," Mark smirked.

Sarah gave a short burst of laughter, stretching out a hand to help Mark up. "Says the man who thought I was a ghost in the graveyard?"

Mark's ears burned pink as he shrugged and reached up to let the woman pull him to his feet. He wobbled, pressing a hand against the lump forming on the base of his skull. It was damp with what he hoped was sweat and not fresh blood. He pulled back his hand and inspected his clean fingers.

"So, Mark Hogarth, tell me why you're here at six in the morning," Sarah continued, crossing her arms over her chest.

The silky blue of her scrubs was the same lovely blue of her eyes. Her long dark curls were bound at the nape of her neck. Though she wore little makeup and had sleepy eyes, Mark couldn't stop staring at her. Her knees were stained a faint muddy brown from where she must've been kneeling beside her grandfather's grave.

"I'm getting my dad's ashes today," Mark murmured, shoving his hands in his pockets as the broad smile on Sarah's face vanished as quickly as a light switch flicked off.

"I'm so sorry," she said. The honest sincerity on her face was so genuine that, for once, it didn't come off as condescending as the others had. "I know how that feels. He was a patient here?"

"Ralph Hogarth. My mother was a patient here as well. Her name was Joan."

"Oh, Joan!' Sarah gasped, sapphire eyes crinkling with bittersweet contentment. "She was an amazing woman. I was with her in her last few days, you know. She was so kind."

"You must've met my dad then. There was no way he wouldn't be with her."

Sarah blinked, her face not changing expression once. "I don't remember anyone else being with her, but it was several months ago."

"Speaking of that," Mark continued, withdrawing the journal from where it rested inside his jacket.

The small notebook was substantial enough that Mark could sense it shifting in his pocket when he moved, a nice comforting weight that pressed against his heart. That journal was all he had left of his father, and he had every intention of cherishing it forever. Between those bound pages rested every thought and wish Ralph had within the last few years.

He pressed the small book into Sarah's hands.

Her nose wrinkled at the sweaty dampness of the leather from being tucked up so close to Mark's moist shirt.

He grasped her hands in his and flipped to the last few pages like he didn't trust her to be as gentle with the notebook as he was.

"Do you know what he's talking about? This was the day he died. It makes no sense. Why would he say it wasn't safe anymore? What was he talking about? Why did he think he could see Joan? I think maybe-"

"Mark," Sarah interrupted, holding up one porcelain palm to stop his ramblings, "if your father was here at the facility, that meant his mental functioning was likely diminished. Patients don't come here for a spa day. They come here because they can no longer live on their own." Sarah glanced at the pages then back at him.

"No, look at this page, this was dated the day after he died-"

"If I had a penny for every resident in there who thought it was either 1956 or 2112, I would have two very heavy pockets full of pennies. Many of them lose grip regarding what day it is. It's sad, but it's a part of life."

She jerked her dimpled chin behind her toward the building, eyes lingering on the dusky tinted glass and hard red brick.

"I think it's more than that!" he insisted through gritted teeth.

"I'm sorry, Mark, I must not be understanding you. What are you implying?" Sarah pursed her lips, her brow still wrinkled.

Mark cleared his throat again and sighed, his head dropping in defeat toward his chest. "Honestly? I don't even know. I guess...it's just so hard to believe he's gone."

Sarah reached over, taking his hand in hers and giving it a gentle squeeze. Her hand was warm and soft against his, and he found himself struggling to release it. When she drew her hand away, his fingers felt cold and lonely.

It was an odd feeling. It was as if the grief were making him more sensitive.

"I know it's difficult. But he's in a better place now. Isn't that what they say?"

There was a speech she was supposed to give in this situation, but she wasn't as talented as the head nurse in giving the grieving family the traditional compassionate spiel. Sarah dealt more with the patients who were still above the ground.

"I guess it's a relief my parents are together again," he admitted, though the words left a bitter taste on his tongue.

His eyes flickered toward the cemetery with a curious crease of his brow. "Hey, how long were you out there?"

"Listen, your eyes are so red they look like they're going to fall right out of your face. Let me call you a cab. Go back to your hotel and rest. Come back at ten. Your dad's ashes are going to be locked up 'til then anyway. Our morgue resident doesn't arrive 'til later."

Scuffling the muddied tip of his shoe on the ground, Mark yielded after noting Sarah's tone did not give him hope he would be able to argue his way into poking around the graves.

"You're right. Thanks."

He didn't want to leave, but he could tell when he wasn't being given a choice. Sarah seemed good at that, giving commands veiled as suggestions. Her intense eyes left no room for argument.

"Go on," Sarah prodded, turning him so he would begin the long trek back down the hill.

She pushed at the back of his broad shoulders, watching as he trudged forward. Sarah smiled and gave a light wave when he paused and glanced back at her once. She pulled out her phone and called for a cab. All the caregivers at the manor had taxis on their speed dial. There weren't many people who visited Springthorpe who didn't want a quick escape.

The lingering fog swallowed him up whole as he disappeared down the sidewalk like he was walking down a giant gray throat. At the end of the path, Sarah could barely see the vibrant yellow of the taxi pulling up to the gate.

As the vehicle sped off, her smile faded off her pretty face until her lips twitched downward and her arms hung like deadened weights at her side.

She turned back toward the nursing home, blue eyes meeting the watchful pair of someone behind the tinted window.

The figure nodded once, and Sarah breathed a sigh of relief, leaning one cheek against the cold metal of the cemetery gate.

CHAPTER THIRTEEN

How were things last night, Ms. Matthews?" Heath Dole asked with the air of already knowing everything that had happened.

This was true, of course; there was nothing that happened within the walls of his facility about which he didn't know. He imagined himself God there, omnipotent and omnipresent. He knew the names of each of his staff and had hired each one by hand, even those in charge of changing bedpans. To anyone who asked, he could tell the birthdate and allergies of each of his two hundred and thirty-seven patients.

Ah, it was two hundred and thirty-six now, he remembered.

The director of Springthorpe Manor stood graceful and tall in the middle of the wide entry hall, his voice gravelly and deep as it boomed along the crisp white painted walls. He tapped the papers gripped between his long fingers on the desk of the nurse's station, reveling in their simple organization.

Heath was the type of man to find joy in the small moments.

He, of all people, knew life was much too short not to enjoy. When one is surrounded by death and dying–and the reminder of what you become past seventy–you can either let yourself sink into depression and cynicism or you can use that knowledge as fuel. Heath had chosen the latter.

A group of some other nurses lingered further down the hall, watching them in a hushed silence of muted whispers. While they were too intimidated to speak to the wealthy fifty-something-year-old mastermind, they were content with catching scraps of his attention and half glances of his ice-blue eyes.

Half of the staff was enamored with him; the other half was afraid of him. Some were both. Heath liked that.

"It was fine! Another perfect night at Springthorpe."

Claire was tiny next to the broad-shouldered, long-legged director. Even his shadow dwarfed her, making her appear more like a toy doll.

Every time Heath asked this question, Claire gave him the same canned response and received the same rumble of thought from the director.

"Chuck told me patient three escaped again," Heath replied.

"She did, but it was no trouble at all," the red-headed nurse replied, taking a long sip of the hot coffee in her pale pink mug and delighting in the sweetness of the fresh half-and-half she'd added in abundance. "I had Ms. Larissa back in her room within fifteen minutes."

"Let's make it five next time."

"Of course," Claire said with a hasty nod of her head. "Nothing else of note happened. Oh, but Mr. Hogarth's son came to get Ralph's things. It was late but expected, given the circumstances."

"Good. So the room is freed up then?"

"It was. We received a new patient this morning."

Back to two hundred and thirty-seven patients it was, Heath nodded.

Startlingly clear eyes, the same shade as a glass pane coated with a touch of frost, swept over the tranquil cluster of elderly residents watching a movie. His eyes were such a translucent shade of blue when he was born, the doctor had sworn the child was blind. They'd all been shocked when little Heath reached out and grabbed the doctor's bulbous nose with strong and focused little fingers. Wincing in pain, the doctor had almost dropped the baby.

Heath's gaze was a laser; it could see right through you.

Springthorpe's patients, however, didn't seem to mind his sharp stare. They paid him no attention.

The volume of the movie being played was so low, Heath couldn't hear the words spoken by the actors. Still, the residents seemed absorbed enough in the film to keep them occupied. One woman's lips twitched along with the beautiful actress's, whispering the lines aloud while the man seated beside her scowled at the soft hiss escaping from her lips.

It was difficult finding ways to entertain the patients at the facility, even with the myriad of classes and activities in which the residents could take part. They were continually rotating the available programs and films. Though it was difficult, it was also necessary. There was nothing more dangerous than boredom. Indeed, Springthorpe had a five-star rating on Yelp to maintain.

"Ralph's son is returning soon to get the ashes," Claire continued, glancing down at the itinerary on her desk. It listed important visitors, scheduled tours, and the nurse's shift changes. "I've made sure everything is prepped for him."

"I'm sure you have," Heath replied with a gruff chuckle. "You're always on top of things, Ms. Matthews, the only one in this place who can get anything done on a consistent basis."

The head nurse brightened, a rare smile lighting her stern face.

It wasn't often Heath Dole visited the facility's large, open rec rooms, but when he did, Claire tried her best to make sure the problem patients were napping or medicated and the best of her patients were placed front and center for him. She hadn't been expecting Heath today, so a few troublemakers had slipped through, but Claire wasn't worried. They'd been quiet as the dead for an hour already. She'd been quick enough to pass out their medications before Heath arrived there.

"What's the boy's name? Ralph's boy."

"Mark. And he's not a boy, Heath. He's at least forty now. We're the same age, I think."

The director chuckled, shaking his head. "It's hard to view our patient's children as anything more than kids."

Heath turned, his scrutinizing eyes sweeping over the clean floor and tidy desk. Though everything seemed spotless and in good order, he'd always been one to find at least something to improve. That was his motto. There was always room for improvement. He didn't believe in perfection, but he strived for it anyway.

"Hmm, make a note we need a few more chairs in the foyer. Some of those are a little rickety. We don't want anyone to fall and break a hip." Heath frowned, kneeling down so one leg of his perfectly tailored slacks pressed onto the floor.

He jiggled a loose leg of a chair and gave a disapproving glance as Claire flushed and scribbled the note. By tomorrow, they would have a dozen new chairs. She'd see to it.

"All it takes is one report, Ms. Matthews, and we'll have fines up the wazoo for a decade."

A gust of wind blew down the hallway as the doors of the facility flung open, sending Claire's itinerary fluttering to the ground. She scurried to pick it up as soft voices spilled over the tile of the hall, echoing off the marble as though the pair arguing were only inches away.

Heath climbed to his feet, dusting imperceptible grime off his pants.

"There is no way Dad would want us to spend hundreds of dollars on flowers for his funeral," Mark groaned. "He didn't even like flowers. Maybe if they made bouquets out of freshly caught fish–"

"It's a respect thing, Mark. I wouldn't expect you to understand at all. He deserves flowers," Liv snapped back.

They turned a sharp corner, marching along in time. Though Mark had taken after their mother and Liv after their father, it was obvious the two were related. Their figures were similar, willowy and lean. Liv was slightly tall, and Mark was slightly short, so they stood head to head.

They came to a swift stop when they spotted the director. Claire stood at his side, her arms crossed over chest, her brows digging down toward her emerald eyes.

The Hogarth siblings went silent, though not before shooting an accusing glare at the other, rapidly advancing toward the majestic gentleman. The sunlight dappled Heath's dark hair, making the few gray strands gleam like spun silver.

Heath's smile grew as he stepped forward, extending a hand to the youngest Hogarth child.

"Hello, Mr. Hogarth. I'm sorry we have to meet again in such sad circumstances."

"Oh, um, good morning, Mr. Dole," Mark sputtered back, shaking the man's clammy hand.

Mark was surprised he was able to come up with the Springthorpe director's name since he hadn't considered seeing him there that day.

Heath took Liv's palm in his, giving it a warm shake. "Mrs. Keller, I was so distraught when I heard the news about your father. I know you two were close. He was an amazing man."

Liv's face lit a deep shade of red that rivaled Claire's hair as she shook her head in silence. Her whole body felt hot and cold at the same time like she was drowning in fiery sweat. She couldn't seem to speak.

Though Heath was not a rugged man, nor was he exceptionally tall, he had a way of filling up a room. Being under his gaze was like being under a spotlight; every flaw and worry was illuminated.

It was impossible for their eyes not to be drawn toward his dazzling white smile, hand-sewn suit, and polished black loafers. He was, perhaps, the most impeccable human being Mark or Liv had ever seen. He hadn't aged a day since Mark had last seen him at the tour of the facility with Joan and Ralph.

Heath Dole was not the type of man to be ignorant of his effect on others. In fact, he delighted in the way his presence could silence even the most rambunctious of children. His twinkling eyes and broad shoulders incited reverence.

"We've already called to have the remains brought upstairs here. We'll have you out of here and back to planning your father's service in just a minute," said Heath.

"Can we get you some coffee while you wait?" Claire offered, though neither Mark nor Liv took her up on the proposal.

Mark's eyes wandered as an awkward silence fell over them, seeking out even the faintest flash of blue eyes around the hall. Liv stared at her feet, shifting from one foot to the other while stealing glances at Heath's handsome face.

It was hard for Mark to believe in just seconds he was going to be holding his father's remains in his hands. It wasn't how he expected to see Ralph again. He'd expected the next time they saw one another to be filled with joy and laughter. He'd thought he'd feel one more clap of Ralph's large palm on his shoulder.

He'd been wrong.

"Oh, look. There we are!" Heath announced, dragging Mark from his thoughts as the director walked toward a young man in deep purple scrubs who stepped out from a small keypad-locked door down the hall.

Mark's throat went tight, surveying the black urn in the young man's clutches.

No. It couldn't be.

He'd thought he would be able to believe it more when he saw it, but it became even more inconceivable by the second.

As Heath turned and walked to take the black urn from the morgue attendant, Liv edged closer to the television, leaning closer to inspect the film being played.

Just like Joan had been, she'd always been a fan of black and white movies. Sometimes she even changed her television settings on contemporary films so she could watch them in monotone hues. It felt simpler. Comforting, in a way.

Liv's head cocked before she turned toward Mark, her lips parting to say something. Her hand rested on the back of the sofa, accidentally brushing against the dark gray locks of a woman seated before her.

The old woman glanced up at Liv with wide, interested eyes, as though she were a raccoon that had spotted a shimmery, shiny penny.

In one split second, the room went from quiet and peaceful to a wild cyclone of screams and torn flesh.

"Wait!" Claire cried, though she was not fast enough to stop Larissa from reaching up and snagging hold of Liv, digging sharp fingernails into the blonde woman's cheek and arms, and dragging her down onto a sofa cushion now sprinkled with fresh blood.

CHAPTER FOURTEEN

The shiny black urn was warm against Mark's arms as he leaned against the wall of the office, his ankles crossed in front of him. The container was lighter than he'd expected, reflecting the fluorescent bulbs overhead with a glare that made Mark's head ache. He'd anticipated his robust father would weigh more than a paperweight. He stifled a yawn, doing his best to ignore the fact he was carrying all that was left of his father. Thinking about it twisted his stomach into knots.

"Mrs. Keller, I don't know how to tell you how sorry I am," Heath whispered, gripping the woman's hand in his and shooting a warning glance toward Claire, who chewed her lip and hovered nearby.

The head nurse hadn't said a word so far, her hands wringing in front of her. She shifted from one uneasy foot to the other, head bobbing up and down with her boss's words.

Mark's eyes flickered around the room, trying to find someplace to set down Ralph's ashes. Though the urn was light, he didn't want to hold it anymore. Every time he attempted to set it down, however, Liv's disapproving glare let him know he was asking for trouble. Not even Heath's distracting blue stare could keep Liv from noticing if her little brother was about to do something she perceived as wrong. Not that she'd offered to hold the urn instead.

"Heath is right, Mrs. Keller," Claire stammered. "I am so sorry. I should have been watching."

Claire was not used to having to apologize for mistakes. Perfection was her forte–or it had been. She hadn't even noticed Larissa sitting squished between Mr. Cooper's broad belly and Mrs. Petty's gigantic bowl of knitting wool.

"It's fine," Liv interrupted, blotting a paper towel to her cheek to soak up the blood from the large gash.

The cut was long but not deep. In a few days, it would fade before vanishing altogether. Though Liv would still have nightmares about being grabbed by jagged claws and biting jaws, it would appear to all the world the incident had never happened.

The door to the office opened behind them as Sarah rushed in, exchanging a startled glance with Mark before laying the small first aid kit on the table beside Liv. She soaked a cotton ball in antiseptic then tapped it against Liv's cheek as the tired-eyed woman shifted in discomfort.

"You know, you're lucky," Sarah teased, pulling back the cotton ball to inspect the cut. She took Liv's chin in her hand, tipping her face one way then the other to get a better view of the jagged red ridges of inflamed flesh. "The last person Larissa challenged to a duel lost an arm."

"Oh my gosh," Liv whispered, her eyes huge as saucers. "Are you serious?"

"She is not." Heath frowned, glaring at the brunette nurse. "Right, Ms. Kramer?"

Sarah winked, slapping a bandage onto Liv's cheek. Stepping backward, she retreated step by step until she was standing beside Mark. Heath still fussed over Liv, no doubt worried about the backlash that could arise from the situation. Mark's sister, however, soaked up the attention like a desperate sponge.

"So, did you get some rest?" Sarah asked Mark. "Did it prepare you for all this excitement? Never a dull day at Springthorpe."

Her eyes wandered to the urn in Mark's hands. He was grateful when she didn't mention it.

"I did." Mark nodded, though that was a lie, and Sarah probably saw right through it.

He'd tossed and turned and fought with his pillows until he gave up. He had managed to eat something, so that was an accomplishment at least.

"Wait," Mark asked, "were you serious about the arm thing?"

"Ms. Kramer," Claire interrupted, "don't you have patients to get back to or are you going to avoid all your duties today?"

"You got it, ma'am," Sarah shot back with the faintest hint of a smirk on the upturned corners of her plump lips.

She raised her eyebrows at Mark as she turned, giving a little shake of her head before stepping out of the room. The door closed behind her, leaving the four others alone. Mark wished he could follow her out the door. She was the only pleasant one there.

"Listen, if you go to the hospital, we'll be happy to cover the bill for you, Mrs. Keller," Heath said, holding Liv's hand in his and bending down so he could gaze into her eyes. "All of this will be taken care of, no matter what. But, and I don't mean to brag, we do have the best staff in the world right here between these walls. Plus, no little scratch could mar a lovely woman like you!"

"Oh..." Liv breathed, batting her eyes in a way that made Mark want to groan and hide behind the urn in his hands. "I mean, she can't help it, right? It wasn't her fault. I should have been more careful. It's not like I need stitches or anything..."

"Bathroom," Mark interrupted, lifting a hand straight into the air like a school child would to call attention to himself. "I need to use it. Where can I find one?"

Claire turned to him with slight irritation fluttering over her green eyes, crossing the room and pulling open the door to point to the left of the hallway. Without a word, she gave a halfhearted jerk of her chin toward an illuminated sign that read *Restroom* in bright white letters above an arrow.

Mark nodded, shifting Ralph from one hip to the other. He stepped out of the office into the long, empty hall. Claire remained still and stiff behind him, watching him from the doorway.

With a glance over his shoulder back at her, Mark turned forward again with a roll of his eyes and walked to the bathroom. He stepped inside, setting the urn on the sink and inspecting himself in the mirror. Though there was no face on the black urn, Mark could feel his father's disapproving stare emanating from the small vessel.

Huge bags hung under his eyes. Bulging red veins curled around his brown irises. Though Mark wasn't the self-deprecating type, he thought, if he saw someone like him on the street, he would've crossed over to the other side.

Ralph would have teased him about it before locking Mark up in a room to get some sleep. Even with both children in their forties, Ralph had still treated both of his progenies like toddlers. To him, they had never grown up at all.

"It's your fault I look like this, old man." Mark smiled, patting the lid of the vase as though he could comfort his father in the afterlife.

He turned on the faucet, leaning down to splash water on his tired face. When he straightened, he patted his face dry with a paper towel and scooped the urn back into his arms. Mark pushed open the bathroom door enough to peek out with one eye.

The door to the office was closed, Claire's tiny, vigilant face gone.

He peered up and down the hall, half expecting the scrawny redhead to leap out at him the second he took one false step. When she didn't, he sighed and slid free of the bathroom.

With a silent apology, Mark set the container down on the floor, tucking it into a corner so it wouldn't be knocked over. A shudder rolled through him as soon as he was free of the jar, and Mark couldn't resist the primal urge to dust himself off as though his father's ashes had somehow managed to sprinkle over him from within the sealed container.

With one last careful glance at the abandoned urn, Mark turned and tiptoed down the hall. He could hear the faint bustle and movement of other patients in their rooms and the quiet chatter of other nurses.

In search of the familiar face of the blue-eyed nurse, he peered into each room as he passed.

Anything was better than being trapped with Heath and Liv while the Springthorpe director tried to flirt away a lawsuit.

He sunk down to his knees as he passed a small, lit office with large windows, the soft voice of the nurse inside drifting into the hallway.

"Anderson…" she said as Mark crept his way around the corner while keeping out of sight. "So sorry…"

The hall in front of Mark was half illuminated and empty. He straightened, stretching and reaching his arms toward the ceiling and rocking one way and then the other. This hall didn't seem familiar from the tour he'd taken with his parents, but that had been some time ago and he'd barely been paying attention.

The rooms were simple enough. Some had boxes of musical equipment or blackboards with foreign phrases. It reminded Mark of an eerie preschool, each room painted with cheery, little decorations but empty aside from the shadows skulking across the floorboards like black snakes.

One chamber at the end of the hall, however, caught his inquisitive eye.

A few half-finished canvases stood in a stocky circle in the center of the tile, the walls pasted with dozens of drawn pictures. Containers of organized pens and colored pencils sat on shelves among stamp sets and messy balls of string.

"The art room," Mark murmured to no one in particular, though he was glad no one responded once he'd uttered it aloud. He glanced behind him and then tugged at the door.

It opened beneath his hand, allowing Mark to slip into the dim room. Even with the bright colors of the walls, paintings, and crafts, it seemed gloomy.

Afraid to turn on the light and get caught, he walked along the perimeter of the room, his eyes following the line of pictures tacked up. He squinted, inspecting each sketch.

The art was basic, like what he and Liv might have done as schoolchildren.

Stick figures were common, dancing across the papers in purple marker and green crayon. Most did not have names or labels to signify who drew the portrait, but Mark kept an eye out for his father's familiar scrawl and the big oversized 'R' that always accompanied his name. The way his father wrote was unique, like Ralph himself had been unique.

By the time Mark had circled once and then twice, he'd found nothing that seemed to be done by his father.

Either way, it was time for him to go and collect the urn before some unobservant orderly or patient could knock it over. Liv would never forgive him if she left that room and found Ralph's ashes scattered along the hall.

With a shrug, Mark turned and walked back to the door, fingers curling around the metal handle. He pulled it, and pushed it, and yanked on it as hard as he could, but it did not budge. Harder and harder he wrenched at it until his fingers ached from the strain.

He pounded a fist against the door, calling out for anyone who may be near.

Pressing his face against the sliver of a window cut into the metal, he couldn't see so much as a shadow in the hall.

The nurse around the corner would never be able to hear him in her tiny, sealed room. No one would.

Mark took a breath, taking a long step back and then hurling his shoulder against the door.

Once, twice, he threw himself against it with such force his shoulder screamed.

On the third attempt, the door flew open before he could reach it.

The momentum sent him flying out across the marble, flailing and crashing into the wall on the other side of the hall. He slumped down to his knees with a groan, his forehead aching with the force of striking the painted concrete brick.

In one day, he'd managed to slam both sides of his skull. His mother had always called him hardheaded, but this seemed like overkill.

Mark blinked hard, trying to clear the little black dots that spun in front of his eyes, dancing in the face of his pain.

He pushed his palms against the wall and tried to force his legs to lift him, but it was so hard to climb to his feet. The black spots spun faster, eating at the edge of his vision as his knees sank back to the ground.

There was no strength in his body. He couldn't focus on anything with the throbbing of his head and the pain in his shoulders.

Every shallow breath he sucked in was uncomfortable. The wind had been knocked from his lungs.

Footsteps squeaked down the hall. Mark grunted for help and tried turning to face the person just as a strong pair of hands shoved against his spine, hurling Mark's face back into the wall.

With a quiet moan, Mark collapsed on the floor in a crumpled heap.

CHAPTER FIFTEEN

The corners of the passages swept past him in a sharp and winding blur as he lumbered forward.

Faster and faster, the man's feet moved until his chest burned and his shoulder hurt from bumping into so many walls he normally could have recited from memory. He escaped deeper and deeper into the welcoming shadows, chest heaving by the time he came to a halt.

A noise to his left almost sent him running again like a startled animal, but there was no easy way for him to escape. Instead, he froze like a deer in headlights, holding his breath and waiting. He was no longer sure where he was in the depths of the endless corridors.

He turned in a slow and nervous circle, shuddering. He was not alone.

"You did so well!" a gentle, sweet voice assured him through the dark, though it didn't stop the rapid beating of his heart caught within his ribcage.

He hung back, cowering from the speaker and hugging his arms tighter around his body with a shake of his head. It wasn't on purpose. He hadn't meant to hurt the man near the art room.

"Take a breath," she instructed him, and he did, sucking in air through his nostrils so deep into his lungs it stung.

Both of his arms remained wrapped tightly around himself and the gift he had smuggled.

"What do you have there?" the woman asked, holding out a hand that glowed like moonlight in the dark.

He jerked backward, shaking his head and clutching the leather book tighter to his chest. He had found it and he wanted it. It belonged to him. They had told him if he found anything, he could keep it.

He squinted through the inky black of the hall. He couldn't see the woman's face. It didn't matter. He knew who it was, but he so liked to see her face.

"Can I hold it?" the woman asked. Her voice was so kind and compelling he couldn't resist her. "I'll be very, very gentle. Promise."

Sighing, he held the book out, allowing the woman to take it into her hands. Instead of inspecting the small book, she closed it and slipped it somewhere he could not see.

With a whine, he reached out to retrieve the book that had felt so familiar in his hands. The woman scolded him like a child. He should have known better than to hand it to her. She always took and never gave.

He would learn someday.

"Here. You lost this."

The white plastic of the familiar ID card glinted in the dark as it passed from the woman's hand to the man's.

He frowned but didn't say anything. He hadn't lost it. It'd been taken.

"Do you remember what else you have to do?" she asked.

She was moving, her voice changing direction. He wanted to chase after her, but he knew the rules. He knew he had to be good. He had to stay and he had to be quiet. Most of all, he had to watch.

He was good at watching.

He nodded, though he wasn't sure if she'd be able to see the slight bob of his chin.

"Good," the woman said.

He could tell she was happy with him. Joy bubbled up inside of him, a slow smile spreading across his cheeks. Making her happy was like his birthday and Christmas all wrapped into one.

He hoped she would give the book back.

"Very good," she repeated. "Keep working as hard as you have, and I'll make sure you get something nice. Isn't that what you want?"

Her voice was more distant now. He had to strain to hear her speak. He reached one of his hands out into the darkness, as though he could snag the hem of her shirt and drag her back toward him, but his fingers only grasped at empty shadows.

Several long minutes of pure silence passed as he waited for her to say something, to continue speaking to him in that soothing way she did. When only the dark quiet greeted him, he sank down to the floor so that his legs were stretched out before him. The tile was cold and uncomfortable under his legs. He stared down at his quivering fingers even though he could not see them.

He would do what she asked. There was no other way.

CHAPTER SIXTEEN

The doughnut was sweet. Blue, pink, purple, and green sprinkles dappled the iced surface of the pastry ring. It was half chewed and cradled by thick fingers.

He leaned back in his comfy leather chair so sharply it squeaked under the movement, kicking up his feet so they rested on the edge of his cluttered desk. With a satisfied grunt, he sucked at his pink sticky fingers and inspected the dozens of tiny screens playing before him in real time.

Elderly residents wandered beneath the cameras of Springthorpe, shuffling and pacing and crying. Nurses raced by with swinging hips and bobbing ponytails. He was alone in this room with his monitors and his doughnuts. He enjoyed being alone.

For the most part, he'd seen very little of importance that day and the day before and the day before that. Nothing exciting ever occurred in the winding halls of Springthorpe Manor.

He set down his half-eaten doughnut on a crumpled old napkin scribbled with numbers before nibbling at a purple sprinkle still clinging to his thumb. He paused. His head tilted, and he leaned down to inspect one of the small screens in the lower quadrant of the monitor–a screen that didn't often get movement.

He clicked it, blinking his glazed eyes as the picture enlarged before his dilated pupils. The screen was bright in the dimly lit room, making little multi-colored dots float around in front of his eyes like miniature hot air balloons.

An unfamiliar man walked down the back hallways, hands in his pockets, peering into every door as he passed. The man with his doughnuts narrowed his eyes, watching before giving a soft humph. It took Chuck a while to place him, but he finally recognized the wanderer as the one who had arrived with the woman who was scratched by Larissa. The thought of the old woman attacking the blonde lady made Chuck laugh so hard he briefly choked on his next bite of pastry. He'd watched that whole event happen as Larissa clawed at the woman like she was a cat and the victim was her scratching pole. He'd replayed it over and over again. It had been much more exciting than the boredom of watching quiet halls.

The man at the computer quieted, brushing a finger over the monitor to wipe away a faint smudge of sticky grime.

Though the man wandering in the hall couldn't see it, the one with the cameras could. Someone followed behind, slipping like a shadow through the corners of the hall. While one of the figures lagged in the dark, they stepped together. Chuck made sure his computer was recording, positive whatever was about to happen would be another fun video to add to his collection.

From where he sat perched in his dark room, the man with his computers could see everything.

There was no privacy in this building. There was no inch of darkness he did not have access to, that he did not see. His cameras infiltrated every room in the manor until there was no such thing as secrecy.

Not for anyone.

The wandering man in the surveillance stream had disappeared into a room. The other figure still lurked outside of it. Both of them waited for the one in the art room to come back out. The man with his doughnuts was sure they both were holding their breath.

Picking up his frosted snack, he gave the doughnut a generous lick to lap up the remaining sprinkles off the sticky surface, though his eyes remained locked on the screen.

If only the doughnut hadn't been jelly filled, it would've been perfect. Chuck pouted, brushing a thumb against the blue polo he wore, the one stitched with two simple words on the breast pocket.

Springthorpe Security.

Fast as a flash of lightning, the figure in the hallway opened the door to the art room, and the man inside ran out as though his pants were on fire, crashing headlong into the hall. Flinching, the man with the doughnut shook his head and sighed, his feet still kicked up before him with the carelessness of a teenager at school.

As the follower approached the crumpled body, the security man gave a final bored yawn and clicked through his other cameras.

He flipped through the screens showing Heath Dole and his guest, the nurses grouped around the front desk, and the patients seated in the cafeteria.

Taking hold of the mouse with sticky fingers, he flashed through the channels, watching the people on the screens pass by in a blur. The disinterested clicking came to an abrupt halt as it illuminated two moving heads bobbing together in a dark hallway.

Two people appeared to be speaking in the dim shadows, lit by the undetectable glow of his camera. He knew the pair. He'd seen them before. He could tell the lights weren't on, the man glancing up and down and around the halls so nervously it made the one watching antsy. They exchanged something, a small parcel switching hands. Chuck frowned and swiped aside his doughnut to write a hasty note on his tattered napkin.

As the pair separated, Chuck sighed and resumed his check of the cameras.

He clicked past the man still collapsed in the hall. He clicked past the now empty office where Heath had been a minute ago. He clicked past the pretty blue-eyed nurse and the red-headed one talking in the lobby until finally, he gazed down at another long, dark length of the hall.

This hall wasn't shiny and tiled like all the rest; it was earthy and deep and shadowed. This was his favorite screen to watch, his camera rotating to sweep over the caged humans lying limp on brown earth.

"Anything of note, Chuck?" a voice crackled through the walkie-talkie latched onto his chest.

Chuck cleared his throat, taking a swig of cola to wash down his doughnut, then lifted the receiver to his lips.

"Nope. Nothing here," he smiled. "Another boring day at Springthorpe."

CHAPTER SEVENTEEN

There were others.

Soft whispers, too quiet to be understood, fluttered around the room like the delicate wings of tiny moths. Their feet moved, sneakers crunching over the pebbled floor.

It was cold and the air was heavy.

Where am I?

The words didn't come.

How did I get here?

Still, there was nothing. Her throat had shut down like everything had shut down. Fingers, toes, neck, it was all frozen.

There had been the white, glossy walls and then there had been nothing. No one cared. No one explained.

"Good morning, Larissa."

The old woman cracked open a heavy eyelid, unable to focus on anything but the large eyes of the nurse in front of her. The young nurse sighed and held Larissa's hand. The nurse's hands were ice-cold, colder than the metallic table Larissa lay upon. She shivered, wanting to ask for a blanket.

The old woman fumbled, trying to tug at her hand, though she couldn't seem to control her own body. There was nothing but the cold here. She wasn't sure if she was bound to the table or if something had happened to her that left her unable to move.

She wasn't in her room anymore. She wasn't in the infirmary. She wasn't in the manor, or rather, she wasn't on the upper floors of it.

Panic rose in the back of her throat. The gentle pinch of a needle sliced through her papery, white skin.

No. No. No! I can't be down here. It's not possible!

The old woman's eyes rolled around, trying to take in as much of her surroundings as she could. Everything blurred; the world spun in front of her.

The drugs made her dazed and confused.

"You misbehaved today, Ms. Larissa," the nurse sighed, stroking the woman's hair and gently cradling one of her hands. "You shouldn't have done that."

Even blinking was hard, like ten-pound weights were tied to Larissa's eyelids. She felt like she was underwater and it was hard to breathe. Her chest became heavy. Her heart strained to keep pumping the thick ooze that her blood had become.

"Time of death is 2:15 p.m.," the nurse announced, dropping the woman's hand so it clunked against the table.

CHAPTER EIGHTEEN

I t was the sputtering of the AC unit that woke Mark.

Once it roared like a beast, shaking the entire floor of his hotel room, Mark's eyes shot open so fast, for a second, he couldn't even see.

He leaped up out of bed as though he were a rocket launching, the blankets that had been tucked under his chin wrapping around his thighs and sending him hurtling toward the scratchy carpet below.

He was able to catch himself before he whacked his bruised face on the floor, pushing himself back onto his knees with a wild, confused look around.

"What the hell?" He breathed, running a hand through his hair and squinting at the red glowing clock on his stand.

2:15 p.m.

He'd been out for hours.

The last thing he remembered was standing in the office with Liv and Heath.

Grabbing the edge of his bed, he pulled himself to his feet only to have a lightning bolt of pain ripple up through the back of his neck.

With a shocked cry, he fell back against the mattress, pressing his hand first to the back of his skull and then to the front. His whole head throbbed. How he'd gotten so hurt and how he'd ended up back at the hotel was a mystery.

It was like that one time he'd gotten black-out drunk in college and found himself naked in his roommate's bed the next morning. A whole chunk of his memory had been ripped straight from his brain with a rusty shovel. At least, this time he was clothed.

Mark climbed to his feet, his toes brushing the yellowing carpet and his body heaving upward as delicately as he could. Swallowing, he groaned and walked to the bathroom.

Pushing the faucet on, he splashed his face with water and bit back a grunt of pain.

His forehead and nose were a nasty shade of swollen blue and sick yellow, his fingers brushing over the tender and bruised areas.

"Damn," he murmured, shaking his head with a wince and walking back to the couch to plop down.

He reached for his phone to call his sister. But it had died and he had yet to get a new charger.

Had it been Liv who brought me back to the hotel? It was hard to imagine her slender shoulders carrying much weight of anything. Mark wasn't a big guy, but he wasn't a waif either.

Frowning, Mark dug his hands into his pockets, seeking out his wallet. The leather met his probing fingertips as he gave a thankful sigh. When he'd blacked out in college, he hadn't the sense of mind to keep track of his wallet. Someone else had used his credit card for a week.

At least he'd matured in some ways.

And at least he'd managed to get some sleep–if falling into unconsciousness counted.

Was that what happened? Had I passed out from pure exhaustion and smacked my face on every desk in the place on the way down?

Dad! Gasping with a grimace, he stumbled toward the wall and pressed a palm against it while his eyes searched around the hotel room.

The urn was nowhere to be seen.

Panicking, he paced the room. There was not a trace of the vase with his father's remains.

Liv is going to kill me. Unless it's Liv who has the urn.

Either way, he was going to hear an earful about it next time he saw her. He wasn't even sure if she was still in town or if she had a flight back home. She had kids, after all, and all the responsibility that went along with them.

He heaved a sigh or a groan–he wasn't sure which–rubbing his head and sinking down to the floor beside the packed boxes he'd collected from his father's room at Springthorpe yesterday.

Mark crossed his arms over the rim of one of the cardboard containers and tucked his chin atop it.

"Sorry, Dad," he sighed, straightening up and taking the taped edge of the box and peeling it back. "I didn't mean to lose you."

He smiled, knowing Ralph Hogarth would've found some vague amusement in the whole thing, except for the fact Mark's face resembled someone who'd been in a fight with Mike Tyson armed with a sledgehammer. Ralph wouldn't have cared if his ashes were with his children or scattered over the Serengeti or in a puddle of rainwater. All he'd desire was for his children to be safe and happy.

The least the youngest Hogarth could do now that he'd lost his father's remains was sort through his father's belongings and pick out something to give to Liv. That way, if he had lost the ashes of their father forever, he'd at least have something pitiful to offer.

Not that Liv would ever forgive him.

He wasn't sure if he'd ever forgive himself either.

Going through the boxes didn't take long. Ralph had always been a minimalist. He never owned more than he needed, donating clothes as he outwore them and passing along gifts he deemed too extravagant. Joan and his children had learned early on that gifts had to be practical, simple, and wise. Gift cards would be given away and luxuries would disappear to friends in need. Ralph was both the easiest and most difficult person for whom to buy presents.

That's why Mark and his sister now hung on to everything. They were used to coming home to find half their clothes and toys gone after school, given away to children more in need than Mark and Liv. At the time, they were too young and selfish to recognize the kindness in the gesture.

To honor his father, Mark sorted Ralph's possessions into specific groups: one heap for Liv that included their old Polaroid camera and one of Ralph's button-downs, which still smelled like their dad; one area for Mark that was an empty spot on the stained carpet; and a third pile of old khakis for the local Goodwill store.

In the bottom of the last box, Mark found something he couldn't believe he'd forgotten about after all these years.

With a laugh, he ran his fingers across the faded teal of the scrapbook cover. Ralph had written in his unique scrawl a simple and sweet title.

A Book of Love—Ralph and Joan.

At every celebrated anniversary at the lake, his parents had taken one photo to commemorate the event. Every year was the same. Mark smiled as he lifted the book and held it in his lap.

He opened it to the first page, gazing down at the young faces of his parents.

They embraced each other, Joan's face half hidden in Ralph's shoulder. She always hated having her picture taken. She much preferred being behind the camera.

Mark turned the pages, tears welling in the corners of his eyes as he watched his parents grow in age and devotion with each flip. Though they became older and more wrinkled and round, their hair color fading and their skin crinkling like crepe paper, the love shining in their eyes never once diminished. The embrace was never forced after an argument or a long drive with two exhausting children. They escaped into one another's arms, even in the pouring rain of their fifth and thirteenth anniversaries.

The photos were beautiful and excruciating all at once.

Mark wished he had one more day with them, one more time that he could hug them both tight and tell them how much he appreciated their patience and love while growing up. He and Liv hadn't been easy children, but he'd never once felt an ounce of their care lessen.

Pausing at the forty-ninth photo, Mark blinked away the tears in his eyes.

They had so wanted to reach fifty years together, and Mark and Liv had both been sure it would happen.

Right after the photo of their forty-ninth year at Lake Jarvis, it became clear the pair could no longer live on their own. The decision to put them into Springthorpe had happened quickly after. Six months later, Joan had died. They'd never reached their fiftieth anniversary. Since Ralph and Joan had wanted so little, it was painful they never celebrated the one thing for which they so deeply wished.

Mark's heart wrenched in his chest. He drew in a deep, guilty breath and tilted his head back to clear his eyes.

As he closed the scrapbook, however, a photo that was stuck between the back pages–instead of in an appropriate slot–fluttered out to the ground.

Frowning, he picked it up and inspected it.

It wasn't a photo he had seen before, though his father was wearing a sweater Liv had given him last Christmas. He recognized it and the obnoxious Santa Claus hat-wearing kitten on the front.

His parents embraced, though it wasn't just love in their eyes, it was something else. Something had made Ralph's mouth taut and nervous in the photo. They didn't stand on that familiar dock at Lake Jarvis, but somewhere that sent shadows over both their heads, obscuring them from the camera. Mark held the photo in front of his eyes, scrutinizing where they were but was unable to discern anything.

Wherever it was, it appeared to be underground, like a cave.

Mark flipped over the photo, inspecting the familiar, jumbled writing of his father on the back.

I always knew we'd make it to 50. Today is my best day because I am with you.

CHAPTER NINETEEN

Ms. Kramer…Sarah…" Claire called, tugging the elbow of the tall, blue-eyed nurse.

Sarah whirled around in surprise and turned a startled gaze back at the petite head nurse who released her hold, arms dropping to her side as she heaved a huge sigh.

Though Claire was ordinarily prim and composed, she was out of sorts that afternoon, her thick hair unraveling from its braid. Claire gnawed at her lower lip, turning the curve of her mouth an angry red, and shifted her feet as she tugged at a loose lock of her red hair. She was acting like a child waiting to be scolded and put in a corner.

"What is it, Claire?" Sarah asked, before shooting a quick glance around.

The other nurses were watching, no doubt taking notes to fuel their gossip farm. With a staff as large and diverse as the one at Springthorpe, rumors took flight in seconds. The last thing either of them needed after all the excitement of the day was for people to be making up stories. Sarah took hold of the other woman's arm and tugged her around the corner of the hallway so they were out of sight of the nosy caregivers and distracted patients.

"Are you feeling okay?" Sarah continued, despite knowing full well what plagued the head nurse.

Everyone in the facility knew what had happened; it was all anyone was talking about all morning. In all the years Springthorpe had been operating, a visitor had never before been injured within the walls. It was unprecedented.

It was surprising it'd happened and Claire was involved. At the same time, once Sarah thought about it again, it wasn't all that shocking. When unusual occurrences happened, Claire was typically the spearhead. However, each time before had resulted in a positive outcome. It was Claire who had set up the cycle of classes to entertain the patients, and it was Claire who alphabetized the food regimens in the kitchen to get the patients' meals out more quickly. This time, it was Claire who'd allowed vicious Larissa to be in the presence of an unsuspecting guest who wound up with a scar on her face–and Mark's sister had been lucky that it hadn't been worse.

Sarah and Claire had both seen Larissa do some damage with her jaws or claws. She was one of the only patients in Springthorpe who didn't have dentures, and she knew how to use those yellowed fangs of hers.

Claire sank down into a nearby chair, shaking her head and running her fingers over her scalp to smooth back her hair.

Sarah remained standing, crossing her arms and leaning against the wall. She wasn't sure why Claire had come to her. They'd never been friends. They'd never seen each other outside their shifts at the facility. Claire was little more than a manager to Sarah. The brunette glanced around, clearing her throat and seeking an escape from the conversation.

"I messed up today, Sarah," Claire murmured, speaking from where her face pressed into her palms. "I really, really messed up."

She peered up at Sarah through her fingertips, redness rimming in her eyes.

"Listen, Larissa is a loose cannon. We all know that. It wasn't your fault."

"She shouldn't have been out. I let a visitor get mauled in front of our director! Heath expects me to keep everything in order, in line. I let him down. I let her down."

Sarah somehow managed to bite back the laugh that bubbled up in her throat, despite knowing full well the situation wasn't the least bit funny. It was odd and a bit surreal to see Claire in such a state. Claire tipped her face back into her hands, shoulders slouching. A nurse passed by, taking her sweet time as she gawked at the crumpled head nurse.

Sarah glared at the young woman, pointing a finger down the hall. The woman frowned back, pouting as she turned on her heel and walked away, though not before casting another lingering glare at Claire. It wasn't just Sarah who was shocked by Claire's moment of frailty.

Usually, Claire was a stoic woman. One could never tell what was going on in her brain.

Today she was vulnerable and fragile, like the little porcelain dolls Sarah used to collect as a child. She'd asked for one every year for her birthday until she was sixteen, when the shelf she'd had them on fell in a minor earthquake. The dolls shattered across the carpet, little flecks of white dotting the floor like stars.

Claire was those shattered dolls now, just as still and lifeless. Sarah wasn't even sure she was still breathing.

"Are you worried about being fired?"

"What? No. That is the least of my worries!" Claire whimpered, sinking down into the chair so that her short legs extended out in front of her.

"No one is going to sue you," Sarah said. Inhaling like she was about to dive deep into shark-infested waters, Sarah settled down in the chair beside Claire's and took the woman's hand in hers with a gentle squeeze. "It was a mistake. Nothing more than that. Even Heath has to admit mistakes happen sometimes."

"Mistakes aren't allowed here. You know that, Sarah."

The brunette nurse didn't respond, her lips tightening. She dropped Claire's hand, leaned back against her chair, and gazed down the hall. Her sneaker tapped against the marble, jiggling along with the tune of the soft music playing overhead. Claire had been distracted by the event with Larissa and Liv. The nurses had taken advantage of the opportunity by playing songs not on her planned playlist of sleepy classical songs.

Back in the rec hall, patients sat back on the sofas and chairs, staring at the screen. The medicines had been passed out, so most of the patients were on a different plane of existence now. They were floating in the sky or having supper with lost family or dancing in front of a full audience. A faint smile curved Sarah's mouth at the thought. She hoped wherever her patients were, they were happy. There was so little happiness in those halls.

"Is Mrs. Keller still here?" Sarah asked, turning her head to Claire, who had straightened up from where she'd sat in her seat and was dabbing powder over her tiny nose and glaring at herself in the small mirror.

Claire's face had hardened over again as she blinked her eyes, pushing back the faintest hint of tears in the corners of her eyes.

For a moment, the redhead didn't bother to answer the younger nurse at her side. Her thin, skilled fingers were dancing over her skull as she braided her hair over again so it lay smooth once more. Not a hair was out of place when she finished.

Clearing her throat and wiping the worry from her eyes, Claire's chin gave a tiny bob.

"Mrs. Keller is still here, somewhere. Heath is discussing Mr. Hogarth's last wishes with her. He's offered to offset the funeral costs...because of what happened." Claire grimaced again and dropped her head in her hands, shoulders slouching deeply. "I saw you talking with Mark earlier. Do you two know one another? Has he mentioned anything at all about what happened?"

"No, he hasn't," Sarah said. "I haven't spoken to him. He left, I think."

"Will you find out how he feels about this place now? If he presses charges…"

In a second, Claire had gone from a marble statue to a puddle in her chair all over again.

Sarah lay a hand on the woman's back, giving it a light and dutiful pat. To her shock, the woman's shoulders trembled beneath Sarah's fingers.

"Hey, listen…" she said before Celeste, another nurse, called out from down the hall for Sarah to help her with a wobbling patient.

"You go. Celeste sounds like she needs help," Claire insisted, her face still buried in her hands. "But please. Check with Mark. Find him?"

With a nod, Sarah drew up to her feet. The head nurse's small shoulders shook with a silent sob.

Sarah took a small step away, watching the doubled-over woman before turning and rushing toward the nurse who was calling for help.

As Sarah rounded the corner and vanished, Claire straightened up, pulled her shoulders back, and lifted her chin high. She smoothed her hair away from her stone dry face and smiled.

CHAPTER TWENTY

The expensive leather chair clung to Liv's legs and made ugly squeaking sounds every time she moved. Compressing her thin lips into a hard line, she resolved to sit as straight and still as she could.

Heath paced the perimeter of his office, circling her as slowly as a shark, gesturing with his hands as he spoke.

His office was how Liv would've imagined it. The walls had been painted a rich mahogany as if to contrast the sterile white of the facility's corridors. A small liquor cart sat propped in the corner. Despite the variety of expensive whiskeys, scotches, and bourbons that rested upon the wooden bar, it appeared rarely used. Heath had passed by the cart a few times, fingering the waxy lid of the whiskey as though he were contemplating pouring a glass. Each time he had moved on without doing so.

When the man spoke in his booming, proud voice, it echoed back against the small walls and hurt Liv's ears. She brushed her hand over the simple rose earrings she wore, tugging at the golden clasp. They were heavy, which didn't help her aching eardrums.

At least her face no longer hurt, though the bandage made her ugly. Heath had tried to tell her that wasn't the case, but there wasn't a person on the planet who could rock a big bandage on one cheek. If Liv were a man, she might appear tough and rugged. But she was a woman–a slim one at that– and it seemed more like she was trying to cover up something grotesque. She was glad her teenager wasn't there, or the girl would've taken pictures of Liv to put all over Facebook.

"Right, Mrs. Keller?" Heath smiled, interrupting Liv's thoughts and making her jump.

She'd stopped listening around the time he mentioned arrangements for Ralph's funeral. It wasn't something she wanted to contemplate right then. The more he spoke, the more Heath's charm seemed to fade, like a veneer slowly polished away. Liv wanted out of the cramped little office with its dark walls.

"You should have it on the grounds," he'd offered a few long minutes ago. "Your father had always loved walking the paths in the morning with your mother at his side. We have a space in the back where the sun makes the marble glow at sunset. It'll be the perfect place to honor his memory."

Liv had nodded along, allowing Heath to spin whatever luxurious tale he wanted to out of the fact her father was gone.

"Right," Liv replied with the hint of a forced smile.

You couldn't peer into Heath's flawless face and do anything but agree with whatever he said. His deep voice was a melody, a siren's call. For a moment, Liv imagined Heath basking on a rock in the middle of the ocean, his naked chest glistening under the sun, the rock warm against his back and palms as he sang aloud and lured helpless sailors to their deaths.

Liv giggled out loud and Heath's dark brow furrowed. Blushing, she cleared her throat and stared back down at her hands as Heath continued his speech.

"We'll cover all the expenses of course, and you'll be able to meet some of Mr. Hogarth's friends from the facility. He was well-loved by everyone."

Gray eyes shifted over Heath's desk, resting on the gleaming black metal of the urn before her. It sat close to the edge of Heath's tidy, long desk, and Liv couldn't stop staring at the thread of wood that kept the urn from plunging down onto the carpet.

They'd found it in the hall only minutes after Mark had vanished from their meeting. He hadn't had to use the bathroom at all. Her little brother had always been a bit flaky, and Liv had heard the desolation in his voice when he spoke about their father's death on the phone the other night. He was not taking the news about their father's passing well. He'd been shaky after losing their mother, but this was on a whole different level.

They were orphans now, though the concept sat strangely in her mind. She repeated it a few times, trying to make sense of the idea, but in the end, it made her sick to her stomach. A year ago, they'd had both parents, and now she and Mark were alone. She and her brother rarely spoke. Aside from the past twenty-four hours, it had been months since the last time she'd seen his name light up her phone. With their parents gone, there would be nothing left that united them. She may never see Mark again.

It might take another funeral to bring us together again.

They didn't have any other family besides her husband and her daughters. She didn't even know of any friends Mark had in New York. He'd moved away for college and never come back.

How would he cope with the loss after we both go back home, almost a continent apart?

"I'm worried about Mark," Liv sighed. The blonde woman clamped her lips together, shaking her head and pressing her fingers against her temples as Heath bent down beside her chair. "I'm sorry," she mumbled, "I shouldn't have said that. I think I'm exhausted."

"What are you worried about?" the director responded, waving away her apology with a dismissive hand. "We have psychologists here, you know. They could have a session or two with Mark while you're both here for the funeral."

Liv and her brother hadn't discussed how or where they'd have the funeral, other than arguing about whether or not to buy flowers. Neither one of them had been willing to broach the topic further than a simple scratch on the surface. To plan the funeral would be to admit Ralph was really gone. She didn't have the money to throw her father the celebration he deserved, and she was sure Mark was equally unprepared financially. So they would have little choice but to take Heath's generous offer.

"There's no way Mark would ever agree to see a psychologist," Liv chuckled. "He's mourning. He'll be alright. It's always a shock when something like this happens, even if you know it's coming."

"You know your brother better than all of us," Heath shrugged, still bent beside Liv's chair. She could smell his cologne, woody and fragrant. It reminded her of a forest on a moonlit night, though there was a faint sourness to it that made her lips pucker.

"Though it is odd he would leave without Ralph's remains," he continued with a thoughtful tap of his finger against his chiseled chin.

"I think he's struggling with this. Living so far away has been hard on him. Losing his wife a few years ago...he's faced several losses recently."

The dark-haired director sighed and nodded. "I can only imagine," he said. "The news was a surprise to all of us. I swear the entire place went silent from the shock of it all. You could've heard a pin drop."

Liv nodded in agreement and gave a tired sigh. "I should track my brother down. He couldn't have gone too far. Maybe he went back to the hotel."

"Of course. You have my number. Give me a call if you want to discuss your father's funeral arrangements or if you want to arrange a meeting with one of our specialists for Mark. I'll have them clear a spot for him right away."

"Thank you," Liv said with a shake of her head, allowing him to help her to her feet.

With a pleasant chuckle, Heath walked to the door of his office. He pulled open the door for her, gesturing her out to the hall. With a final shake of their hands, Liv plodded toward the front door.

Nurses bustled past, sometimes pushing patients in squeaky wheelchairs, as classical music played lightly overhead, making her sleepy.

She couldn't wait to get back to the hotel, check-in, and rest.

Liv was halfway down the hall before her entire body went stiff, her purse almost dropping to the floor.

"Oh, crap..." She uttered, whipping around on her heel and darting back down the hall toward Heath's desk where Ralph's ashes still rested. She'd forgotten to bring the urn with her.

The door was heavy and Liv had to use both hands to push it open. Behind the stark doorframe, she could hear the rumble of the manor director's raised voice as he roared at someone.

When she stepped into the room, he fell silent, eyebrows shooting up toward his salt and pepper hairline.

"Mrs. Keller," he said in surprise, hanging up his cell phone and setting it down on the desk and files and papers. "Can I help you with something?"

Blushing with embarrassment, Liv gestured at the urn without a word. She paused, head cocking to the side as she inspected a photo that was half tucked under a file on Heath's desk. She tried her best not to stare.

"Is there something else you need?" he asked, folding his hands in front of him.

Liv shook her head, tearing her eyes away from the little pigtailed blonde child in the photo, and picked up the urn.

"No, no. I'll be on my way," she said with a forced smile.

He nodded, standing up as Liv escaped down the hall. He frowned at the door as it closed behind her.

CHAPTER TWENTY-ONE

Mark turned in a slow circle, staring over the disheveled items left behind from his father's boxes. Though he'd never considered himself a neat freak, even he knew the hotel room was a mess.

The cardboard containers themselves had been ripped apart as Mark searched for any other clue to the mysterious photo he'd discovered. He'd found nothing other than a sticky note in Ralph's khakis with a phone number to an out of town Indian restaurant. The stack of pants once neatly folded lay turned inside out and strewn about, the scrapbook sat on the floor flung open to an empty page Mark had accidentally ripped, and the other assorted toiletries and items had been tossed into the corners of the room.

Mark stood in the sea of his chaos, observing it all with frantic but exhausted eyes.

There had to be something, some clue as to what that photo meant. He felt sure of it.

It was clear now his parents had been together at some point after Joan was pronounced dead. They had to have been.

But where were they? Was it possible they were still there in the darkened depths of whatever cave in which they'd been hiding?

Kneeling, Mark flipped open the scrapbook, turned to the back page where he'd stuck the photo, and inspected it once again. No matter how much he stared at it, begging his parents trapped behind the glossy film to speak, the picture remained silent and secretive.

Where were they when it was taken? Nothing made sense to Mark.

"Dad, what is going on?" Mark wondered aloud, as though he expected to hear the sage rumble of his father's familiar voice.

Mark brushed his thumb over the strained smiles of the pair. Their arms were wound tightly around one another. Their embrace was different than in the other pictures. Though the love and tenderness were still there, they clung to one another as though they were afraid the other would vanish forever. Joan was pale as a sheet, glowing in the flash of the camera. Her eyes were squinted from the brightness. She was dressed in an outfit Mark didn't recognize, ill-fitted sweatpants and an oversized shirt. Joan had always been the type to dress primly, dotting rouge on her high cheekbones and never going without her lipstick–especially when she knew a picture was imminent. In the photo, she didn't wear a trace of makeup at all, and her short hair was unusually long and mussed. Ralph kept one arm tight around her, the other outstretched to hold the camera, his face grim.

Mark closed his eyes, dropping the photo face down on the white paper sheet of the album. He could hardly keep his eyes on the pair in the picture, the anguish in their eyes was tangible.

Something had happened and it wasn't good.

"I'm going to figure it out," Mark promised them, his teeth gnashing. "If you're out there, I'm going to find you."

An abrupt knock at the door of his hotel room made Mark's hair stand straight, his eyes narrowing on the thin wood. Without a noise, Mark carefully closed the photo album and pushed it under his bed.

Moving with the slow deliberation of a cat stalking its prey, he crept to his feet and paced across the floor. Though the room was small and cramped, it felt miles long. He tried to cross the carpet silently. The old floor creaked and moaned with every delicate step he took. Whoever was out there would know he was inside. Mark pressed a brown eye against the peephole; however, he found the glass too fogged and dusty to see anything of note. He could only see a figure outside shifting back and forth.

For a moment he considered not answering, but, when Mark took a step back, the floor creaked so loudly the figure outside stiffened and pressed his or her face against the peephole, attempting to see within.

He had no choice now.

With a sigh, he wrapped his long fingers around the doorknob and twisted it open. He cracked the door open so he could peer out into the quiet hall. In his hours there, Mark hadn't heard anyone else walking back and forth in the hallway. He hadn't even seen any trace of the cleaning crew. However, when he'd woken, he found the drapes drawn back and the bathroom tidied.

"Oh my goodness," Sarah Kramer yelped as she stared at Mark's bruised and battered face with an expression of mixed horror. "Who did you get into a fight with?"

Mark's fingers flew to his face, brushing over the tender welts on his nose and forehead. In the excitement of finding the photo, Mark had forgotten the pain in his skull. Sharp discomfort flooded back as the pretty nurse gawked at him with those sapphire eyes. The ache between his ears made it feel like his entire brain was bruised.

"Honestly, I don't remember. I don't even remember coming back here."

Sarah frowned, reaching forward to sweep her warm hand against Mark's cheek. He froze at the gentle touch, eyes going wide, his heart stopping in his chest. She snapped her hand back, clearing her throat as her eyes dropped to the side before returning to him.

"Let me have a look at you. I'm a nurse, remember? I want to make sure you don't have a concussion."

"I don't have a concussion," Mark said, rolling his eyes.

"You don't recall coming back to your hotel, Mark," Sarah replied, pretty blue eyes flashing. "That's hallmark evidence of a concussion. Let me in. Any nausea? How's your balance?"

Mark edged backward, swinging the door open so Sarah could enter his cluttered space.

The willowy nurse took one step inside the hotel room, her gaze sweeping over the explosion of Ralph's possessions. She turned back to Mark and her brow wrinkled with raw concern.

"What's going on in here?" she asked, sticking her hands in the pockets of her white coat. She glanced at the door as though she were reconsidering entering.

Mark stared at her for a long, frightening minute.

Sarah could see his brain churning behind his reddened brown eyes, his mouth a straight, hard line on his face. He was contemplating something and Sarah was apprehensive about what it might be. There usually wasn't anything good about an expression as stark as his.

"Listen, Mark. I'm worried about your head. Let's have a look."

"Not now. I need to show you this," he muttered in response, crouching down to grab the photo album and thrusting it into Sarah's hands.

She opened it, resting it on one of her forearms. She shot an uncertain glance at the man still kneeling, then peered at the photos.

"This is so sweet!" she gasped. "Look at how young they are!"

Mark flipped to the back of the book, pointing a rough finger at the last photo as Sarah glanced up at him in bewilderment.

"What?" Sarah asked.

"This is recent. Dad got that sweater last Christmas."

"Okay?"

"Look at the back."

"Oh my gosh, they were together fifty years? I don't think I know anyone who's been together longer than a decade."

"My mom died before that anniversary, Sarah. She died six months after their forty-ninth. They couldn't have taken that photo. Where are they? Do you know where that could be?"

Sarah's smile faded as she stared down at the dusky photo, running a finger over Joan's hesitant smile. Mark could see it on the nurse's face; she was well aware of the strained emotion in the picture. It was etched in every line of their weathered faces. Ralph and Joan were terrified of something or someone.

"Like I said before, Mark, patients get their dates all confused. I've got no idea where they are, but it could be anywhere. We take our patients out on field trips all the time." Sarah shrugged, though her voice pitched higher than usual.

Mark wasn't sure if she was trying to convince him or herself.

He reached forward, resting one hand on Sarah's elbow. She stared at him, lips pursing then opening then twisting closed. Raking her brain for any possible explanation of the photo, Sarah gave a small shake of her head and focused back down at the pair. Though it was true the excursions the patients took were frequent, it was always to parks or museums—never to dark and creepy tunnels.

"This photo was taken at your facility, Sarah. I know it was. And it was taken after Mom died. I know that's the truth, and combined with what Dad wrote in his journal…"

Mark stopped, slapping one hand against his chest over the empty pockets of his jacket. His eyes roamed the room and the mess on the carpet.

"Sarah, the journal. It's gone!"

CHAPTER TWENTY-TWO

The woman just arrived."

He spoke into the phone with a hushed and hurried whisper, holding it cupped against his ear as he angled his body away from everyone else.

The man's eyes scanned the small space around him, one polished shoe clicking against the brown painted tile. He chewed his thumbnail. He'd kicked the troublesome habit months ago, but, whenever he had to make calls like this, the old compulsion resurfaced again like an aching tooth impossible to ignore.

He shoved his hand deep into his silk-lined pocket with an irritated grunt and shifted the phone closer against his cheek.

People roamed in front of him, poking at stale cookies that had been left out for a week and flipping through outdated brochures of all the fun events held outside the local vicinity. There was nothing to do nearby. There were no sights to see and no attractions to visit. They didn't even have a chain restaurant within the confines of the small town. There was only the one pizza place which had been known to reuse uneaten pepperonis. That was his favorite spot to recommend to the unlucky tourists stuck in the town from either a canceled flight or a visit to Springthorpe.

There were never more than a dozen people there, but, on that day, they all seemed to want to bother him.

He was a patient guy–always had been. That's what his mother had said about him anyway.

His brain churned from the phone call, and his eyes paused at the little, framed photo he kept on the desk, taking in her bright and cheery smile under strands of long dark hair blowing over her face. His fingers smudged the glass over the photo, blurring her familiar face and pink lace dress.

It'd been Easter when he'd taken that picture. It'd been their last Easter together. He was glad he had that photo now.

The person on the other end of the line was silent, as was typical. The quiet breathing breezed through the phone. The sound made him antsy. He drummed his fingers against the back of the receiver. The tapping beat through the phone, dancing over the line and closing the distance between the two speakers.

He didn't know much about the person on the phone. He'd still never met the person. He hardly even knew what was expected of him.

The quiet that lingered on the phone during these calls became painful. He wouldn't go as far as to label these short talks as conversations, as he did most of the talking. He was grateful the calls were few and far between–or they had been until recently.

Clearing his throat, he leaned over the counter and pressed one elbow on the hard wooden surface. He wasn't sure how to stop himself from rambling. He rambled when he was nervous. He was never sure what the person on the other end of the line was waiting for him to say. There wasn't any praise or disapproval, just the occasional muted grunt or sigh. When the person did choose to speak, it was never pleasant. He reminded himself the quiet was good.

When the person didn't hang up, the concierge supplied more information.

"She asked what room Mark Hogarth was staying in, then raced off up the stairs. She should be with him right now. I thought you would like to know she's one of the nurses," the concierge continued, pushing dark hair away from where it hung down into his eyes.

He inhaled a breath and held it, waiting for the person to reply. When no reply came, Stanley let the breath flow through his lips, counting to ten as he did so. His heart felt heavy in his chest, beating against his ribs with the steady power of a hammer.

Thump, thump, thump.

There was never a goodbye in these calls or even a notion of gratitude. When the person received what was wanted from the concierge, the phone was hung up and the line went dead. He'd be left with sweat collecting on the nape of his neck and a hope the phone would never ring again. It was an empty hope. The phone always did ring again with another request or another hiss of a sigh.

The person continued to wait. He could hear something faint in the background. Music was playing. Jazz. His mother had loved jazz.

He tilted his head upward, as though he could see through the two thick floors of the hotel separating him from where he knew Mark was staying. Curiosity festered inside of him.

What was so interesting about this Mark that all these calls had to be made? He wasn't sure the brown-eyed man was worth all of this trouble.

"Oh, sir," a woman interrupted the concierge's phone call, leaning against the desk and pointing a finger toward the bus schedules. "Do you know when the next bus will arrive? The time slots are all blank. We want to go into town and see those cute little boutiques that are in those pamphlets over there," she went on. "I have this friend named Betsy. Anyway, I want to get her a sun hat she can wear while she's gardening. She's a lovely gardener. You should see her roses. They're huge. Like grapefruits!"

The hotel concierge blinked hard, trying to make his expression appear as if he cared about the blathering woman in the floral dress. He knew he'd failed. He could see it reflected in her mystified eyes as she trailed off into uncertain silence, her smile now frozen on her bright pink painted mouth.

"The buses are out of service. That's what the red sticker on the schedule says, doesn't it?" he barked with the politeness of a garbage dump hound dog and pointed at the small red label crossing the empty time slots. "You've got eyes on your face. Learn to use them."

The woman balked, eyes widening at the crude tone of the concierge. "How rude!" she exclaimed, ruffling up like an irritated bird and shooting a scowl at the cluster of her baffled companions. With a shake of her head, she turned and shuffled back to the plate of old cookies. Her waiting friends exchanged low grumbles and glared over at him as though he'd shouted personal insults about all their families.

The concierge groaned as the person on the phone made a gentle tsk of his tongue. He wasn't supposed to be rude. For a second, he'd forgotten he was on the phone.

"Now, now, Stanley," the caller said as the concierge's face drained of color, the phone almost falling from his hand, "service is our priority."

"I'm so sorry," Stanley replied, unsure if he was trying to say it to the caller or the woman, tripping over his words as he tried to backpedal.

Leaning toward the offended lady to apologize, he reached out a hand to grasp at the sleeve of her fluttering dress. Stanley hoped it would be enough for the caller to forgive him. Before his fingers could brush the cotton dress, though, a tremendous bang echoed in the hall, followed by the stomping of hurried feet.

The door to the stairwell had burst open, and Mark and Sarah flew into the hotel lobby.

All eyes turned toward the breathless pair, regarding them with a mix of startled surprise and suspicion. Going silent, even the person on the phone seemed to know something strange was happening. The music was gone. Over the phone line, not even a breath was audible to Stanley anymore.

"Have a good afternoon," the concierge smiled into the phone, dropping it back down onto the receiver, and cleared his throat.

His heart still raced, echoing in his ears. He could barely comprehend his thoughts. He was going to hear about that later. He shouldn't have hung up in the middle of a conversation. Stanley knew the rules. That was two strikes in one conversation.

"Hello, Mr. Hogarth. How are you doing?" Stanley's voice flowed out from his lips in a surprisingly calm manner.

He'd expected his voice to falter, to be high-pitched with worry, but instead, it sounded as calm and collected as ever. His heart settled. The phone would ring again and next time he would do better.

"Mark, you need to stop and take a breath," the dark-haired woman following after him insisted. "You need to think about what you're doing. You're going to come off as crazy!"

"The police," Mark gasped, breathless from the run down the stairs and the adrenaline surging through him. "I need to call the police."

"Mark!" the nurse cried out, eyes blazing. "Wait for a second and listen to what I'm trying to-"

"No, Sarah, I don't have time to argue about this! My parents could be alive. They could be hurt. They could need help."

The off-duty nurse bit her lip and lifted her hands in a helpless act of frustration. "I understand you think something might be going on, but you can't just..." she trailed off, aware of everyone's eyes on them. She cleared her throat and dropped her voice. "You can't just make a scene. Not here. Not in this place."

Other people in the hotel lobby gathered around, murmuring to themselves at the mention of the police. With a loud gasp, the woman in the fluorescent skirt grasped at the cross dangling down her neck. Her bulging eyes turned toward Stanley and then back to Mark.

"What's happened?" she gulped, still half chewing one of the stale oatmeal cookies. "Was someone hurt?"

Mark didn't seem to hear the woman. His attention was rapt on Stanley and the phone. Sarah shook her head and turned toward the woman. Concealing a groan, her practiced nurse's smile lit her lips as she reached out and patted the woman's shoulder.

"Not at all. It's nothing to worry about. Right, Mark?" she added, prodding him.

Mark didn't answer, his eyes locked on Stanley. He wasn't going to listen to the nurse at his side.

Shame, really, Stanley considered. Sarah Kramer was a smart woman. He knew that from observation. He'd seen her plenty of times and hadn't needed to speak with her to know how keen she was.

"Please, the phone," Mark said. "I have to get in touch with the cops. They need to see this. It's about Springthorpe Manor. If something is going on there, the police can fix it."

The suited concierge smiled, pushing the handset across the counter toward the wild-eyed man. Mark looked like he hadn't slept in years, his face so battered he didn't seem like the same person who had arrived yesterday. He appeared more feral animal than human. Every breath seemed to shake through him like wind through the branches of a tree in the middle of an ice storm.

Stanley felt sorry for him. He'd never seen a bloody and unconscious man dragged through his empty hotel lobby before. The concierge hadn't been sure Mark would ever end up on his feet again.

When the nurse popped up at his desk twenty minutes ago, Stanley had held his breath and waited for her scream when she found his unconscious body. Mark was much stronger than Stanley expected.

Stanley didn't respect him for that; instead, it made him pity Mark further.

Being stubborn wouldn't get you far here. It'd get you killed. Less than twenty-four hours there and Mark Hogarth had already made an enemy more powerful than he could ever imagine.

While Mark lurched to the phone and dialed, Sarah's head cocked to the side as she gazed at the concierge. "Your eyes..."

She slid closer to Stanley, who kept his polite smile and lifted one brow.

He hated this part of his job, the awkward conversations and the trite questions. It was endless. Stanley adjusted his nametag while he waited for the woman to finish her train of thought, brushing his fingers over the rigid plastic.

Sarah observed him, her chin resting on her palm. "I didn't notice before that they're two different colors."

CHAPTER TWENTY-THREE

The patients swarming the nurses reminded Liv of the shark feeding frenzy exhibit at the aquarium back home.

They circled and begged for their medicines as the nurses doled out little paper cups with names written on them. The patients gulped them down. Some of the elderly didn't even wait for the water to wash the large pills down.

Had Mom or Dad been one of those sharks, circling for another quick fix to dull the pain in their bodies and their hearts?

She couldn't imagine them acting that way. Then again, Liv had trouble imagining them here at all. She'd visited them often at first. She claimed she did it as often as she could. She blamed the ever-lengthening time between visits on her children, her husband, and her job, but none of them really had come in the way. The truth was, she didn't want to see them. Every time she visited, their faces had shone a little duller, their speech had become a little slower, their stories had become a little more rambling.

Even with what she knew, that little ball of guilt she carried with her every day, it was still a struggle to accept it.

"Who do we have here?"

Someone interrupted her thoughts. She was grateful for that.

Liv glanced over her shoulder, taking in the old man standing at her side. He leaned on a walker with bulky forearms, his back slouched over like a steep stoop. Unlike the other patients, he didn't seem interested in the medicines. He was dressed differently as well, wearing a pair of faded and wrinkled scrubs instead of pants and a shirt.

He saw her eyes skim his attire, a grin brightening his pale face.

"I work here," he beamed. "Can't you tell?"

Liv offered a polite smile, the same one she used when her children told her they did something good at school or finished their homework.

"I'm sure you do."

He nodded with an excited grin. For a split second, Liv did miss her daughters. Then, visions of grubby hands and temper tantrums danced in her head, and she felt relieved again for the break from her family.

Nurses and orderlies passed by, uninterested in the conversation between the visitor and the old man. The medical staff walked in clumps of two or three with their heads bowed together as they pored over charts and files. Liv had meandered from one end of the hall to the other, searching for her father's room. She hadn't wanted to enter the room. It'd be too painful to see another person in there, living in the space her father had considered his own. She'd wanted to go there one more time in an attempt to recall the last words Ralph had ever said to her.

Her father had patted her hand with his cold one, his face so distracted Liv could barely carry on the conversation with him. It'd been only a month ago, but she'd known he hadn't had much time left, not with how distant and worried his expression was. She should've told Mark how bad it'd gotten. She couldn't now. He'd never forgive her. He'd never forgive her for any of it once he found out.

"Are you alright, dear?" the stranger continued, his voice gravelly and low, like two rocks scraping together.

When Liv turned to face him, his dull brown eyes widened round as glassy saucers, and he pushed himself up a little straighter. His fingers curled around the cool metal of the walker, leathery knuckles blanching a ghostly white.

"Ralph?" he said in clear shock. "Is that you?"

"I'm his daughter." Liv smiled again.

She smiled when she was nervous. She couldn't help it. She'd seen the smile reflected back at her once in a work meeting when she'd caught sight of herself in the window across the room. She'd been grinning like a manic clown, her lips stretched so thin across her face they almost disappeared.

She wasn't sure whether she should be offended that the senile old man had thought for even a second she was an aging grandfather. The man was a patient here, so she shouldn't take too much offense, she reasoned.

Trying to work her mouth back into a normal line, she extended a hand. When she was younger, Ralph had taught her how to shake hands.

"Smile like a lady, shake hands like a man," her father had said with a grin, grasping her small hand in his firm, warm one. She'd hated that saying of his, but she'd loved the attention.

"Daughter. Huh," he echoed like the word didn't fit right on his tongue.

She didn't know who this man was or why he was so interested in her.

For at least thirty minutes, she'd been standing rooted to the same spot in the manor's hallway. If she had moved, she would have had to consider her father's funeral and how they'd have to plan it and hold it in a facility he'd probably despised. There, in the middle of a busy hall, she could pretend for a little while longer it wasn't something she was forced to consider. The last thing she'd wanted to do was ponder what flowers he would have liked best–the answer of which was none–or, with her suitcase still missing, where she was going to find a black dress, or what various out of touch family members were going to be insulted that they hadn't received an invitation to the gloomy affair.

The urn rested nearby, quiet and condescending, watching her every move. She avoided it and wanted to handle it as little as possible. If only Mark had taken the thing when he'd left.

"Oh, his daughter?" he repeated once more, recognition lighting like a small flame in his brassy eyes. "Of course, you are. Liv, isn't it?" He sounded as though he wasn't sure why she was introducing herself, as though he'd known all along who she was.

Liv wasn't sure if he was toying with her or being serious. She cleared her throat, glancing around as though she were hoping someone would come and rescue her from the awkward conversation.

When her eyes trailed back up to the tall, bent oak of a man, he was still staring at her.

He gazed at her, analyzing her while also looking through her.

Everyone at Springthorpe was like that. It wasn't just the elderly patients. The nurses, too, all seemed to ignore her. She was used to being invisible. Her father had been the only one to ever really see and understand Liv. Still, the way the people moved–as though the halls were full of water and their arms and limbs were weighed down–was eerie. Like trains on a track, they focused on nothing but moving from one place to the other.

She could sense the miserable pull of the gravity there. The air was heavier inside than beyond the locked doors. Liv had the urge to run outside and gulp in all the fresh air she could, but she recalled the cemetery looming right by the front gate, so she changed her mind.

"Liv?" the man asked. "That's your name, right?"

"Oh. Yes. That's me," Liv responded in surprise, dropping her hand back down to her side when the man continued to ignore it. Her arm ached. She wasn't even sure how long she'd had it stuck out in front of her, hanging in the air. She was having trouble focusing. It was probably jetlag, though it wasn't like she'd crossed any time zones. The flight had been only ninety minutes, so it had taken her only a few hours to get there.

"I knew it," he grinned.

She hadn't expected him to know her name. She hadn't expected anyone, not the head nurse nor the director of the facility, to know or remember her name. It always surprised her when someone spoke it out loud.

"Ralphie talked about you all the time. His little Liv."

"Ralphie?" Liv said, unable to keep the shock from blooming over her typically expressionless face.

Her father hadn't ever been one to care for nicknames. It felt odd and foreign to hear someone refer to him with one. She wanted to ask him not to say it like that again.

"Yes, yes, Ralphie. How is he now?"

The man's eyes were a tawny brown, like a penny left out on the sidewalk for too long. The irises were dingy, feathered by pale white lashes that fluttered against his hollow cheeks. His bald head was shiny, reflecting the overhead lights like a disco ball. He was pale and gaunt, a tacky cardboard skeleton cut-out at Halloween.

He gazed at her in such an unfocused way she almost had to peer over her shoulder to make sure he wasn't talking to someone else, yet his eyes were piercing. She could sense his laser gaze, burning down to her bones. He could see all of her, every inch exposed, all the pages of the book of her soul strewn out in front of him. She couldn't help but sense he was privy to her innermost secrets, though she'd barely breathed a full sentence in his company.

She wished she could ask her father who this man was and why he insisted he was Ralph's friend. Ralph had never once mentioned him.

Liv cleared her throat and tucked a thin, stray lock of blonde hair behind her ear. She wanted to leave. She wanted to find Mark. She wanted to get on a plane and fly home. She'd rather be with her girls who weren't interested in her and her husband who didn't care for her than be stared at so intensely that she had to clutch at the hem of her shirt to make sure she wasn't naked.

"Actually, I'm here to set up my father's funeral. He passed not too long ago." She spoke faster now, trying to hurry through the unpleasant topic. She hated saying that. She hated admitting her father was gone.

Unable to stop herself from glancing toward the ebony urn on the chair, her eyes darted toward the small container. Even that short glance made a shudder roll up her spine. She turned away again with a jolting shake of her head.

The man went still, his eyes narrowing on her with that same burning intensity. Though his eyes were faded like yellowed newspaper and caked mud, they glinted as sharply as knives.

"That's Ralphie in there?" he asked, his eyes unblinking and round.

Liv wasn't sure he'd blinked even once since approaching her.

His whole body had gone still, a snake readying a venomous strike.

For a moment, Liv was afraid as she gave a silent nod, but then the storm passed over the man's face and serenity settled back on the man's weathered cheeks. Liv couldn't tell how old the man was, but he seemed ancient, like a silly caricature of Father Time. His flossy white beard curled around his chin.

"That's too bad," he sighed, the exhale whistling through his missing teeth. "My name is Graham Jones. I knew them both before. I work here, you know."

He stuck out his hand briefly, as though he wasn't sure why he did it. Before Liv could shake it, he'd curled his fingers back around his walker.

"Joan loves daisies," he continued, pointing at the catalog tucked into Liv's arms with the flowers strewn over the cover.

For a funeral book, it was vibrant, with pretty flowers, leaves, and swirly letters gracing the cover and pages.

Graham stroked his chin, then gave a little nod. "They grow in the cemetery between the dead oaks. You should bring her some. I bet it would cheer her right up."

Liv arranged a polite smile on her face she hoped didn't look too agitated, hugging the catalog closer to her.

She started to tell Graham that Joan was gone as well but she thought better of it. She didn't want to see his face change from pleased to riled again. She wanted to leave. She regretted having stayed at the manor to sort through the funeral packages they offered. She wanted to go back to her hotel room, call about her missing luggage, lay in the bed, and eat or cry or yell.

"I should be going," Liv said, reaching down to scoop her father's ashes back into her arms along with the funeral catalog.

The metal of the urn was cold and hard against her. It was difficult not to imagine how cold her father's skin must have been when they found him. Her throat felt tight. Liv had to force herself to swallow or she was sure she would not have been able to breathe.

"It was nice to meet you," Graham continued, scooting his walker a bit closer to her. "Don't forget the daisies for Joan."

Liv inched back then gave a prim nod. She turned on her heel, taking one step before she heard Graham take another after her.

Over her shoulder, his eyes rounded once again. His face drained of color as though he'd seen a ghost float right through the halls of Springthorpe Manor.

"Ralph?" he called in surprise, reaching toward Liv with a wrinkled hand as she backed away and strode toward the front of the building. "Is that you, Ralphie?"

CHAPTER TWENTY-FOUR

Officer Brian Schumacher regarded the situation splayed out before him with tepid curiosity.

Calls to the town police station were rare around there. So rare, in fact, the force consisted of fewer than a dozen, and that was including the two receptionists and the intern who brought them coffee on the odd days he came in. The deputies on duty had played seven rounds of rock, paper, scissors to determine who would be lucky enough to leave the station.

The last call had been a month ago. Lucille Abbott across town had lost her cat again. No one had played rock, paper, scissors for that call.

Schumacher gave a faint chuckle. It was just a matter of time before old Mrs. Abbott was sent to Springthorpe and out of their hair.

Folding his arms across his bulky chest, Schumacher leaned against the painted hotel wall and pretended to focus on the man speaking. Instead, he was scouting the hotel. He'd never been in there before. He'd have to bring his wife sometime for a little local getaway. She didn't care for the town. Most people who were unlucky enough to live in the shadow of the retirement home didn't, and they had to travel for at least thirty minutes to go out for a drink.

"If you look at this picture," the brown-eyed man instructed, sticking it up to the officer's face as Schumacher jerked backward, "you'll see what I mean! This tunnel or cave or whatever this is in the photo, it has to be part of the facility. My mother was down there after I was told she died...maybe my father is as well!"

Schumacher suspected drugs. A person didn't appear as ragged and worn down as Mark Hogarth did without drugs.

Their community was so small and disjointed they'd never before had to deal with someone with a drug problem. The closest high school was over twenty miles away, so they didn't even get to bust teenagers sneaking out after their curfews to pass a joint in the park. There was rarely anything exciting to do or investigate.

The officer shot a glance toward the dark-haired concierge who shrugged, then moved on to the woman standing beside Mark. Her eyes were bright and blue, but her brow was furrowed in concern. She kept nudging Mark, trying to hush him, but he insisted on babbling on about some crazed theory that his dead parents were still alive.

Schumacher hadn't taken any names or any statements. Mostly, he'd been excited to use the lights on his patrol car for a reason other than being late for dinner.

Springthorpe Manor had its own security squad, so the local police station never really had to take any calls regarding it. Schumacher had been inside once to escort a grief-stricken family member who refused to leave. He could still see Mrs. Andrews' face in his mind. Her gaunt, stricken eyes were painted on the inside of his skull. After dealing with that situation, he'd been glad Springthorpe called the police in for aid so infrequently.

Mark was still speaking, explaining something he'd found in a journal that had since been lost or taken–assuming it ever existed in the first place.

"My parents, they could still be alive. If they are, we need to help them. We need to find them."

Perhaps it wasn't drugs affecting the poor man, just grief. When Schumacher was younger and his pet Dalmatian had died, for months, he'd continued expecting the animal to greet him at the door or show up underfoot.

He knew how hard it could be for some people to accept a loss in their lives. He'd taken a course about it when he was training to be a deputy. He'd done all his training in the city and, when the only job offer he received was in this town, he'd been hoping to be able to work for Springthorpe. He imagined it was a perfect, cushy job, standing around while old people prattled on about their great-great-grandchildren. Instead, he was stuck hunting for illegally parked cars and drivers rolling through stop signs.

Schumacher knew he was supposed to be gentle and kind to the grieving man, but the other officers were calling in for pizza at the station and he wasn't going to miss the free meal. There wasn't time to humor Mark any longer. The roughed-up man needed sleep, not someone pretending to be interested in his delusional accusations.

"Listen, Mr. Hogarth, I'm going to tell you what I see," Schumacher stated, cutting off the rambling man. "I see someone who is devastated about his parents. Losing both of them within six months must be heartbreaking for you. You need rest and a good, hot meal, not a full-on investigation into a picture you found that may or not be recent."

"But the picture and the journal together-"

"What do you want me to do? Are you trying to report that journal as stolen?"

"Well, no, but…" Mark already felt foolish enough about misplacing his father's ashes.

"If you don't want to make a report, I'm not sure why you called me out here," the officer continued, sweeping a hand back over the walkie-talkie hanging from his belt.

He wanted to call in and ask if they had any pepperoni and mushroom slices left.

"This picture!" Mark said in irritation. "Have you even looked at it? Where are they? Why is Dad wearing that Christmas sweater?"

Schumacher laughed. The boys back at the station were going to love this. The closest they'd ever had to a call like this was when a patient at Springthorpe had swiped a spare nurse's uniform, slipped out the door, and called from the payphone down the road to report her socks had been stolen.

"Springthorpe is a tight ship. It's well-staffed. They have state-issued inspections every month, and that doesn't include the weekly tours they give to anyone who wants to check out their place. All family members are welcome to visit whenever they like." Schumacher recited from the pamphlet he'd read about the facility when he was still in training. "There is nothing suspicious about it. You're searching for any shred of hope that your parents aren't deceased. I'm sorry. But they're gone. It's time for you to move on."

Mark took a deep breath and gave a small shake of his head. "Please, Officer, listen for a minute-"

"I've given you more than a minute, Mr. Hogarth. I'm leaving. We may have people calling to report something of actual significance," Schumacher said, holding up his hands as though to create an invisible wall between them. "You're wasting our valuable time. Please, Mr. Hogarth, if you ever feel like calling again, leave a message with the operator."

Still chuckling, Schumacher turned on his heel and left the hotel while Mark's arms sagged to his sides.

CHAPTER TWENTY-FIVE

I can't believe it..." Mark muttered, dropping down onto the lumpy couch and crossing his arms.

The cushions were hard under his legs, poking all the tender, sore spots on his body. He felt like he was bruised and brittle all over. *How many times have I fallen?*

Irritation simmered inside of him, making him forget his discomfort as his blood ran hot and fiery through his veins. He could feel it tingling all the way from his toes to his fingertips, pulsing between his ears.

"I swear, the cops in this town," he started, lurching forward so that his arms were pressed to his knees, "are they all so condescending? He didn't even bother to listen to a thing I was trying to say."

Sarah observed Mark with a calm stare, her arms crossed over her chest.

Her white coat lay folded over the back of the couch. She wore her simple blue scrubs. They matched her eyes, which remained locked on the slumped man on the couch.

"What?" Mark snapped when Sarah continued to be quiet. He'd learned in the short hours they'd known each other that was not her typical behavior. "What is it you want to say?"

"Oh, are you finally ready to listen to me?" she replied, arms sliding away from where they were crossed so her fingers could coil at her sides.

Eyes narrowing, she leaned into one hip. Mark knew he was going to be scolded. He felt like a kid in the principal's office.

"Well?" she prompted. "If I'm going to bother with this, then I need you to listen to me."

"If you have something to say to me, Sarah, just say it," Mark sighed, running a hand through his hair. His fingers brushed over dirt and matted blood. His palm was smeared and filthy.

"When I say I need you to listen to me, I don't mean I want you to hear the words I'm going to say and then dismiss them because you don't like it. I need you to hear me. Really, really hear me. If you think anything is strange at Springthorpe, and if you think you can do anything about it, then-"

"What do you mean, *if* I think something strange is going on? You don't think this all points to something, Sarah?" He regarded her, straightening up on the couch and frowning. "You don't believe me?"

The thought hadn't crossed his mind, which made him feel foolish. The woman's stare softened as she gave a sigh and walked over to the couch. She sank down beside him on the small sofa, their knees touching.

"It's not that I don't believe you, Mark. It's just I've worked at Springthorpe for years, and I've never had any reason to believe anything's off. The nurses can be a little cold at times, but they do care about the people there. Your parents received excellent care, probably near the best in the country."

Mark gazed at where their thighs pressed together, the soft fabric of Sarah's scrubs smudged by the dirt from the cemetery earlier. She'd never changed.

He wanted to argue with her, to wave his photo around and insist what he knew in his heart to be true, but he bit the argument down on his tongue.

"What were you going to say?" he asked instead. "What do I have to do to convince you, to convince anyone about this?"

"First of all, you need to calm down," Sarah replied, laying one hand on his knee. His mouth pinched at her words. His eyes jerked toward her at the simple touch. The contact was comforting and gentle. It allowed the frenzy of his irritation and sadness to diminish.

"It's hard to be calm when I know something is wrong," he said.

One of those gentle smiles crossed her lips and it silenced him. The words he was going to say fell dead on his lips.

"I know," she said. "I know."

They observed each other. Sarah pulled back her hand and folded her hands in her lap. The small patch where her fingers had rested on his leg felt cold without her presence.

"What do I need to do?" Mark asked again. "How can we go about this?"

"I want you to go into that bathroom and give yourself a good look in the mirror, Mark. Is anyone going to believe you when you look as crazy as you do? I know there's a handsome man under those bruises and those wild eyes, but not everyone is as lucky as me." She smirked and Mark hoped he wasn't blushing.

When she gestured toward the bathroom, Mark gave a slight nod and climbed to his feet. With one lingering glance back at Sarah, he marched through the doorway and pulled the door shut behind him.

As he turned on the light, dull yellow rays flickered, illuminating his face with a strange and sallow shadow. The bathroom was small, fitted with a miniature shower so cramped Mark wouldn't have been able to fit behind the curtain without knocking his face on the rusted faucet. He leaned against the sink, resting his palms on the cool white porcelain as he inspected himself in the hazy mirror.

Sarah was right.

Between his black and blue face, swollen nose, and bloodshot eyes, Mark seemed more like one of the patients of Springthorpe than a newspaper editor from New York.

Turning the knob on the sink, Mark cupped his hands under the running stream and dunked his face into the icy cold water. He washed away the crusted blood on his lip and under his nose, watching as the clear water ran red with his dried blood. The chill of the water felt soothing against his bruises like he was bathing in ice.

He ran his wet hands through his bedraggled hair, washing away the dirty muck. He watched the crimson swirls vanish down the sink. *How did I manage to get so injured?* It couldn't have been just any trip and fall that had so severely banged up his face. *And how had I traveled back to the hotel?*

Giving a shake of his head, he sighed. There were too many things about this place that didn't make sense. There were too many questions that didn't add up.

He had to focus. All that mattered to him right now was figuring out the truth about his parents. If they were out there, he was going to find them.

When he straightened, he pressed a towel against his face and smoothed his hair, then took a deep breath and regarded himself once more.

Though he was still beaten and bruised, he was calmer now, his eyes less crazed. The cool water had helped with the redness of his sleepless eyes, and he no longer appeared to be a rabid beast waiting to attack someone.

Once he changed out of his wrinkled, stained clothes, he would be much closer to his former self.

If he was going to help his father and discover what was going on at Springthorpe, he had to be more composed. He couldn't let it get under his skin. There was too much on the line. His whole soul told him there was something wrong at that place, and he'd been the one to put his family there in the midst of it. Therefore, he was going to have to be the one to fix it.

With a heavy sigh, one he felt in his aching back and heavy shoulders, he pushed open the bathroom door and stepped back into the hotel room.

Sarah was standing there, her hands wringing in front of her. At the creak of the door, she whipped around to face him.

"Mark," Sarah said, swallowing a thick lump in her throat, "I think I have an idea."

CHAPTER TWENTY-SIX

This is a little unusual, sir," Cynthia James offered with a
stiff shrug as she stood in the middle of the office.

The room was cool. A portable AC unit sitting on
the windowsill blew steadily, vibrating with a low hum that
shook the window. Over the noise, she could hear birds
chirping outside, flittering this way and that between the small
trees of Heath's private flower garden. It was a lovely little
scene, the grass green and the butterflies colorful. Beyond the
garden sat the graveyard, separated only by the metal fence.
Though the flowers were delicate and vibrant pastel hues, the
fence was harsh and it glared under the sun.

Cynthia had never been asked to be seen by the
Springthorpe Director before. She'd only been working at the
manor for a few months, but she'd learned the less attention
you received, the better off you were.

If the head nurse never had to turn those stone cold green
eyes at you, you were a lucky, lucky worker. Cynthia was
afraid of Claire. Then again, most of the staff were. She'd been
told to be fearful of Heath, too, as well as some of the patients
and some of the nurses. Cynthia had been told to fear everyone
and everything and to stay as small and nondescript as she

could if she wanted to have a long career there, which she did. The money was good.

Cynthia had once tried to have a conversation with the grouchy head nurse. She had failed miserably. Apparently, asking Claire whether she preferred ham sandwiches or turkey had not been a suitable conversation starter.

The director of the manor was frightening in a different way. He was so handsome, Cynthia wanted to turn away. With his eyes upon her, she felt like she might faint.

Heath smiled at her, and her heart nearly exploded as he gave the young psychologist a comforting nod of his head.

"Ah, yes. I know it's quite a unique situation, Ms. James, but this is a special case, and I believe you to be the perfect one to handle it."

"You say the gentleman is struggling with his father's death?"

"Exactly. His sister came to me in a panic. He's not sleeping, you see, acting erratically. I've had several reports from the staff that he's frightening them. The sister, Mrs. Keller, is worried he'll get into trouble if he doesn't get a grip on his emotions."

Cynthia swallowed, her hands going clammy. "And you think...you think I'm the one who can help him? We have a trained grief counselor, don't we?"

When Heath smiled that stunning smile again, it was enough for the young psychologist to forget her nervousness.

She only ever worked with the patients of the facility, never their family members. She liked helping the elderly men and women who lived there. They often told her sweet stories about their children or their pasts. It was a cushy gig, to be honest. There was a reason she didn't work with more coherent patients or have a practice of her own, after all. She'd come close to flunking out of grad school. This job had been a godsend.

Her schedule was full, her time always taken by a rotating list of patients who came to her–drugged and smiling. Cynthia asked them questions supplied by the nurses. As far as she could tell, the questions were generic. She did perform a few tests on mental ability and a few on reasoning, but, mostly, she just listened to them talk. The patients rarely had troubles beyond feeling sad that a family member hadn't visited.

"We do, but I am positive you are the one up to this task," Heath replied without hesitation. "Our grief counselor is tending to a different matter at the moment, and we're going to be holding Mr. Hogarth's father's funeral here due to the unfortunate events that occurred," the man continued with a clear of his throat. "So we're going to need the young man to be present for that event. Don't you think?"

The psychologist gave a hasty nod, not that she would ever dare to disagree with Heath Dole.

"So, this is Ralph and Joan's son?" she asked, fidgeting with the clipboard in her hand.

She'd had a few conversations with Ralph, but Joan had been gone by the time Cynthia had started working there. Since he wasn't one to speak about himself, her memories of Ralph Hogarth were faint. He hadn't seemed to like their sessions much, but Ralph had always spoken so tenderly about his departed wife that Cynthia had enjoyed seeing him each time so she could hear a new story. Even in his decline, he'd had a way with words. He was able to paint the picture of their lives so that, even though Cynthia had never known Joan, she felt like she had.

"He is. His older sister, Liv Keller, is the one who asked me if there was any way I could help him. She was desperate, you see."

Cynthia gave a small nod, jotting down a note on the clipboard. "And it'll just be him at the meeting? Not his sister? I heard her cheek was ripped clean off." Cynthia gulped and clamped her jaws down so hard she bit her tongue and made stars dance in front of her eyes.

She shouldn't be spewing gossip to her boss.

To her surprise, however, Heath laughed and Cynthia relaxed, offering an apologetic smile.

"I'm afraid her cheek is still very much intact, Cynthia."

"I'll have to use the art room, sir," Cynthia said, messing with the slipping curls of the bun at the back of her neck. "My office is being renovated this week, so that's where I've been holding my appointments. The patients, they like to color sometimes while we speak."

Heath's perfect smile faltered, his eyes narrowing.

"I can always find somewhere else. Our classes are so full right now that it'll be hard but-"

"No, no, Ms. James. If that's where you've been holding your meetings, that will have to do. I'll have the grief counselor send over some questions to ask Mr. Hogarth about his stability."

Cynthia gave a sharp nod of her head though her voice was much less confident. "I'll go prepare now then, I guess."

As the door closed, Heath slammed a firm finger down on the glowing button on his phone set, addressing the person who had been listening in on the entire conversation.

"Make this happen," Heath growled, his fingers curling into hard fists, "and make it happen now."

CHAPTER TWENTY-SEVEN

Claire arranged herself, pushing her hair back from her round face and crossing one leg over the other.

Though her stature was small, she was regal in her chair, her neck long and straight, her fingers intertwined over her knees. Even in the murky darkness where they sat, she settled upon the padded benches like a queen.

The hall she'd chosen for them to meet was shadowed and quiet, tucked away from the bustle of the front lobby. It was the only place Claire had been certain would be free of nosy nurses, rushing orderlies, and the wandering eyes of patients. Despite the massive span of the facility, there wasn't much space within the corridors that didn't have wandering eyes and eavesdropping ears. Everyone in the manor hid a weapon behind polite smiles and stiff greetings. Everyone wanted something and was willing to do most anything to get it; the three hiding away for a secret meeting were no different.

Mark and Sarah, seated at her side along the bench, both stared at her with mixed expressions of uncomfortable silence. They seemed much less at ease than Claire was. Mark sat in tense silence, his jaw gritted, as though he was worried about what would spill out had he not clamped his lips. Sarah was much stiffer, her ankles crossing and uncrossing, hands folding then unfolding. Her eyes, however, were focused on the head nurse. Though she was tense, her armored poise rivaled Claire's. If Claire was the queen of the dusty bench, then Sarah was a warrior.

"What happened to your face, Mr. Hogarth?" Claire asked with a quirk of her eyebrow that told him she was hardly interested. "Did Ms. Larissa get a hold of you, too?"

Mark couldn't help but be caught off guard every time Claire spoke with that sugary-sweet southern drawl. Her face was so hard and her mouth was so curt, he expected her voice to ring out with the sharpness of a knife against his eardrums.

Sarah and Mark exchanged a startled glance, uncertain if stoic Claire was attempting to crack some sort of a joke.

While Sarah remained silent, Mark attempted a strained chuckle.

"No. I'm not sure what happened. I think I passed out." He shrugged and smiled again, though he watched her face for any sign of a change or a shift of the shadows on her cheeks.

Not even the corners of her mouth twitched. She was a statue, unmovable.

"Hmm," the head nurse replied, bright emerald eyes sweeping toward Sarah this time. "I assume you've been with Mr. Hogarth all afternoon and that's why your patients never received their lunches?"

Sarah's cheeks burned red as she cleared her throat and shifted from one side of her seat to the other. "I asked Celeste to cover for me. After we talked, I wanted to make sure Mark was okay."

"Well, she did not cover for you," Claire shrugged, "and she's not going to be the one to get in trouble for it."

Sarah had to resist rolling her eyes. Claire was back to normal after her small meltdown. The blue-eyed woman should've known Claire's open vulnerability wasn't going to last long. Asking her for this meeting might have been a mistake.

"That's fine, Claire. We're not here for me to have a performance review."

"That's true. Why are we here?" Claire gazed at Mark, her thin lips in a line.

Her eyes were unreadable, masked behind a thick layer of condescending apathy. She spoke like a robot, like everything she said was prerecorded. There was no note of slight surprise or interest in her monotonous southern drawl.

"Claire, I thought you could help us figure out something," Sarah said. "We don't know what to make of this photo, but I thought you might know something about it. Mark has reason to believe it was taken after his mother passed."

Sarah's eyes met Mark's, gesturing with her chin toward Claire. When Mark hesitated, Sarah placed a hand on his knee and smiled.

Claire took in the slight affection of the gesture. Her nose wrinkled.

"I don't have time to mess around, Ms. Kramer," she grumbled. "Unlike you, I have to get work done. You asked to meet, now get to the point."

Mark heaved a sigh and leaned over toward Claire, stretching a photograph toward the waiting woman.

"I found this in my father's things," he explained, letting her take the picture into her hands.

The arranged disinterest slipped from her stony face as her eyes widened. She stared down at the picture, then, with a heavy swallow, Claire shoved the photo back into Mark's hands as though it had burned her fingertips.

Mark could sense Sarah's whole body go rigid beside him, her eyebrows lifting in surprise.

"You know what this is, don't you?" Sarah asked Claire.

Mark didn't miss the startled awe in the nurse's voice. She'd been so sure Mark was wrong about there being any shadowy tunnel of doom beneath the facility, but the instant recognition on Claire's face was a clear signal something was amiss.

"Yes. I do," Claire replied, "but I don't know how Ralph and Joan would ever have found it or why they would be there."

"What is it?" Mark insisted. "Are they alive? Are they there?"

Sarah leaned forward, eyes rapt on the head nurse. "Claire, you have to tell us-"

A loud bang rocketed from down the shadows of the hall as Claire leaped to her feet, widened eyes sweeping the darkness as she gave a firm shake of her head.

"I can't. Not here. What you have in your hands could kill you. Think long and hard about that." Claire pushed past the pair, her shoes clicking down the hall as she ran to check on the commotion.

Mark and Sarah stared after her in shock before Sarah turned toward Mark and grabbed his hand. She'd been so suddenly filled with confusion and apprehension, she felt as though she could turn into a balloon and float away. Disbelief etched onto her beautiful face, she clung to him, a grounding force.

Her lips parted, then closed, her voice failing her. Mark gave a short shake of his head. He didn't need to hear the words. He could see it in her eyes. She believed him now.

More than ever, Mark was sure his instincts had been right. There was no more self-doubting. Mark and Sarah had discovered something significant. Even if his parents were no longer alive, there was something terrible happening at Springthorpe.

"We're going to get to the bottom of this," Mark whispered, though he wasn't sure whether he was speaking to himself, Sarah, or the spirits of his parents.

"We will," Sarah assured him, climbing to her feet with a nervous glance behind them.

The winding corridors and shadowy rooms of Springthorpe felt foreign to her like she'd never truly paid attention or taken in what was going on.

What was happening in the facility that had sparked such panic in Claire's eyes?

Oblivious to the blinking red light from the camera in the corner, Mark and Sarah paced down the hall after the head nurse.

CHAPTER TWENTY-EIGHT

A black and yellow butterfly fluttered from one flower to another. Its wings were long and sweeping and spread from its small, brown body. Tiny leaves danced under the microscopic breeze of its wingspan. It was the largest butterfly she'd ever seen in her life.

The little girl leaned closer, her elbows resting on the dirt as her small body stretched out on the glossy green grass. Her neon turquoise leggings fit sloppily, hanging too loosely around her waist. They'd told her she'd grow into them in time, and she liked the bright color which reminded her of home.

Her big eyes narrowed on the butterfly, watching with interest as it burrowed into the depths of the pink petals.

Sneaking up onto her knees, she held her hands out to her sides and then swept them closer, trapping the large butterfly between her fingers. She squealed with surprise at her victory, feeling the wings and antennae flutter against her small fingers as she drew it to her chest. She peered down through the tiny crack between her thumbs, though she couldn't see the insect trapped in the shadow of her hold.

A man's face appeared in the window facing where she sat. He leaned forward against the glass so that his forehead was pressed against it. It didn't seem to frighten her; instead, a bright smile lit her round face.

"Hi!" The little girl grinned with a faint giggle, opening her hands to the sun so the butterfly could slip free of her fingers.

Instead of flying away, the tiny creature fell limp onto the grass beneath her knees. It struggled for a moment before its wings went still, moving only from the faint breeze of the afternoon.

When she gave a quiet gasp and lifted her chin back toward the window, the man was gone. Tears pricked the corners of her eyes as she gazed at the motionless insect, the mournful silence broken by the faint buzzing of cicadas and bees in the distance.

The man stepped out the side door and onto the soft grass of the garden, fixing her with a sad gaze. He didn't speak much, and she didn't mind.

"I didn't mean to," the girl whispered, her voice thick with sadness. "I didn't know I'd hurt it. I thought I could take it back with me when I went down below. I thought he could live in my room with me."

She pushed her blonde curls away from her face as a single tear slid down her cheek. To the butterfly, she whispered a quiet apology that was lost in the wind.

In her time playing, her hair had come loose from the sparkly pigtail holders and fallen around her shoulders. Twigs and blades of grass clung to her hair from where she'd bounced across the small koi pond and failed to balance on the stepping stones leading from the wild roses to the milkweed. She loved this time in the afternoon when she could play outside and sit in the sun and sing as loud as she wanted. The other times she had to be quiet.

The man gave a silent nod while easing his body down onto the ground so he was seated at her side.

"Do you want to play for a little while?" she asked, trying to keep her attention from the downed insect. "I braided you a crown like you taught me."

He held out one large hand, letting the girl place a braided daisy band in his palm. The tiny flowers had been woven together in a circle. When she'd first arrived, the twists of the branches had been clumsy and rough, leaving the leaves and stems ripped and torn. She'd become good at it now, the crowns more intricate. She'd made three today; one for herself, and two for her friends.

She was never sure which of them would visit, but they always did. She liked when they would come and play with her, but she knew it meant it was soon time to go back inside. She preferred being outside to play, but being below was fun somedays as well.

At night, her friends would come and read her a story. Every day was a new story with pretty pictures and glittery words. There were stories about princesses and dragons and scientists and fish. She also had coloring books and all the candy she could eat. It was to make up for what she had to go through when the day was not a fun one.

When they'd told her they wanted her to play with them, she'd thought they meant on the swings or the slide in the playground where she'd used to play. She hadn't known they would take her on a field trip. She wasn't sure where her mother was or why she hadn't come to visit, but there were so many games and toys for her to play with there, she didn't miss her too much. Only at night when she couldn't sleep. They told her she couldn't have a nightlight, which made her sad. At home, she'd had a butterfly one that lit up with a pretty pink glow. In her new room, she could only close her eyes and pretend it was there with her, lighting the corner of the tiny room. She didn't mind that her room was smaller than her old one, and she didn't care that they didn't make her pancakes on Saturdays like her mom did.

She'd stopped asking when she was going to go home because it made her friends so sad.

Crawling with its wobbly legs, the butterfly lying between them moved its wings as the girl's eyes widened in joy.

"He's awake!" she cried, clapping her hands. "Mr. Graham, he's awake!"

Graham Jones grinned at the girl, ruffling her mussed hair as his daisy crown dipped down over one eye.

CHAPTER TWENTY-NINE

The taxi rocked, sending Liv Keller's shoulder jostling against the faded black interior of the door.

She supposed she could've walked back to the hotel. It was a nice enough day, the sun peeking out through the haze of cloud and fog that clutched to everything from the ground to the small homes to the tips of the streetlamps. Though it was still afternoon, the lights in the tall lamps glowed, making an aura of hazy gold shimmer like lightning bugs.

Shifting back to the center of the seat, Liv cast a careful glance at the man driving her taxi. He didn't speak; his eyes remained on the road. He hadn't said two words when he pulled up in front of the manor. Without meeting her eyes once, he'd gestured at the meter in the front of the taxi. When Liv had agreed to the cost of the fare, he'd pulled away from the curb and rounded the bend.

Though the heat was on in the taxi, Liv shivered and shrank down into her heavy wool cardigan. She'd have to thank Mark when she saw him again for reminding her to bring a sweater.

Under the arm of her sweater, she ran a hand over her forearm, fingers brushing against the bumpy flesh. Her whole body still tingled from the strange conversation she'd had with Graham Jones, like her veins were trying to crawl out from beneath the layers of her skin and muscle.

Though the entire town was making her feel uneasy, there'd been something in Graham's dingy, copper eyes that stayed with her, like she could sense him watching her all the time.

There was something wrong with that man, she was sure. And it wasn't just the way he had referred to her father as Ralphie.

The urn sat next to her, buckled in as safe and secure as she'd buckled her children into their seats back at home. When the taxi lurched to a stop, the cold metal bumped into her side, jabbing her with the golden rimmed lid and making her jump. She grimaced, poking it aside with a finger and shaking her head.

Pressing her face close to the window and squinting, Liv peered into the haze outside.

The only hotel within the town limits, the building was old and stout. Green vines tangled high up its walls. Its windows were tinted so no one could peer inside. Old-fashioned, red blinking letters settled over the teal awning. *Stalwart's*, it read, the initial 'S' only partially lit.

The driver tapped the meter. The red numbers on the dark screen scrolled along, charging her nickels and dimes for every second she put off walking inside.

"I'm going," she said. Her voice broke the heavy silence of the cab so sharply it made her wince. "Thank you."

Robotically, he stiffly stared straight ahead as Liv handed him some cash.

Shuddering, she fumbled over another thank you to the taxi driver and climbed out of the vehicle, hugging her purse tightly against her side with the urn tucked up under her thin arm.

The mist was so cool and thick it was tangible. Tendrils of smog ran sharp nails down her back as though the bulky sweater wrapped around her thin form was nonexistent. It was Thomas's sweater, too large and heavy and too scented with scotch he had spilled on the sleeves. She had tried to fall asleep on the airplane but couldn't because the scent of alcohol made her head ache.

An owl hooted from where it sat perched on the hotel awning, its glassy yellow eyes locked on Liv. The afternoon sun was fading, the heat of afternoon ebbing into the chill of the evening.

While she couldn't be sure her brother was also staying at the hotel, she doubted he would have found a room anywhere else. She hoped he was here resting so she could hand over the urn she was still toting around and then begin to track down her bags. She wouldn't be able to relax with the black metal of the urn staring at her from across her room. She'd rather leave it with the concierge than take it to her room with her.

Shielding the mist from her gray eyes, Liv heaved a sigh and shoved the door of the hotel open so she could slip inside.

Warmth embraced her, stroking her hollow cheeks and pulling her further inside over the soft carpet of the lobby. For a second, the change in brightness blinded her, forcing her to blink her eyes hard to persuade the black swirling dots to melt away. The main room of the hotel was decorated with the same elegance of a gaudy costume diamond ring. The colors were a little too vibrant, the gold trim of the paintings and baseboards too gleaming. It was kitschy, borderline tacky.

Liv didn't like it. That came as no surprise to her.

"Hello, ma'am," a man said from behind the desk as Liv swiped at her still fuzzy eyes. She turned to face him with a quip not to call her 'ma'am.'

The words, however, fell flat on her tongue. Sucking in half a breath, Liv went still, staring at the concierge as though she wasn't sure who he was.

Shoving limp strands of blonde out of her wide eyes, she rubbed again at her closed lids. When she finished, black mascara tracked sideways across her cheek.

Standing as stiff and silent as the taxi driver had been, the man continued to smile, the kind of smile that seemed to be painted on his face.

"It's you," Liv said, drawing her purse closer to her chest. A few coins spilled out, bouncing around her feet on the carpet. "You're that man from the airport."

"I'm sorry, ma'am," the man with the different colored eyes replied. A cool smile graced his lips. "I've never been to the airport."

"But I saw you there today," Liv insisted. "This morning. My luggage was gone."

"That's terrible to hear. Are you checking in?"

Liv paused, stealing a glance at the swinging entrance door like she was considering escaping, but she was exhausted. Everything down to her bones hurt. She needed to lay down and rest for a while. This was the only hotel nearby, and she wasn't about to get in another taxi to travel twenty miles to another hotel.

"Yes, I'm checking in," she sighed, edging closer to the desk. "I made the reservation already."

A glance around the quiet lobby told her she probably hadn't needed to do that. There didn't seem to be many others there. Liv could hear the faint flare of jazz music, but she couldn't place from where it was coming.

The concierge's fingers moved like lightning, fluttering around the keys like a hummingbird would flit from blossom to blossom. She watched as he typed, trying to recall how the man at the airport had done so.

It turned out, there wasn't much difference, though Liv wasn't sure how many different ways people could type. His hands seemed so similar. He had small palms with long and tan fingers that could've been a pianist's.

At Joan's behest, she'd taken piano lessons when she was small, but she had neither the grace nor the interest to stay with it for long.

Liv's eyes drifted up, sweeping over the polished nametag clinging to his black-suited lapel.

"So, Stanley, you've never been to the airport?"

She tried to determine how long it would've taken to get from the airport to the hotel as well as to recall how long she'd stayed at Springthorpe. Time, however, seemed to blur together. There was no morning, afternoon, or evening; there was just weary grief. She was pretty sure the man would've had time to finish at the airport, change, and reappear at the hotel.

"Not once. Not much a traveler," he shrugged. "I like my feet to stay on the ground. Planes make me nervous."

Liv forced a civil smile, unconvinced by his cavalier tone. He extended one of those doll-like hands of his. Her hotel key rested between trimmed nails.

"Third floor. Room 318," he announced.

The key was a simple square of red plastic with the word *Stalwart's* emblazoned in cursive yellow across the front. Like the carpet and the décor, it was garish. At least she wouldn't have to worry about misplacing it.

It was only as Liv turned to walk toward the elevator that she paused and turned back over her shoulder.

The concierge was still watching her, that frozen smile back on his lips. He met her eyes as she turned. His gaze hadn't turned away for an instant.

Why was it in this town she could go nowhere without feeling seen? Liv thought. For a woman who had spent her life disappearing, this was disturbing.

"I never told you my name," she said, the words making a shiver roll up her back. "How did you know what room I had?"

"We've only got the one check-in today," he shrugged, "It was easy to guess. By the way, the elevator is under maintenance. You'll have to take the stairs."

Liv didn't answer, giving a slight shake of her head and entering the stairwell. Pausing on the first step, she watched as the heavy door slammed behind her, sending a low boom reverberating through the passage. Not a fan of physical exertion, she paced up the steps.

By the time she arrived on the third floor, she was already damp with sweat, her purse dangling from her hand. Upon entering her room, she glanced around and turned to the closet. She set the urn within the small space, sliding the white wooden door closed in front of it.

That way, she could try to pretend it didn't exist. It wasn't like she was going to be putting her clothes in there anyway, not with her luggage missing.

With a sigh, she straightened and inspected herself in the nearby mirror noting the bandage on her face and hoping her skirt wouldn't wrinkle over the next few days she would have to wear it. She slipped out of her black kitten heels, her feet brushing the rough carpet, when the bedside phone rang.

Was it Stanley? Was he going to admit he'd been at the airport and, for some reason, hadn't wanted me to know?

That same feeling bubbled up in Liv, the one she'd sensed when Graham had approached her and the one she'd had in the taxi–the one that was as constant in that place as the fog.

Telling herself she was being silly, Liv walked over to the phone. She lifted the receiver and pressed it to her ear.

Though Liv's lips opened to speak, it was the caller who broke the silence first with a familiar tone that made Liv sink onto the corner of the quilt-covered mattress.

"Tonight, up here. Tomorrow, down below," the distinct voice chuckled into the line before it went dead.

CHAPTER THIRTY

Mark paced the hall, hands stuffed in his pockets, chin tucked down into his chest, face puckered in intense concentration.

From where she leaned against the wall, Sarah's glazed eyes followed his path.

Four years. She'd been working there for four years and never thought anything out of the ordinary was happening within the walls of that facility. She had felt safer and more at home there than she did in her one-bedroom apartment in the city.

What had that photo of Mark's parents meant? Why had it incited such fear in the head nurse's green eyes? What did any of this mean?

Mark whipped around for at least the hundredth time, pacing back down toward the front of the hall.

To save power, the lights on the corridors were programmed with emergency lighting only. So the halls were dim. The well-lit areas were on the other side of the building, where most of the classes and programs were being held. Mark's shoes squeaked with every step he took, the sound echoing around them.

Turning her blue eyes in his direction, Sarah watched as he passed her once more. His lips were moving as if he were talking to himself.

She worried that he might lose his cool again. If he did, they could kiss goodbye any chance of finding out what was going on at Springthorpe. She'd expected Claire to laugh at the picture, or at them, for assuming there was anything foul about it.

That was not the case, however.

Sarah shifted from one foot to the other, waiting for either her brain to sort the sense out of this mess or for Mark to come up with some genius plan.

At the moment, it seemed like neither was going to happen.

The squeak of Mark's sneakers turned into a squeal as he whipped toward the waiting nurse.

"Mark?" she said, pushing up from the wall as a slow grin twitched at the corner of his mouth.

When he smiled like that, with bright and clear eyes and a boyish smirk on his lips, it made Sarah's heart skip a little beat. She cleared her throat, trying to shoo away the silly thought, and shifted from one foot to the other.

"You know," Sarah said, her mouth moving quicker than her mind, "when your face heals up a bit, you're going to look like a real badass."

"If a badass gets his face all beat up from passing out," Mark retorted. "And I don't think that's how it works...But, Sarah, I think I've got it," he continued, his hands slipping out of his pockets as his arms crossed over his chest. His smile widened a bit more, his chin bobbing with a nod. "I have an idea."

"Let's hear it, Sherlock," Sarah quipped back, tossing her hair over her shoulder. "How are we getting to the bottom of this?"

"The art room," he replied, "what can you tell me about it?"

Sarah paused, head cocking to the side, "The art room?"

Mark nodded, eyebrows lifting.

"Well…" Sarah paused, tapping a finger to the slight cleft of her chin. "It's…got colored pencils in it."

Mark laughed and rolled his eyes. "That's all you got? Nothing else?"

It was the first time she'd heard him truly laugh, the kind of laugh that ripples through the chest. Before that, his forced chuckle had held the weight of uncertainty and grief.

"And art supplies. And paper."

He stepped closer to her, shaking his head as he waved away her straightforward suggestions.

"The concierge at my hotel told me to look at the art room. He said it might interest me, or something."

"That's nice," Sarah responded. She worried that Mark had suffered another breakdown. Or maybe it was his concussion acting up. "But what does that have to do with anything?"

"Maybe nothing," Mark smirked, in that same striking way that made Sarah's throat go tight. "Maybe everything."

Even bruised and blemished, he was a handsome man. Sarah could see the traces of Joan in him, from the sparkle of his brown eyes to the lopsided smile on his full mouth.

Sarah bit the tip of her tongue trying not to make another comment about it.

"Can't argue with that flawless logic, Mark Hogarth," Sarah said, rolling her eyes. "I'll take you there. We're already pretty close. It's down this hall."

The woman brushed past him, her fingers warm on his elbow as she gestured for him to follow.

When she stepped in front, Mark couldn't resist touching the spot of his shirt her fingers had grazed. It was still warm from the touch of her hand on the fabric. It was odd, what that sensation did to him. He could feel warmth not just on the pads of his fingers but also somewhere deep inside of him, somewhere he had forgotten for the longest time.

He tried to place the feeling, but Sarah's blue eyes glinted in the darkness.

"You coming, Sherlock?" she asked.

Mark gave a quick nod and followed the dark-haired woman as she turned and wove her way through the inky black of the halls. The darkness made Mark feel like a child again, hiding under his sheets and fearing the creatures of the night. With every turn they made, he wasn't sure what was waiting for them. He couldn't shake the feeling something was about to leap out at them.

"I'm sure we'll be able to convince Claire to talk to us soon about that picture," Sarah considered as she walked, her white jacket fluttering around her thighs. "I still can't wipe that expression of hers from my mind. It's like she was afraid of something."

Mark was glad for the break in the quiet.

"Or someone," Mark murmured in response. "We just don't know who yet."

Sarah gave a small shake of her head, pointing down the hall. She tried to make a list of anyone at Springthorpe Claire would fear, but she was unable to identify a single suspect. Claire was fearless.

"The room is right down here."

As Sarah charged on, Mark's footsteps stalled.

"Hey, wait," Mark called, stopping in the middle of the shadowy hall as Sarah frowned at him in confusion.

"Why?" she murmured, pointing over her shoulder. "Like I said, it's just over here."

"It's not that," he replied, his voice dropping into nervous quiet.

Mark's tension made Sarah edgy as well, her eyes darting around the shadows like she was expecting to hear someone chasing them.

"Um, listen," Mark said, rubbing his jaw as he tried to sort through the whirlwind of thoughts and emotions swirling in his brain. He inspected his shoes, noting they were still covered in dirt, before running a hand through his hair.

"Sarah, I want to thank you. I know you didn't believe me before, and you may not believe me still, but it means the world to me that you would help. That you're here."

Sarah laughed, blue eyes like jeweled beacons in the dark hall as she trotted back to his side.

She reached out and pressed her hand against his cheek, letting it linger for a second before her arm dropped back to her side. Her fingers left electricity dancing over Mark's cheek, causing him to suck in a slight breath of surprise.

"I do believe you, Mark," she responded. "I don't know what that photo means, and I don't know what we'll find, but if your parents are out there, we're going to find them. If they're not, we're going to figure out what happened."

He nodded in firm resolve. "You're right," he said. "We'll figure this out."

While he wasn't sure how they were going to do that, he was hopeful that the art room would hold a key. And now he had a companion in this.

"Here, like I said," Sarah said, "around this corner is the-"

Mark gasped as they stepped around the corner. He took a slight step to the side, reaching out a hand and pressing his palm against the wall as though he needed the wall's assistance to stay standing.

"What's wrong?" Sarah asked, retreating to his side and slipping an arm around his waist. "Did you hear someone?" she hissed.

"Just, Sarah, I need a second." He rubbed at one of his temples, wincing.

Something clawed at the back of his brain, making his whole head throb. There was something important about this place in the hallway–and not just because of the art room.

"Holy crap," Mark whispered, staring with wide, glassy eyes down the hall. "Sarah, I've been in the art room. Someone attacked me. That's how I ended up back at the hotel."

"Wait, Mark, what?"

He rushed forward, pushing into the room and taking in the vibrant markers and rainbow-colored pencils. It was all the same except for one significant difference.

"The pictures..." Mark whispered, turning to Sarah. "There were dozens of pictures hung up on the walls. I saw them!"

Sarah turned in a slow circle, taking in the barren walls. She rarely stepped foot in the art room, but she'd seen the pictures before.

"I don't know what to tell you," she said. "I don't know anything about the decorations here. I don't know where they would have gone or why they'd be taken down."

Mark circled the room, staring at the barren walls. All that remained of the drawings was a single piece of tape with a torn edge of a paper. He reached forward, running his fingers over the small, transparent adhesive strip.

It was gone, all gone. There'd been something here that would have given them a direction, Mark was sure of it. He'd had his chance to figure out what it was before, and now he'd lost it forever.

It was a dead end.

Mark gritted his teeth, yanking the remnant of tape off the wall. It couldn't end like this. Not when it was just beginning.

Behind them, the door creaked. Both Mark and Sarah whirled in surprise, Sarah's hands curling into fists and lifting in front of her like she was ready to attack someone. Mark, meanwhile, stumbled to the side and knocked over a box of crayons that spilled along the sparkling tile.

Claire appeared in the cracked open doorway, the sliver of a woman so tiny and frail. Her eyes were still wide, but her jaw was set.

"You two," Claire whispered, her pale skin glowing like the moon through the shroud of darkness. "The cemetery. Look for the daisies. You'll find what you need to know."

She slipped back into the hall. Mark ran after her, tripping not only over his own feet but also the crayons.

"Wait, Claire!"

"I can't say any more," she hissed, lips curling back from her teeth. "They're watching. Always."

"My father. My mom. Are they alive?"

Claire stared at him, her glassy green eyes a mirror that reflected Mark's troubled face.

"You saw the ashes," she said, before turning on her heel and melting away among the shadows.

CHAPTER THIRTY-ONE

I told them," Claire said into the radio while leaning against the wall of the room as three nurses shifted papers around in front of her, "just like you asked."

She crossed one ankle over the other and smoothed a pale palm down the front of her jacket. It was spotless, a clean and bright white that matched the clean walls and the sharp overhead fluorescents of the small office space.

The trio of nurses shifted in precise and synchronous movements; one sorting, one signing, the other filing. Their gazes did not waver. No one was willing to chance being caught in a moment of distraction. They focused with laser intensity on their papers, making sure everything was perfect before they passed it down the line. The box at the end of the table was large and so heavy it'd taken all three of them to heft it up onto the heavy wooden surface. Claire hadn't helped, though one critical eye remained on the trio at all times.

"Ladies, come on now," Claire groaned, flicking her red locks back from her forehead with one hand while the other still held the radio against her cheek, "you're taking too long for all of this. Hurry up."

The radio crackled with static and Claire gave a faint nod as though she understood the popping noise, sliding it back onto the band of her fitted pants.

One of the nurses swiveled where she stood, holding out a single sheet of paper with black type and markings littering the front. The other two glanced at her and then back down at the documents before them. They couldn't continue their tasks until the third returned to her position.

"This is Larissa's report?" Claire asked, settling down into a cozy rolling chair and curling her body into it with the poised elegance of a cat.

Her green eyes narrowed, inspecting the words printed in the margins. "Is she not responding to our experiments?"

"She is not," one nurse said, giving a faint sigh. "I don't think she's going to be of much use down below."

Claire didn't answer. This wasn't good. They'd had high hopes for Larissa. Her brain was a fascinating thing. Unfortunately, the old woman was not the first hopeful subject to have disappointed them. She wouldn't be the last, either.

"We need your approval for these as well," the young nurse said, gesturing toward the pile.

The girl paused, taking a moment to fiddle with the nametag pinned to her chest while the other two grimaced. *Celeste*, it read, *Celeste Janikowski, RN*.

It wasn't really her name, not her first name anyway. But Sharon was so mundane and bland compared to Celeste. They'd told her it didn't matter when they hired her. It wasn't like she had a medical degree. Why would it matter if she chose to go by her middle name?

Claire arched a delicate eyebrow, judging the young nurse before she leaned forward to inspect the papers. A spreadsheet stretched over the pages, the columns filled by pencil. When Claire viewed it again in an hour, it would be type-written and free of errors. Everyone in this room knew the cost of a mistake.

"This is the next group?" Claire asked, running a finger over a list of names delineated before her.

"Hmm...switch Kelly Turnbull and Edward Vance. Edward has been showing some signs of hallucinations. Leave Kelly up in the main room for now. She has a brother who visits her."

The young nurse nodded, giving a slight sigh as she rubbed the eraser end of the pencil on the paper. Celeste had spent three hours of her own time the previous night creating the list and studying the patients' living relatives, visiting schedules, medications, and expected life remaining. It'd been draining.

She couldn't even sip a glass of wine while she did it, in case she missed the smallest detail.

She wasn't sure why she bothered working so hard. It wasn't good enough for Claire. Nothing ever was.

"Where is Edward right now, anyway?" Claire inquired, slipping her pen out of her pocket to bend down over the paper and make a slew of changes and corrections.

She didn't miss Celeste's lips twist into a pout, her arms folding in front of her.

Claire rolled her eyes at the paper.

"He's eating a late lunch. Then he has a session with the new psychologist."

"Perfect," Claire stated, signing her name at the bottom of the paper. "What should his time of death be, Sharon?"

The girl winced at the misuse of her old name, Claire's eyes blinking at her grimace.

"He returns to his bed by seven thirty." Bouncing up onto her toes, the wide-eyed nurse replied without correcting the head nurse.

"Fantastic. Time of death will be recorded as 8:00 p.m. Does he have any family? Will we have to arrange an urn?"

Celeste shook her head, eyes dropping to the side. "No. Not this time."

"Even better."

Claire flipped through the rest of the stack, signing her name on the death certificates for the not-yet-deceased.

When she finished, she leaned back in her chair and beamed up at the young nurse.

"On your way, Sharon. I want the art room full next month."

CHAPTER THIRTY-TWO

The hummed melody reverberated through his throat and tickled at his thin lips as he closed his eyes and bobbed his head with the simple rhythm.

The origin of the song he'd so often hummed finally came to Graham Jones.

It'd been driving him crazy to have the song stuck in his head, playing on a constant loop while he strained to recall where he'd heard it.

He'd thought perhaps it was a song played in the background of the black and white movie they showed daily in the main rec room of the facility, but he'd watched the film three times now and hadn't been able to place the tune. He thought it could be music that a nurse had played over the speaker system while Crotchety Claire was out of the facility. That's what some of the nurses called her anyway. He, for one, thought she was nice. But he did consider Crotchety Claire a funny name.

A faint chuckle warbled through his chest before he stifled it with a slight clearing of his throat.

An hour earlier, he'd slipped into room 36C again while the new patient who dared sleep in Ralphie's room was meeting with a counselor. The last time Graham had heard the familiar song had been in that room.

The woman with the kind brown eyes used to sing the sweet words, stroking Ralphie's hair as his head rested in her lap. His whole body would be still as she calmed him from the panicked nightmares that made his chest rise and fall. Ralphie had experienced many bad dreams, and Joan was the only one who could soothe him. Ralphie would gaze up at her with those gray, watery eyes while she ran tender fingers through his silvery hair.

Graham had been jealous, but he didn't say anything. He didn't have to. Soon after, both he and Joan had been taken below while Ralphie was left behind. Then, while Joan stayed below, Graham had been let free to play with Ralphie as much as he wanted to.

Some of the words came to mind, and Graham wanted to sing them out loud as his heavy shoes crushed the brittle green grass, but the pretty red-headed nurse had asked him to be very, very quiet.

Graham loved to play. The games she asked him to play were so exciting he could barely contain himself sometimes.

She had asked him to pretend to weigh so much he could barely move as he edged down the halls among the others. She had asked him to listen and to go as long as he could without speaking. She had asked him to explore the winding tunnels, play with the little blonde girl in the garden, and even play chase with Ralphie's son in front of the art room.

Graham had played too rough that time, but Crotchety Claire had assured him that Ralphie's son was okay and that she would have him sent back to his hotel to rest.

The most recent game he was asked to play was even more fun than the rest. He was so glad to be out from the dark down below. It hadn't been any fun down there. Those games hurt his mind and made his body ache. Though he had lots of friends down there, he liked to play in or outside the manor instead.

He danced between the trees, lifting the heavy stick up in the air as he spun in a little circle. The sharp bits of painted metal tacked into the dense wood glinted in the afternoon sun. Graham smiled. He'd made it in the art room. That was another game Claire liked to play; arts and crafts were her favorite.

Now he would get his chance to share it.

Realizing he was making too much noise, Graham bent down behind a withered old oak in the graveyard, feeling the familiar gaze of Springthorpe's tinted windows behind him. He was sure she was in there right now, watching him play his game and making sure he followed the rules. He wanted to turn around and give a happy wave to her. But he didn't. He pressed his palm against the tree trunk and leaned around the side.

The pair walking several yards ahead of him were talking in low, hushed voices that danced in the cool breeze. He closed his eyes and listened but couldn't decipher what they were saying.

The brunette woman shivered, digging her hands into her pockets as Ralphie's boy slid out of his jacket and wrapped it around her shoulders. *So nice, just like Ralphie.*

Graham knew who the female was. She was one of the nurses who worked in Springthorpe. She was kind to Graham. She'd even given him extra cookies with his dinner last week. She'd winked a pretty blue eye and told him not to tell.

He'd grinned at her, a toothless, happy smile and nodded along. He was a good secret keeper. He had so many that his brain was full. He'd saved one of those cookies tucked it into a handkerchief at the bottom of his sock drawer. It was stale and crumbly now but Graham didn't care. He kept it with the other items he'd found or received that were precious to him. He liked collecting things.

It was Ralphie who'd taught him to hide things. He was such a smart man. He didn't like to play the games as much as Graham did. That was why he'd had to go, Graham thought, and that's why Joan had to go.

That was why Sarah and Mark both had to go, too.

He understood the game. He understood the rules.

Sarah and Mark paused now, glancing around them as though they could tell they were being followed. Graham held his breath and counted to ten. By the time he got to seven, the pair had turned around and continued on their way.

They were going to the daisies, Claire had told him, and they wanted to play with him and his shiny new toy.

Graham could barely wait.

CHAPTER THIRTY-THREE

The road was cracked and uneven as Liv ran.

She squinted as her thin body hurtled through the fog, her eyes staying on the looming building of Springthorpe Manor in the distance. It wasn't dinner time yet, but it was quiet as the dead of midnight outside. The tranquility was broken by the patter of Liv's heels on the pavement and her gasping lungs dragging short breaths down her scratchy throat.

She was glad she had her sweater when she escaped the hotel and its red-papered walls. She'd felt them shrinking in on her after that phone call, squeezing her tighter and tighter.

She'd recognized that voice the second he spoke.

Her family was all in danger and it was her fault.

Her toe caught on a large, jagged crack in the sidewalk, sending her tumbling head over heels across the sidewalk before she could react enough to stick out her arms.

A shrill cry escaped her lips as she skidded across the hard pavement, lying limply on her back for a few minutes. The sky overhead was gray. There weren't any clouds in her view. It was a long, pure blanket of gloom for as far as she could see.

She couldn't stay there. She knew that. Her time was running out. Rolling over, she felt the concrete scrape across her skin, tearing at her knees until blood speckled the front of her pants.

Biting her lip, she whimpered and crawled up to her feet, grasping a nearby fence for help.

The homes were all the same, little cookie-cutter places with blinds over the windows and curtains drawn, and they stretched down the lane.

Liv stood on the sidewalk and clung to a dingy white picket fence. The house before her was covered with a thin layer of dust. Vines curled around sidewalks that had never been stepped on; garages sat so still that Liv was sure they'd never been opened.

Her throat went tight as she turned to another house beside her and then to those up and down the road. There were no newspapers on anyone's driveway waiting for the owner of the house to come home. There were no trucks or vans parked by the curb.

There were no people there. There was nothing but unending quiet.

It was an entire town constructed to pretend there was life there.

Knowing what she knew about this place, Liv wasn't sure why this shocked her, but it did. It made her brain spin, like she'd just stepped off the carnival ride that spun you around in tight circles over and over again until your whole body was forced to the wall and you couldn't lift your head. Her eldest daughter had loved that ride. Liv could hear her excited squeals in the back of her mind even now.

Will I ever see my daughters again? Liv thought.

Tears pricked the corners of Liv's eyes.

She'd made so many mistakes, she wasn't sure she'd ever be able to right them. She wasn't sure she'd ever have a chance now.

She had to get to Mark. She had to get him out of that place before it was too late.

It was already too late for their parents, but at least Mark could survive if she could make it to him in time. But she didn't know where he was. She'd tried calling him and he didn't answer.

Had they already captured him?

Trying to ignore the sharp pain in her knees, Liv pushed away from the fence and walked toward the manor in the distance. Mark was there, she hoped.

Hobbling forward, she turned, only to find she wasn't alone.

She'd taken too long and her heart sank like a lead weight into her stomach. She inhaled but her lungs stung, and she could only breathe in sharp gasps.

"Hello, Mrs. Keller," Stanley whispered from where he stood next to a sleek black car, his eyes grim. "You didn't think we could let you go, did you?"

Liv took one faltering step back, but Stanley's hand moved down, exposing a gun at his waist.

"It was you at the airport, wasn't it?" she breathed.

He gave a faint nod. "It was supposed to be standard stuff, just keeping an eye on you, like the others. If you had behaved, you'd have been on your way home already. Now, don't make this harder than it has to be. Don't you want to see your parents one more time?"

CHAPTER THIRTY-FOUR

She woke up in a cage.

With her eyes closed, Larissa inhaled, breathing in the heavy scent of dirt, damp, and decay. It stung her nose and made her gag.

A tremor rolled through her, and she blinked hard once, then twice, before realizing her eyes had actually been open since she'd awakened. With a soft whine, she held her hand before her face, wiggling her fingers. Through the dense, inky black she could barely see the slight movement. Her sight hadn't been stolen. The place was so dark she couldn't see two inches in front of her face.

When they'd first taken Larissa, the muscles of her arms had ached where they'd injected her with chemicals. The tubes and needles had left her skin pocked, pricked, and wounded. They'd taken so much blood for testing that she'd become dizzy and passed out.

Now that she was awake, everything felt strange, like her brain had turned to mush and her thoughts had to tread through the muck of her mind. She hadn't been like that earlier.

Larissa had always prided herself on being strong. She could see well, her teeth were free of rot, and she could walk better than the others. That hadn't been enough to keep her from ending up there. Like all the rest of them, she had been discarded.

After a while, she shifted, rolling onto her stomach, causing lazy, pulsing throbs of pain.

She cried out but the sound slurred on her tongue.

What have they done to me?

The floor was frigid against her palms, as if it were made of ice instead of clay. She shivered, the tremor rocking through her spine once more. After it passed, she reached out, finding herself surrounded by cold metal bars.

How long have I been down here? Though it hadn't yet been a full day, to Larissa, it already felt like weeks.

She heard others around her. Some cried, some laughed, some sat in the corners of their cells, rocking back and forth, the edge of their hospital gowns fluttering across the dirt floor.

She tried not to imagine how long some of them had been stuck here, how many needles, procedures, and frightening nights they'd had to endure. She'd never seen anyone who was taken come back–except the one. She'd thought she had been safe upstairs. But, apparently, no one was safe.

Larissa shivered and ran her hands over her hospital gown. Her clothes were gone, as were her shoes. All traces of who she was before were stripped. A numbered plastic band encircled her wrist.

A loud, mechanical hum made the earth rumble beneath her body. Blinding lights flickered on overhead. Someone screamed. Larissa whimpered, curling into a ball and hiding her face in her hands. The lights hadn't switched on one by one, slowly lighting the long tunneling hall; instead, the massive, bright lights all came on at once, blinding anyone who happened to have their eyes open. Many begged for the lights to be turned off, but no one listened to them.

Nervousness bubbled up in Larissa. She wished she was a bird; she wished she could grow wings and soar out of this tunnel. She'd done so well in avoiding it for so long. She hadn't been able to help herself when that woman came back.

Larissa hated many people, especially that woman. She'd had to claw her to punish her for what she'd done–allowing Joan to be taken below.

A man's groan echoed as two researchers dragged his body down the tunnel. They pulled him by his arms. He was missing a shoe as his feet and hips dragged along the ground, and brown dirt smeared down the front of his Christmas sweater and dirty khakis. Larissa lifted her head, shielding her aching eyes as she squinted through her fingers against the blinding light. The researchers' white coats seemed to glow in the pure bright light.

The man, though, Larissa recognized. Her heart dropped into her chest at the sight of his battered body.

"Wait..." she tried to speak.

A woman lingered outside of Larissa's cage. Larissa didn't like this woman. She knew her, though the name escaped her. Her brain was so tired it made her eyelids grow heavier and heavier.

The woman leaned against the metal bars, arms crossed over her head, her long braid disheveled and unraveled at the end. Larissa squeezed her fingers together to block out the sight of her, pretending she hadn't seen a thing, especially not the woman's bright red hair and white skin that glowed as bright as a bone bleached white in the desert by the sun.

"What are you looking at?" the woman asked, her drawl drenched in rich, southern molasses.

"Nothing," Larissa croaked back. "Nothing. Nothing. Nothing." Her whine trilled higher and higher until the red-headed woman slapped a hand against the bars.

"Shut up," the woman hissed. When Larissa glanced up again, the woman's green eyes were locked on her.

"My son, I want to see my son. I want to go home…" Larissa whimpered, struggling through the words as though they stung her tongue with each syllable.

"Sweet Mrs. Stalwart," the woman sighed, leaning through the bars to grasp the elderly woman's frail chin in a tight hand. Her untrimmed nails dug into the woman's flesh as Larissa gave a sharp cry of pained surprise.

The elderly woman blinked hard, trying to focus despite the ringing in her ears. It was so hard to listen, to understand what was happening.

The redhead smiled, her teeth as white as her colorless face, nails gripping harder on the woman's face. "No one here goes home."

CHAPTER THIRTY-FIVE

You look like you know where you're going," Mark panted, chasing after the beautiful brunette nurse as she ducked and snaked through the trees and artfully skipped over the raised tendrils of thick roots.

Mark followed after her, though he was less adept at slogging through the thick, damp earth of the cemetery. He was used to zigzagging through the crowded, firm pavement of a New York sidewalk.

Walking was difficult on the soft earth, which tended to cave beneath their feet and melt away like they were walking through snow instead of grass. Sarah wove them a careful path between the gravestones, being mindful and never stepping over a resting body. She knew it was respectful to avoid the gravesites, but she also couldn't shake the image of a skeletal hand lurching up through the crumbling dirt and twisting bony fingers around her ankle.

She shuddered, rounding another grave with high precision.

Being surrounded by the graves was unsettling, as though they were being watched by thousands of undead eyes.

Mark could see why he'd thought Sarah Kramer was some ethereal ghost or cemetery fairy when they'd first met.

The fog clung to her white jacket like a cloud, her steps so light and deliberate she appeared to be floating.

How did she manage to be so pretty in the middle of a graveyard?

"I think I know what Claire was talking about..." Sarah murmured like she was afraid to disturb one of the buried bodies. Since Mark's footsteps were noisy enough for her to know he stayed close behind, her eyes only focused ahead of them. "By Grandpa's grave, there's a little patch of flowers. The trees are so thick over the cemetery it's hard for anything but weeds to grow, but there's a little clearing beyond the headstone where a patch of daisies grows. I always thought that was why he chose that spot."

"He chose it?"

Sarah gave a distracted nod, coming to a stop beside a tall, bent oak. It draped over her head, dusting the top of her skull with its dangling yellow and orange leaves. When she turned to him, a few of the brittle leaves fell free, sprinkling her hair and shoulders with bronze confetti.

With an awestruck shake of his head, Mark's eyes widened at the sight below, his hands slipping into his pockets.

"Wow." That single syllable leaped to his tongue. Standing beside her in a daze, Mark whispered, "This...wasn't what I was expecting."

He felt there were certain words you used when a friend brought you to a close relative's grave; however, the appropriate words escaped him.

"I know, it's gaudy," Sarah said. "But he was so good to Springthorpe that they wanted to honor him. I couldn't exactly say no, especially when they gave me a job."

A mammoth mausoleum loomed before them. A curious redbird perched at the top and eyed Mark and Sarah cautiously. The bold, roman script read *Henry Kramer* across the top.

Romanesque in design, the building seemed to be made of slick, gleaming marble that had slightly weathered. Four massive columns rose high up on either side of the gold-plated stone door. Bushes of tended roses sprouted up along the side walls.

"All this for a man who wanted a tree," Sarah clicked her tongue.

"Haven't you been calling this a headstone?" Mark asked.

She arched an eyebrow. "Semantics, Mark Hogarth."

"Why?" Mark asked with a slight shrug of his shoulders. He gestured with his palms at the humongous tomb, repeating the question because he couldn't process it.

The tomb was as big as his city apartment.

"He was one of the founders of Springthorpe," Sarah said, reaching out to press her hand to the marble structure. "Heath Dole was his brother-in-law. My grandfather married Suzette Dole, Heath's sister."

"You're related to Heath?"

"Is that how that works?" Sarah asked, crinkling her nose in slight apprehension. "It doesn't feel like it. Maybe because my grandma died when my mom was a little kid. I never knew much of my family aside from Grandpa. He was all I had." Sarah paused, reaching over to stroke one of the roses. "And he would've hated all of this."

Mark smiled, reaching over to rest a gentle hand on her shoulder. She plucked the flower and held it cupped in her palm, burying her nose among the soft petals as they tickled her.

"I know how it feels to lose someone you love, Sarah. I know how hard it is."

She nodded, moving closer to him so the hand on her shoulder slipped down her arm.

"Grandpa died so suddenly I never had a chance to say goodbye. I always wanted a second chance at that. Hopefully,

Mark, we can give you the opportunity to see your parents again."

She extended the rose to him and Mark tucked it into the small breast pocket of his shirt. Sarah reached out, pressing her hand against the short stem of the flower that rested over Mark's heart. She tilted her head back and smiled at him.

He couldn't help but smile back as he brushed her bangs from out of her beautiful blue eyes. Her face turned to rest against his palm, and she could hear the quick beat of his heart against his ribs. It thudded loud as thunder between his ears, drowning out all his thoughts.

Sarah stepped back, away from Mark's touch, a coy smile on her mouth as she peered toward the daisy patch blooming past the tomb. Mark followed suit.

They were here...so where were their answers?

The nurse glanced around, goosebumps prickling over her arms.

Something was off. Sarah wasn't sure what it was. Usually, being beside her grandfather's memorial made her feel comfortable and safe. This time, however, she couldn't shake the feeling of impending dread.

Mark moved closer to the building, inspecting the smooth and polished marble. It was immaculate.

"Does Heath pay to have it refurbished too?" Mark asked, pressing his hand against the smooth stone of the closed doorway. It was heavy and cool against his palm.

"I've never been in there," Sarah whispered with a stark shake of her paling face. "I don't know if I can-"

Laughter rippled through the trees behind them as Sarah ducked closer to Mark, one hand curling tight around his elbow.

"What was that?" Mark whispered, his eyes wide in confusion as he squinted through the foggy haze.

Everything went silent. A shudder rolled long and slow up Mark's spine, his hair standing on edge.

The stillness was broken as leaves and branches were crushed under the running body of a tall, older man lurching through the trees.

"Let's play!" he yelled, charging toward them so fast Mark couldn't even muster a shout of panic.

Clenched in the man's hand was a long, rough plank of painted wood with bits of sharp, gleaming metal protruding from it.

Without thinking, Mark clutched at Sarah and tumbled hard against the mausoleum door which gave way under the pressure of both falling bodies and sucked the pair into its dark embrace.

CHAPTER THIRTY-SIX

Yes," Heath said into the phone, his heels propped up in front of him on the desk as he leaned back and forth, the heavy leather chair creaking with the movement. "I called earlier about hosting a funeral here at the manor. I'm afraid the family has reconsidered, and we no longer need the bouquets."

He inspected his perfect nails, holding his fingers flexed out in front of his face as he laughed at whatever inane thing the florist on the phone prattled on about.

Heath was well adept at making people feel more important than they were, at making them think his suggestions were their ideas. It was a skill honed from his early childhood. With his first choppy sentences, he'd convinced his mother to give him all the cookies in the large tin high up out of his toddler reach. He had eaten so many that day he grew to hate them. Heath hadn't touched a cookie since.

"Mmhmm, of course," he continued when the blathering became too much to handle. "You know how quickly these matters change. We will certainly call you for our next event."

Another charming chuckle reverberated over the phone as he wished the florist a pleasant afternoon and hung up with a roll of his icy eyes.

Leaning forward, he scooted a crystal glass across the mahogany surface with the tip of one long finger, taking the bottle of scotch from the corner of his oversized desk and pouring a much-needed drink. Rarely were his days at Springthorpe overly stressful, but the last twenty-four hours had been precisely that. He looked forward to the day being over, returning home to his king-sized bed and Egyptian cotton sheets, closing his eyes, and forgetting the day had ever happened.

His lips curved against the rim of his heavy goblet. He gave a soft sigh that clouded the clear glass. After downing the entire drink in one long, steady gulp, he plopped the glass back down. He wasn't the type to waste twenty-five-year-old scotch, but it was a special day. The alcohol flooded his throat with a warm fire, sinking all the way down to his stomach. He closed his eyes, lips puckering from the sharpness of the warm alcohol.

He rocked again, fingers pressing into a steeple over his lap as a pleasant smile stretched across his face.

His plans were coming along. Despite the bumpy start, all would soon be well. The drink had clarified his decision, making more apparent the path he would have to take.

It wasn't too late to sweep this all under the rug. He was the only one now who could take care of this mess.

At least he would no longer have to deal with the funeral of Ralph Hogarth.

He hated hosting funerals at Springthorpe. It wasn't good for morale for the other patients to get even a whiff of death. While deaths did happen—with alarming frequency at times—his staff did their best to keep quiet about each passing.

Straightening from his desk, Heath stretched his legs and walked the short perimeter of his office to the well-organized bookcase at the side of the room. He stood over it, running his fingers over the edges of each title until his hand came to a stop over the worn edge of a leather-bound journal.

The book was familiar, the corners of the cover curved and frayed. He gave a thoughtful grunt, his eyes narrowing as his finger hooked around the cover's binding, when his phone rang once again.

Distracted, the lean man stalked back toward the desk, sinking into his well-used chair and kicking up his legs as he poured himself another tall drink of liquor. He still had more calls to make, and he had to track down that psychologist and tell her to forget about the appointment with Mark.

"Oh, hello, Mr. Moore," he said into the phone. "Thank you for returning my call. I wanted to discuss the automatic payments I have on my bank account to a Mrs. Liv Keller. I would like to stop those. Her services are ending with me today."

CHAPTER THIRTY-SEVEN

Mark had been expecting heavy, dank air laced with death and dust, but the inside of the tomb smelled pleasant.

Nothing about this mausoleum indicated there had ever been a dead body within its small walls. Though it was massive and overwhelming from the outside, it was cramped on the inside, and pitch dark. The scent of roses was thick.

While he pressed against the heavy closed door of the mausoleum, straining to hear the laughter of the strange, frightening man outside, Sarah stood stiff as a statue at his side, one of her hands grasped hard on his shoulder, as though she'd topple over without the support.

Pressing his ear against the marble, Mark held his breath and listened, though he couldn't hear anything other than his heart thundering like crazy. The internal thrumming was so loud and powerful that he could sense his body shifting with every raucous beat. Adrenaline coursed through his veins, making his skin prickle. It felt like fire was surging through him, giving him a thousand different commands at once. Part of his brain told him to run, while another part told him to stay hidden. Another portion of his brain told him to grab Sarah and give her the biggest kiss he'd ever given anyone in his entire life because, somehow, they were still alive.

When he blinked, he could still see the metal of the large wooden plank crashing toward their heads.

Was this stranger the same one who'd attacked me in the hall of the art room? How many loose assailants were wandering free around the grounds of Springthorpe?

Claire had sent us out here and we'd been attacked. But was that her fault? She'd said someone was always listening, so maybe her message had been intercepted.

He turned his back against the door and sank to the ground. His fingers swept out along his legs, feeling the ridges of the marble tiled floor of the tomb, as he blinked over and over, trying to convince his eyes to adjust to the dark. It was cold, colder than it was outside. Though there were no windows to let in fresh air or light, the air wasn't stale.

He curled his legs so that he was seated cross-legged, hoping his eyes would adjust to the darkness soon.

Sarah was a blurry figure swaying beside him, fingernails still digging into his shoulder. Her grip was hard and firm, though that didn't surprise him. He wouldn't have been surprised to peel back the delicate layers of Sarah's milky skin to find metal bones beneath. She seemed that strong.

Mark inhaled, still surprised that the air was not musty or dank.

"You've never come in here?" he asked.

Sarah shook her head, or he thought she did. He still couldn't see her clearly.

"The last time I saw my grandfather, he was smiling. He was happy. I wanted to keep that image for as long as I could. I didn't even look in his casket at the wake."

Mark nodded, then grunted in agreement, though she couldn't see him either.

"We were the only family we had. Now I'm all that's left," Sarah said, her hand moving from his shoulder.

Sarah moved away from him, her feet scuffling on the dustless floor. As immaculate as the outside of the tomb had been, the inside was even more carefully cleaned.

Reaching out her hands, she squinted hard and grazed her hands over the ledges and walls, feeling for a casket or wrap or skeletons, anything that belonged to her grandfather, but her fingers met only empty air.

"I don't think...I don't think Grandpa is in here," Sarah whispered, her jaw clenching so hard a vein throbbed up her temple. "What...? Where could he be?"

"That guy, Sarah, who ran at us. Do you know who he is?" Mark asked, still seated on the ground.

"Where's my grandfather?" Sarah asked instead, her shrill voice rising. "Where is he?"

She moved from corner to corner now, bouncing around like the ball in one of those old pinball arcade games with the bright, flashing lights. As her eyes adjusted in the darkness, the truth became clear. There was nothing in this place. It was an empty, open square and they were trapped inside while a man stalked the outside with a weapon that could bludgeon both of them to death.

"I can't believe this," Sarah whispered, clutching at her heart as it palpitated with utter bewilderment and disgust. "Where is his body?"

Mark stood and stumbled to her, his eyes adjusting more slowly. While she could see the shapes and outlines of the square box, he could see only her tall, slender form. He grabbed her shoulders, pulling her toward him, and pressed his forehead to hers so he could see the gleam of her sapphire eyes.

"Do you think..." he paused, mulling his words. He wasn't sure whether he should finish his sentence.

Sarah furrowed her brow and gazed at him in confusion.

"It's just that...Do you think it's possible he's alive, Sarah? Like my parents might be?"

She bit her lip so hard she winced, her soul twinging with a torrid mix of hope and despair at the thought of her kind, intelligent grandfather being trapped somewhere deep and dark and scary.

He'd died several years before. *Was it possible he was being held prisoner this whole time?*

Sarah didn't say anything, shaking her head and the thought from her mind. She didn't want to consider that. She couldn't. They had to focus and decide on their next course of action.

"I can't believe Claire sent us out here," she sighed. "Do you think she set this up or what?"

"Well, we never made it to the patch of flowers," Mark replied. "I don't know if that's what she wanted…or if this was." He grimaced as he gestured toward the outside of the tomb where their predator probably still prowled.

"Do you think she's alright?" Sarah's voice went soft like she was afraid to say the thought out loud. "If she wasn't the one who arranged for our…guest, then do you think that person might've hurt her for telling us to go here?"

Mark walked around, searching the walls of the tomb. He ran his fingertips over the slick surfaces, walking in a slow circle. He didn't answer her question. He didn't want to think too hard about what might've happened to the stern head nurse. Not when there was nothing either of them could do about it.

The first step was getting out of the mausoleum.

"What are you doing?" Sarah asked, her gaze following Mark back and forth around the tomb. "Do you think Graham is gone?"

"Graham?" Mark asked, eyes narrowing as his finger caressed a knot in the otherwise smooth wall.

"That was Graham Jones out there. A patient."

Sarah frowned, leaning into the door and listening. The walls were so thick and heavy it was impossible to hear anything out there. Graham could've been shouting at the top of his lungs and they wouldn't hear.

Mark gave a low grumble, keeping one hand on the nearly imperceptible bump in the wall as his other hand spread out over the wall. There was another bump in the marble about six inches from the first.

Though he couldn't see the pattern with his eyes, he could see it in his mind. He'd seen this before in his father's journal.

Ralph had left that odd triangle of smeared dots on the journal's last page on purpose, not haphazardly. It was a reminder of how to get to Joan.

Mark pressed the notches as hard as he could, feeling them hesitate and then give beneath his force. Mark reached toward where he knew the third button would be located, pushing it in.

His father had been there, inside the tomb.

"Sarah..." Mark whispered in awe, stepping away, though the woman's back was to him and she wasn't paying any attention to him.

She muttered to herself, working up the courage to crack open the door and check outside for Graham.

"Sarah," Mark said again, eyes going wide as the marble came to life with a gasping moan. "Sarah, look!"

She whipped around, releasing a shocked cry as the wall slid downward and exposed a dark tunnel before them.

"It's the same one..." Mark whispered as Sarah crept to his side and peered down the dark depths.

"That picture, Mark, it was taken down there," she finished his train of thought.

CHAPTER THIRTY-EIGHT

L iv couldn't tell where she was.

The light was so bright it made her eyes sting even when they were closed. The backs of her eyelids burned red as if blood or paint had been splashed over her face.

She had approached the black vehicle and then everything went dark. She had awoken with no recollection of anything between.

She'd never made it to Mark. He was in danger and he wouldn't know it until it was too late.

She'd done this. She'd done this to all of them. She'd managed to doom her entire family.

"I did...everything you asked." Liv gasped hard for each breath.

Though a heavy blanket was stretched over her body where she was bound to the table, she still shivered. She couldn't seem to move except to shift her body one way or the other.

"Everything?" a woman asked, leaning over the table. Her small pointed elbows pressed into the padding, sharp green eyes gazing down at her. "I don't know if that's quite true."

With more effort than she'd ever exerted as a teenager at one of those jazzercise classes she'd been dragged to with her mother, Liv gave a cramped bob of her head. Even the small movement sent the room spinning around her. She hissed, groaning as bile rose up the back of her throat.

It was quiet, aside from the occasional beep of a machine hooked to her arm and muffled noises from outside the room. Liv couldn't tell if it was just the two of them or if there were other people inside the room, too.

Am I at Springthorpe?

A faint noise drifted into the room. It was the sound of a child's laughter, and it seemed familiar to her. The soft, whimsical giggle conjured the image of blonde pigtails in the back of Liv's mind.

She gasped, peeling her eyes open, her lids fluttering as the bright light poured painfully into her pupils. "The girl," she wheezed, "that's the little girl who's missing."

"She is indeed."

Confusion rippled through Liv, making her stomach twist and her heart ache.

Why had that little girl become tangled up in all of this? She is innocent. This makes no sense.

Liv turned her head, gray eyes meeting green.

"Claire, did you take her?" Liv asked, the words wavering in Liv's weak throat. "Did you steal that little girl?"

The woman nodded without hesitation, her red braid tumbling over her bony shoulder as a triumphant grin spread over her mouth.

"Why?" Liv's said as her eyes drifted shut again. The effort used to keep them cracked open turned out to be too much in her weakened state.

"Why do any of us do anything, Mrs. Keller?" the redhead sighed in retort, stroking Liv's limp hair as tears leaked from between the pale lashes. "Why did you do what you did?"

Had her tone not been so condescending, the sugary sweetness of her southern accent would've been comforting.

"I gave you my mom. You took my dad. I kept my mouth shut about all of it. I never told anyone," Liv sniffled, dragging in another raspy breath. "I did what you wanted!"

The woman laughed with a short bark. "What was that thing Joan used to say? Sometimes your best isn't enough."

Liv's heart shattered in her chest, the tears leaking more quickly.

Why are they doing this? Why did I agree to this in the first place? Why, why, why?

Liv opened her mouth to question the situation further but could come up with no question that would give her all the answers she sought. There was no answer that could quell the heat of her guilt.

The hand on Liv's hair went still, and when Liv opened one watery eye, she found herself swallowed in blackness. She strained against the chunky metal chains around her wrists and legs, slamming her hands against the stiff table beneath her.

"Stanley said I would see Mom and Dad again. He said I'd get one last chance-"

She spoke to nothing and no one as a heavy door slammed shut somewhere in the corner of the room that Liv couldn't see.

She squeezed her eyes closed, fingers balling into fists so tight that blood welled against her palms where her short nails dug in.

She deserved this. She deserved every second of this misery. No one was ever going to find her. No one was going to figure out where she'd gone. The hotel camera would show her leaving in a hurry and never returning.

They'd never find her. Her girls would lose their mother. And it was all her fault.

CHAPTER THIRTY-NINE

Sarah's hand was warm in Mark's clammy one. Their fingers interlaced firmly together, their hands swung between their bodies like a pendulum.

They held one another tightly, navigating the thick blackness of the tunnel in silence. Sticking close to the wall, Mark kept his free hand running along the rough, rocky earth. He couldn't tell in the darkness whether he was touching rock or concrete, but every foot they wound through the never-ending darkness made his stomach twist further and further into anxious knots.

Mark found it difficult to imagine anyone being down there. He couldn't envision how it must feel to be trapped in the bleak shadows. The guilt of putting his parents into this situation made him sick.

How didn't I know when I signed Dad and Mom up for this place that it would be trouble? Why hadn't I been able to tell?

"Mark!" Sarah gasped, dragging him up against the rough wall. She tucked up under his arm, pressing her hand against his mouth to keep him from questioning her aloud.

Curling his fingers around her wrist, he tugged her fingers away from his lips so he could furrow his brow at her instead.

"I saw someone. Something. There's light around the next corner," Sarah whispered in his ear, her blue eyes round and worried. "There's shadows over there. People."

His father could be mere feet away. Mark wanted nothing more than to grab him and haul him out of there as fast and as far away as they could get.

"Come on, Sarah," Mark whispered, twining his fingers back between hers.

She swallowed, nodding and squeezing his hand. Her eyes darted toward the light as they tiptoed through the shadows.

The path they followed took a winding turn, the tunnel turning into a ledge as they crept past a vast, black hole in the ground. Together, they peered over it, staring down into the bottomless pit. It appeared to be the entrance to hell, all cracked mortar and rugged edges. Mark wasn't sure how deep underground they were, but the pit seemed like it went to the other side of the Earth. It was terrifying to think they may have taken a false step into it.

Sarah made a small sound of confusion, kneeling down over the edge to peer into the darkness.

"There's something…Mark, there's something down there." Sarah flattened herself on the dirt floor as though she were on thin ice.

Mark joined her, kneeling at her side and peering down while holding onto one of Sarah's legs. Mark couldn't tell what it was. "Be careful," he cautioned.

"I think it's a shoe," Sarah murmured, inching along and reaching down to grab it from the ledge it rested on. She grasped the dirty shoe briefly before losing her grip. The shoe tumbled down into the pitch black hole.

The pair held their breath and listened for the sound of the object hitting the ground, but they were met with only silence.

Shaking her head, Sarah climbed to her feet and gestured back toward the light shining in the distance.

Mark took a step and Sarah matched his quick but careful pace as they darted around another corner. They stuck close to the dark walls and wove together along the long tunnel until they hung at the edge of the lighted area.

They stumbled upon something that made Mark's stomach twist with such violence he thought he was going to vomit.

Sarah, likewise, gave a strained grunt as her hand slapped to her mouth.

"They're in cages like animals," Sarah breathed, voice muffled against her trembling fingers, her shoulder collapsing into the side of the darkened wall. Her eyes swept over the elderly people trapped behind metal bars.

She recognized many of them, which sickened her even further. Who knew how long the rest had been held hostage? They each were pale as ghosts and just as fragile, barely more than skin and bones. Their bodies lay strewn on the dirt floor or curled up in the corners of their cages.

Practically every day, Sarah had visited her grandfather at his tomb, the gate to this hell. This had been happening just below her feet. In some way, just by working at Springthorpe, she had helped this happen.

Unknowingly, Sarah had had a hand in all this madness.

All was still and quiet under the sharp lights, except for the sound of soft steps approaching from ahead.

"Claire!" Sarah gasped into Mark's ear. But Mark had spotted something even more interesting–a familiar Christmas sweater across the room.

His father was there. Ralph was alive!

CHAPTER FORTY

Graham twined the daisies together as he settled down in the patch of flowers.

He tilted his head up, frowning at the gray clouds. He hoped it wouldn't rain. He didn't like the rain because it meant he wouldn't be able to stay outside and play. Pouting, he wound the delicate green stems together, manipulating the fragile petals with such tender hands not a single flower fell out of place.

With a smile, he placed it on his head and then glanced at his watch. Four o'clock. It was getting late. He'd already missed lunch because he became so caught up in his playing.

Adjusting his flower crown, he turned to gaze over his shoulder at the manor.

Crotchety Claire didn't like it when he didn't finish his tasks, but Ralphie's boy wasn't around anymore, and Graham wasn't going to follow him into the tunnel. Graham had recently come out of it himself, and he wasn't going to put himself back inside. The thought made him shudder. He climbed to his feet, abandoning his wooden plank out of boredom. He would come back some other time to collect it.

He scuffled off between the trees, bending to pick up shiny rocks or pretty golden leaves that called to him. He tucked the collectibles into his pockets until they were stuffed full.

Every few steps, he would pause and turn back toward the mausoleum, wishing Ralphie's boy and the nice nurse would come back outside. He wouldn't have minded sharing his lunch with them. They could have had a picnic together.

"Graham, what are you doing out here?" a voice asked, as Graham turned to face the man standing at the gate of the cemetery. "Aren't patients supposed to stay inside?"

Stanley stood before him, hands in his pockets, mismatched eyes dark and mindful. Graham didn't argue with him that he was a worker here and not a patient.

Middle-aged and quiet, Stanley rarely ever appeared at Springthorpe Manor, but Graham had heard from him often. Graham liked it when Stanley called him and told him all of his secrets. Graham would listen over the phone so he could relay the information to Crotchety Claire.

Graham knew Stanley had a temper—one that had to be kept in check. It was alright. Everyone had to be reminded of the rules of the game now and then. They were lucky Graham had memorized them all.

Graham grinned, leaning against a tree and gazing out from behind it.

He liked Stanley and the clean black suit he always wore. Graham wished he could dress up as nicely as that. He didn't say anything, choosing instead to watch the dark-haired man before him.

Stanley glanced around, noting the still quiet of the manor, then turned back toward the old man with the copper eyes.

The pair regarded each other in silence, trying to figure out what the other knew.

"Why are you here?" Graham eventually asked.

Stanley rarely came to visit.

"Business. And to see my mother."

Graham laughed, shifting from foot to foot so that he peered out from the other side of the tree. The bark was rough against his fingers, but he didn't mind. He dug his nails lightly into the bark, peeling a piece free and watching it tumble to the ground.

"What's so funny?" Stanley asked, no trace of amusement on his stern face. "You going to stay out here tonight?"

Graham gave a shake of his head, his toothless smile widening. "You can't see Larissa." He grinned. "No way, José!"

Stanley crossed his arms, lifting an impatient eyebrow. He didn't have time to spend with an old man who was convinced he was a child. He'd already dropped off the woman, Liv. He had to get out of there and get back to work at the hotel.

"Why do you say that?"

Graham chuckled and cocked his head. "Yesterday up here, today down below!" The old man cackled. "That's the way that Springthorpe goes!"

Stanley's body went stiff.

CHAPTER FORTY-ONE

D ad...Dad!" Mark whispered, heaving himself against the bars of Ralph's cage as he stretched an arm toward his father.

Ralph lay in a heap on the ground, his chest rising and falling, his eyes open and staring upward. He was really there. He was alive. Mark wanted to pinch himself to make sure he didn't imagine it. He blinked hard once, then twice. He could still feel the rough earth under his knees, and he could hear the soft wail of the others in their cells.

The entire place was a torture chamber. Patients sprawled about in clothes much too flimsy for the chill in the air. Mark's stomach lurched one way, then the other. He felt like he was at a zoo. A sick, repulsive zoo.

"Can you hear me?" he whispered, wishing his father would turn his eyes in his direction just once, that he would speak his name.

Was it anger, disorientation, or hopelessness that silenced him? What had been done to him? Mark wondered.

Sarah wrapped her arms around herself, gazing up and down the long hall. Claire had vanished into a room on the other side. Though they were alone for now, she doubted it would last very long. She knew how things in Springthorpe were run. It was a tight ship.

She couldn't believe this had been happening right under her feet. She'd had no idea at all.

What was all of this? What was the purpose? Who was behind it all? Who was running this hellhole? Was it Claire? Was it Heath? Was it someone else?

She couldn't begin to comprehend it.

The old man in the cage grumbled something, his head shifting toward Mark, gray hair hanging over his face.

Sarah knew the signs of exposure and dehydration. *When was the last time he'd been fed or given a drink?*

With another watchful peek up and down the hall, Sarah returned to Mark's side and fiddled with the lock. A digital keypad with pneumatic doors, there was no way they were getting into the cell without the code. She was worried messing too much with the lock would trigger an alarm.

They were out in the open. Anyone could see them. The people in their cells paid them no mind, crying and groaning to themselves. They were drugged. There were so many of them in the cells Sarah couldn't count them all.

If Claire cracked open the door at the end of the hall, they'd be sitting ducks. She doubted they'd ever have a chance to return to the surface after that.

Sarah grasped Mark's shoulder. She didn't have to say aloud what he already knew. They were running on borrowed time.

But how was he supposed to convince himself to leave? Sure, he'd found his father...but where was his mother? Was she here as well and cold, wet, and frail? Sarah thought.

Clinging to the cold metal bars with one hand, Mark stretched his other arm as far into the cell as he could. His arm ached and his shoulder felt like it was about to pop, but he was only centimeters from touching his very alive father.

Mark had been devastated by the news of his father's death. Again, he regretted not spending more time with him. Sarah was right; he had a second chance now. He had to save his father, and his mother, too, if she was there somewhere as well.

He wouldn't leave Springthorpe until he had both of his parents in his arms.

"Dad?" Mark whispered again, his voice begging and pleading for any response. "Are you okay?"

It seemed like such a silly question, asking the exhausted and injured man if he was alright, but it was all Mark could conceive to ask. His mind was in such a delirious jumble.

When Ralph moved, rolling onto his side, Sarah stiffened, her fingers digging into Mark's shoulder.

She recognized him. She knew this man. She hadn't known his name at the time, or she had and had since forgotten. Her time spent with him was minimal but distinct.

"Mark…" Sarah said, giving his shoulder a gentle squeeze. "We have to leave now. We have to find the code. We have to set these people free."

Mark shrugged his shoulder, letting her hand fall away from his body. *How am I supposed to turn around and abandon my father again? Isn't there anything we can do now?*

Ralph was whispering, his lips moving. Mark and Sarah strained to hear, falling silent in an attempt to listen to the simple words passing through dry, cracked lips.

"I can't…I can't hear you, Dad." Mark gritted his teeth, his arm falling back to his side as he clutched the bars with renewed anger. The old man was two feet away from him, yet Mark could do nothing to help him.

Ralph drew in a sharp, painful breath, one of his hands pressing into his chest where his heart palpitated.

Finally, he was able to speak.

"Run."

CHAPTER FORTY-TWO

Cynthia James was in a tizzy when she finally spotted Mark Hogarth and one of the nurses sprinting over the lawn.

She'd spent the last half hour driving the nurses in the lobby crazy by asking whether or not they had recently seen Ralph Hogarth's son. Escaping out of sight, the man was as elusive as a minnow in a pond.

It was maddening, especially when she had a job to do.

The pair moved fast, bursting through the cemetery gate as Cynthia gave a slight sigh. She clicked her tongue and sauntered out the lobby doors. The air was crisp, blowing her thin, dark bangs into her eyes. She shoved the hair out of her line of sight.

"Mr. Hogarth!" she called, recognizing him from Mr. Dole's description of the middle-aged man—wild brown eyes, bruises, despair etched into every inch of his face.

This was definitely a man suffering and in need of some intense grief counseling. While that wasn't her forte, she trusted Heath knew best.

"Mr. Hogarth, hello!" she called again when he ignored her, lost in deep conversation with the beautiful nurse at his side.

The two of them walked closely together, faces almost touching, so absorbed in whatever it was they were discussing. She hoped the nurse wasn't worsening Mark's sensitive condition. The loss of a parent is never easy, not on children nor grown adults. That was Psychology 101, which she had passed with ease.

Lifting her hand, she gave a little wave, hoping to summon him over to her.

There was no way Cynthia was going to be ignored. Heath Dole had asked her to do one thing and she was darn well going to do it. It wasn't often she was asked to do much of anything. She was prepared with her folder and her colored markers, though she wasn't sure he'd be as interested in those as the elderly patients were, and she'd cleared the art room for the hour.

"Mark Hogarth!" she shrieked, stamping her foot as both the nurse and the man skidded to a halt and turned toward her with wide, startled eyes.

Sucking in a deep breath, Cynthia tucked a lock of hair behind her ear and beamed. "You and I have an appointment, sir. So, if you'll come with me-"

"I'm sorry, that'll have to wait," Mark responded through teeth clenched with sheer emotion Cynthia recognized. She pitied this man and his devastating loss.

"No, whatever it is you have planned will have to wait, Mr. Hogarth. You're mine for the next forty-five minutes."

"What's this about?" Sarah asked in bewilderment.

Sarah knew who Cynthia was. She was brand new in the halls of Springthorpe and eager to prove herself useful.

Cynthia gazed at Sarah from down the length of her hook nose, pinching her lips this way and that before turning her attention back to Mark as though the blue-eyed nurse wasn't there.

Sarah lifted her eyebrows, arms crossing over her chest.

"The director of Springthorpe Manor is concerned about you, Mark. He's worried the loss of your parents is negatively impacting you and those around you."

"And?" Mark interrupted, his eyes were blazing and impatient.

"And I would like to have a session with you."

"I really can't right now-"

"What is it that's so urgent you don't have forty-five minutes, Mr. Hogarth?" She frowned, tapping her fingers on her folder as she waited for him to explain.

Her eyes, however, told him there would be no argument that was going to get him out of this. He felt like a kid in the principal's office waiting to hear his detention sentence.

When he offered nothing but a slight gape of his mouth, she nodded and gestured at the doors. "If you'll follow me to the art room, please."

Mark's next argument died on his tongue. *The art room*. He could try and glean some information while he was there.

Sarah prodded him with a tiny nod of her chin, gesturing after the walking psychologist, who paused at the door to the manor, waving Mark inside.

"Go," she whispered, "I'll go to Claire's office. We'll meet soon."

CHAPTER FORTY-THREE

This is like my art class back in high school." Mark smiled, easing down into the comfortable chair across from the small table where the psychologist sat and gazed at him with observant eyes.

With brown eyes, brown hair, and a few brown freckles on her tanned face, the young woman before him was utterly forgettable. She was the type of woman you would meet once and then forget her name. In fact, it escaped him now, though she had mentioned it once or twice on the walk over.

The art room was identical to when he and Sarah had been there earlier in the day, though the pencil cases had been moved around. The walls were still barren and devoid of any artwork.

What had been there that was so important? And who had taken it?

For a moment, Mark almost stood up and paced, but then he focused. He was there to be judged by the psychologist. She could probably kick him out of the manor if she deemed him too unstable.

He made it a point to relax, his hands folded on top of the table, one of his ankles perched on his knee. When he smiled, the woman scribbled a note on her pad. He shifted, trying to get a glance at it, but she angled it away.

"Except at my school, the teachers would hang up the students' works all over the walls. It was so cheery," he added with a laugh he hoped sounded real.

"Yes…" the psychologist frowned, eyes flittering over the walls. "They used to have those here as well, but they're obviously gone now. I haven't been here for very long. It's possible they change them out every so often."

So, she has no idea where the pictures have gone, Mark thought.

Mark worked to keep the smile on his face. If he wanted to get out of there as soon as possible and return to Sarah and his father, he couldn't show this woman an ounce of volatility. He'd been hoping she could point him in the right direction about the missing artwork. Perhaps there was still some other information he could learn.

"What did you say your name was again?"

"Cynthia James. I'm the resident psychologist here."

She'd wanted to add "the only one, in fact, not counting the grief counselors," but she knew that would sound boastful.

"You're young!" he noted. The fresh-faced woman didn't appear old enough to drink legally yet. "I bet your parents must be proud. Is this place a dream to work at?"

The young woman flushed and gave a slight nod of her head. "They are, and it is. I still can't believe I got the job here. I bet there were so many more qualified people." She mused, before clearing her throat and turning her attention back to her papers.

She was supposed to fill out several forms, the typical, generic information as well as some additional questions that would judge his mental state and whether or not he had any delusions. Grief brought out the strangest manifestations in people, even long dormant psychological disorders.

"Um, so, Mr. Hogarth-"

"Mark. You can call me Mark." He grinned again, Cynthia's eyes darting up toward him as her cheeks flushed pink.

They hadn't told her he would be handsome, so ruggedly good-looking. It appeared he'd recently gotten into a fight of some sort, but boys will be boys, she figured.

Cynthia had become very comfortable working with the elderly patients. So, she wasn't used to such a nice-looking guy beaming at her in such a friendly way. She wasn't sure what his sister must've been worried about. He seemed calm and collected to her.

"Okay...Mark."

"So, you're the psychologist here?" he continued before she could make sense of the questions that had been prepared for her. "Do you meet with many of the patients?"

"I've met with quite a few, at least half of the residents here," she replied. "Mark, how would rate your grief on a scale of one to ten?"

"That's quite the caseload for one psychologist! I bet it gets overwhelming."

Cynthia giggled and shook her head. "No. Not really. I have many people helping me. The staff organizes my notes for me in the computer system, so the important bits are always easy to retrieve later."

One of his eyebrows quirked upward, though he quickly concealed it with a brush of his hand through his hair. Mark gave a thoughtful hum, tapping his chin. "Did you ever meet with my father? Ralph Hogarth?"

"I did," Cynthia responded, leaning back in her chair.

"He was an amazing man, wasn't he? So sturdy. Like an ox," he said, gazing down at his clasped hands.

"But warm," Cynthia offered. "I came on the team shortly before..." she paused, grimacing as she hadn't meant to turn the conversation in this direction, "before he passed. I only had a few chances to meet him, but he was always so kind."

Mark nodded. "Did he talk about me, Ms. James? What else did he talk about?"

"Cynthia," she returned, a soft smile on her lips, "call me Cynthia, Mark."

She closed her folder, forgetting all the questions she was supposed to have Mark answer. They didn't seem relevant. She could see Mark for what he was. He wanted to hear about his father, to hear what his last days entailed. The questions could wait for another time. She was sure Heath would understand.

"How was he?" Mark continued.

"Well, as I'm sure you know, the Alzheimer's was difficult for him."

Mark paused, the smile melting off his mouth. "Was it?"

Cynthia gave a soft sigh and a nod, fiddling with her pencil. It tapped on the table, punctuating the silence. Mark held his breath.

"It was bad even when I first started here, but toward the end, he was living in delusions, Mark. He didn't interact with the others. He was frequently solitary, rarely leaving his room. He was lost in his stories. All he had was the past."

CHAPTER FORTY-FOUR

Getting into Claire's office was surprisingly easy.

The head nurse liked privacy, so it made sense her small space was secluded.

In the hall adjacent to the art room, Sarah could hear the muted sounds of the conversation happening next door. Though she was curious about what the pair were discussing, she focused on her mission. Besides, Mark deserved a little privacy. Even if he was in there to see if he could find out any information, a little therapy had never hurt anyone.

She was sure there would be something in the head nurse's office that would let them figure out what was going on in those dark, hidden away tunnels. Claire would have it tucked away somewhere, and Sarah had no choice but to do everything she could to discover it.

At the very least, Mark's father was alive, and perhaps his mother, and possibly even her grandfather. Sarah paused, shaking her head. She couldn't let her mind wander yet. She still wasn't sure how to feel about that possibility.

A shudder twitched up her spine, the musk of damp earth still clinging to her hair as she cracked open the closed door and slid inside.

Afraid to turn on the light and draw any unwanted attention, Sarah crept down beside the desk and used the light of her cell phone to shine a path forward.

The office was as clean and organized as Claire was, everything put in its place. The head nurse had a small green fern placed on the corner of her desk, the lush leaves stretching toward the ceiling.

Sarah sank down so she was crouched on the floor, running her fingers over the smooth wood of the desk and trying the drawers. Each one was locked.

So much for easy, Sarah sighed, chewing her lower lip.

She gave a rough tug at the lower drawer, the large one, but it didn't budge.

A patient person, Sarah presumed, would have scoured the office for the key. But that patient person didn't know Claire, who would never leave such a precious thing laying out in the open.

Sarah was going to have to do this the old-fashioned way, but she would have limited time after that. The next time Claire returned to her desk, it was going to be obvious that someone had been in there.

From here forward, it was a countdown.

Sitting on the floor and grunting, Sarah pressed her sneakers against the bottom of the desk, curling her fingers under the small lip of the drawer handle.

She took a deep breath, straining her ears for any sound of someone walking up the hall, and then thrust her legs out against the desk while jerking the drawer as hard as she could. With a snap of the broken lock, the heavy wooden drawer lurched backward, flying over Sarah's head and crashing into the wall behind her.

Sarah gave a yelp and a gasp, crawling on her hands and knees to the pile of papers.

There were several folders, one of which was labeled *Patients* and another marked *Test Subjects*. She gathered it all into her arms, heart thundering against her ribs.

Any second now, security was going to burst into the room. She already heard the psychologist's raised voice in the art room as Mark tried to keep her attention.

Sarah scooped it all up and burst from the room only to have someone grab her arm and drag her into a nearby hall.

CHAPTER FORTY-FIVE

Heath Dole shifted in his leather chair, his crystal scotch carafe half empty.

He hadn't meant to drink so much—he rarely did on a workday—but one glass and then two had just not been enough to calm his stressed nerves.

Smoothing a hand over his throat, he felt the lingering burn of the alcohol seep down through his chest. The way his veins throbbed was a pleasant feeling. His cheeks were flushed a slight hue of red. He always turned pink when he drank.

The red light of his phone blinked, and he leaned forward over the leather-covered journal lounging open across his desk to click the button. He pushed the diary aside, glancing over the file of papers Claire had left for him to sign. Picking up his favorite fountain pen, he pressed the point to the tip of his tongue and signed them. His work never seemed to end.

"Hello," he said, still signing papers as he lifted the receiver to his ear. "I've decided what I'm going to do about our little…problem. Just this one last task and we will be back on track again. Isn't that grand?"

He didn't wait for a reply. He didn't care to hear what the other person had to say. The alcohol made him even more impatient than he usually was. He'd already made up his mind so the matter was more or less over. Besides, what was one more notch on his belt when there were already so many others who had fallen into his death hole?

"She's caused too much trouble for me. First taking that child...she's starting to believe she runs this place. I've humored her for too long, and you know the truth in that. She's out of control. There's no putting her back in a cage now. She'll find a way to escape. Again. And it will lead to more trouble. Again."

Heath rocked in his chair, drumming his fingers on his knee as he gave a patient sigh. "I know how much she means to you, but this must be done. You know that, don't you?"

"Have a nice afternoon," he concluded when the person on the phone sat in silence. "I'll see you soon."

With a happy whistle curling his lips, he slapped down the phone receiver and poured himself one last celebratory drink of his expensive scotch. He could barely taste it anymore, he'd had so many that afternoon, but the latest drink wasn't due to stress—it was a celebration.

When he finished it, he climbed to his feet and gave a glance around his tiny office. Of his many offices sprawled out over the vast span of the facility, this was his favorite. It was where he performed his best work.

He approached the door, twisting the golden knob and shoving it open before him. When he stepped out, he lifted a hand to shield the glare of the bright lights from his eyes.

As they always did, the patients in their cages moaned and groaned and wailed, begging him to set them free.

Heath ignored them, brushing the dust off his shoulders and breathing in the damp, earthy air. He had a task to complete and then he'd be free of at least one of his troubles.

CHAPTER FORTY-SIX

"Shhh!"

A rough hand shoved against Sarah's mouth, pushing her lips back hard against her teeth and silencing her before she could scream.

With a grunt, Sarah clenched long fingers around the person's wrist, twisting and bringing her knee up between his legs. The man yelped, though the pain only made him shove Sarah harder back into the wall, momentarily knocking the breath from her lungs before she cried out against the sticky palm.

She clutched the papers harder against her chest, trying to hide them inside her white coat, but the person seemed disinterested in them.

When he leaned closer with a groan of pain, Sarah recognized the fervent, mismatched eyes.

"Stanley...?" she whispered in shock against his hand, though the name was muffled and came out more like a grumble than a word.

The concierge was trembling. His whole body shook like he was vibrating from the inside out.

It made her jaw chatter the way he was holding onto her, sending little shockwaves through her brain that made it hard to think.

Sarah wasn't sure whether to be afraid of him or pity him.

"What's going on?" Sarah hissed, shoving his hand away as some of the papers flew to the floor, sinking to the ground like fallen butterflies.

She bent to scoop them up. Stanley stood stiff and rigid in front of her.

"They said they would keep her safe," he whispered through clenched jaws. He sucked in a breath, squeezing red-rimmed eyes shut.

She recognized his expression which was the same look Mark had when he'd first popped up outside the cemetery that morning.

"Who said they would keep her safe?" Sarah asked, shoving the files under her arm and placing a tentative hand on the man's shoulder.

He winced at the touch. His tears sparkled in the dimness of the hall.

"My mother. Larissa Stalwart. Claire promised she wouldn't be taken. I couldn't take care of her anymore when she became sick, but I couldn't afford the costs here. They said I could work it off and she'd be okay. As long as I did what they said, she'd be okay."

"Taken?" Sarah asked, though her stomach was twisted into hollow, heavy knots.

"To those horrible tunnels they have. To be experimented on...they said she'd be safe!" he repeated, forgetting his order to be silent as he stamped his foot and punched the wall.

Sarah flinched and grabbed his wrist. "Is that what's going on down there? Experiments?"

Stanley nodded. "It's disgusting, but they said-"

"What do you know, Stanley?" Sarah interrupted, not wanting to hear the same diatribe again. "How can we get them out?"

He collapsed against the wall, sinking to the ground.

"I don't know. They didn't trust me with much. I was their errand boy. I listened. I let them know when things happened. I kept the police distracted."

"Is it just you?" Sarah asked, holding her breath.

She felt dizzy and thought she could pass out at any second. This was bigger, so much bigger than she'd initially thought.

Stanley shook his head. He whispered, "There's an army of us. We're everywhere. You're being watched all the time, Sarah. You and that friend of yours. You can't trust anyone. Not even yourself."

"Not even myself?"

Stanley shook his head again, his chin falling on his chest. "Everyone is an eye for this place. Whether they mean to be or not."

"Mark said you told him about the art room. Why?"

"I wanted him to calm down. I wanted him to stop looking. I thought if he viewed that picture Ralph drew, he would be comforted enough to stop." He paused, chewing his lip.

"Picture?"

"He drew it of him and his wife. I saw it once. They were hugging under the night sky."

Sarah didn't answer. It sounded like the photo she'd seen that Mark carried around. Sarah doubted they were standing under the night sky, rather under the dark earth.

"The tunnels, have you been down there?"

He didn't answer, a soft wail of sadness coming from his throat as he buried his face in his palm. "Mom, I didn't mean to..."

Clutching the folders against her, Sarah shook her head and stepped back.

There was a raucous noise from down the hall, just outside the art room.

"Oh my goodness, someone broke into Claire's office." The breathy voice of the psychologist rang out down the hall as curious feet pattered closer. "Call security now!"

CHAPTER FORTY-SEVEN

Sarah's blue eyes glinted from across the hall as Mark stood staring into Claire's empty office.

He wasn't sure whether to be relieved or cross there was such a mess in there, but at least she'd escaped without being caught. He'd stalled Cynthia for as long as he could, asking more and more questions about his father, but Cynthia had eventually burst out of the art room to see what had crashed in the room next door.

Claire's office was a mess, and that was putting it lightly.

The door hung open, exposing a half-toppled desk. One of the drawers had been ripped out, laying in a damaged heap on the floor. A potted plant had been knocked off the desk along with several other papers covered in dirt.

Apparently, Sarah was hardly subtle. Mark kind of liked that about her.

As Cynthia had continued panicking, pacing up and down the hall, and speaking into a radio, Mark had retreated to the shadows of a side hallway, where he fell in beside Sarah.

A limp figure sat on the floor at her side, its body rocking back and forth like many of the skeletal figures in the cells down below had. Mark was about to question who the crumpled person was, but then he recognized the suit.

"What's Stanley doing here?" Mark asked. "Is he alright?"

"His mother is Larissa. The one who clawed Liv. Apparently, she was in one of those cells."

Mark pursed his lips. He knew all too well what suffering Stanley was experiencing.

"Are you alright?" Mark asked, but Stanley just stared at him, shaking and frozen. Mark shook his head, turning away.

"Anything?" Mark whispered to Sarah. "Or did you destroy her office for fun?"

Sarah rolled her pretty blue eyes and gestured to the files in her hands. "Only partly for fun."

She paused, peering around the corner and down the hall as a security guard with a stained shirt appeared at Cynthia's side.

"We have to go. Now! Stanley?"

He ignored them, letting out a soft warble of pain and burying his face in his hands again.

Mark and Sarah exchanged glances before Sarah gave an awkward pat on the concierge's shoulder and then grabbed Mark's hand, dragging him further down the hall. Faster and faster they ran until Mark was having trouble keeping up. They passed room after empty room. Mark kept expecting Sarah to choose one for them to hide out in, but she refused to stop.

She was a fluid runner, her body more athletic than he'd initially realized. Though his heart burned in his chest and his abs clenched, she didn't seem bothered in the slightest.

They rounded a few corners, but Sarah didn't stop moving until they exited a small, hidden door in the back shadows of the manor.

Dim light welcomed them as they burst outside, the clouds so dense and gray that Mark expected a thousand gallons of rain to be dumped on them any instant. The air was thick and muggy, sticking to Mark's clothes like he was wading through glue.

A spattering of gravestones and wilted flowers sprawled around them, and he could see the familiar rusted gate nearby. They were behind the building on the far side of the cemetery. Through the thick wall of trees beyond them was the entrance to the tunnel hidden in the mausoleum.

"What's going on, Sarah?" Mark panted, leaning over so his hands pressed to his knees with a grunt.

He needed to work out again. He'd love to have Sarah be his coach. She was so lithe and quick.

"I wanted to get out of there." Sarah replied, not even breathless after how far and fast they'd run.

She turned her head toward the red walls of the building. It appeared more like a prison than a sanctuary for the mentally ill. The tinted windows were ominous. Anyone could be peering down at them from inside, watching them. Stanley had been right. There were eyes everywhere. She could sense it, crawling over her skin. How hadn't she noticed that before?

"What'd you find?" he asked, gesturing at the files.

Sarah continued scoping around, making sure there were no stray people wandering through the graveyard before she knelt down and lay the papers out on the soft, fading green grass. They were in scattered order now and crumpled from her zealous clutches, more than thirty sheets in the first folder. Because she had dropped them, Sarah couldn't be sure the papers were even in their right folders. She hoped something in this pile would help them in some way.

Mark picked up some of the papers, sorting through them while Sarah did the same at his side.

The pages didn't make any sense to him. They consisted of two lists of names, one on each side of the paper. It seemed in random order to him. For all he knew, it could've been groups of patients with an allergy to peanuts.

"Wait," Sarah breathed, drawing a curious glance from Mark as her eyes narrowed on a spreadsheet. "Mark, this has your parents' names on it."

He took the paper, inspecting it. It was much more interesting than the one he'd been studying.

In neat print, *Test Subjects* labeled the top of the paper. The list was in alphabetical order, and everyone was assigned a number and a date. Next to Ralph's name was written the date of four days earlier. Above his row on the paper sat Joan Hogarth, assigned the date of her death, a few months prior.

"Oh no," Mark dropped the paper like it burned him, shoving it aside.

"Take a look at this, Mark," Sarah said with a shudder, holding out a stack of crumpled papers.

"Death certificates."

"Your mom and dad both have one," she continued, "and Claire signed all of them."

"She's the one," Mark sighed, running a hand through his hair. "She's behind this. She imprisoned my parents for whatever it is that's going on down there."

"Research," Sarah said. "That's what Stanley said."

"What kind?" Mark asked, but the woman just shrugged.

"I can't be sure. Knowing Claire, it could be anything. It could just be for fun. Should we talk to the police?" Sarah asked.

"Somehow, I have a feeling they won't believe us," Mark replied. "Not until we have more proof. Let's go back down and take pictures on your phone. Then we'll go right to the station. They'll have to believe us."

CHAPTER FORTY-EIGHT

The tomb was serene and silent as they approached, the door still ajar from when they'd run free of it an hour earlier.

Sarah gazed at it, her full lips contorted on her face. The papers were tucked into the inner pockets of her white coat. Mark had tried talking her into hiding them, but Sarah had refused. She wasn't giving them a chance to disappear like the pictures in the art room and Ralph's journal already had.

"I can't believe they'd turn my grandfather's memorial into…into this," she whispered, hands curling into fists. "He'd have hated all of it."

"We're going to make this right somehow," Mark assured her. "We're going to get those poor people out of there. We have to take some photos on your phone first. That's the only way that cocky cop is going to hear anything we have to say. He's already nearly convinced I should be locked up here."

It was going to be harder than anything Mark had ever done to go down into those tunnels, see his father again, and then have to leave him behind once more; nevertheless, it was the only way Mark could think of to get him and the others out of there. Surely, with the police at their side, this whole thing would be over before dinner.

Mark wondered whether it was possible, after all this time, that he'd see his mother and father together again. The thought was bittersweet and painful. They'd have another chance at being a family.

Sarah grinned, and, for a moment, Mark forgot their dire circumstances as he studied her kind face.

"Are you *sure* you don't belong in there?" she quipped, making Mark laugh.

It felt strange to laugh right now, but he wanted to hold onto that feeling forever. They were about to go into the tunnel again, after all, and Mark wasn't confident they'd be able to make it out. One mistake and they, too, could be locked up in those cages.

"Let's go," he whispered. "My dad is waiting for me." He paused. Sarah's face was grim. "Sarah, you never really knew my dad as a patient did you?"

Sarah quieted, her eyes hesitant, then gave a serious sigh.

"I did know him, Mark. Only a little. But I did. I didn't realize it was him at first." For the past several months, she hadn't been able to get him to speak to her or to say his name. He hadn't said anything at all.

Mark grimaced, running a nervous hand through his hair. What the therapist had said was right. He could read it on Sarah's face. He didn't want to hear it said aloud. He didn't want to know how far his father had degraded. He wanted to get Ralph out of his cage.

He extended one hand toward her, the tips of his fingers twitching. As worried as he was about what was going to happen in there, the thought of having Sarah at his side made him stronger, more capable.

She slid her hand into his, interlacing their fingers, and then pushed open the door so they could gain access.

The interior of the tomb was as dark and empty as it had been before, the walls rising sharp and high. Though the entrance to the tunnel had been closed, Mark opened it with no trouble.

How many times had Dad traveled down this way? How had he become stuck below?

As they crept further into the tunnel, the soft hush of speaking voices echoed from down the corridor.

"Who is that?" Mark whispered to Sarah, whose face had gone pale and drawn.

She tugged him down the hallway, pressing close to the shadows of the wall and motioning for him to stay as still and silent as possible. Judging by her face, he knew he wasn't going to like what they found.

Since the pair had traversed the tunnel an hour earlier, they knew the layout, where to step and where to stay hidden from the light.

"You started this, Ms. Matthews," a man's voice echoed.

Mark sucked in a shocked breath. *Heath Dole. Of course.*

Mark spied around the corner. Two people stood on the other side of the large hole in the tunnel.

He wasn't able to peek for long, but he did see Claire's bright red braid as she laughed and stepped further away from the manor director.

"Heath, what are you trying to say?" she said. "Of course I started this. Without me, you'd be nowhere. You'd have nothing. You're lucky I've helped you. I could've taken you down in an instant."

"Don't be dramatic Ms. Matthews. It doesn't suit you," Heath responded, approaching the woman. "We got as far as we did due to science, not your…offerings."

"My gifts have propelled your research ahead by lightyears," she snapped back, "The serums you can make-"

"You've been nothing but trouble since the day you stepped foot in here. I have been lax with you, Ms. Matthews. I have allowed you to get away with too much. I apologize."

"Heath Dole never apologizes," she shot back. "Isn't that what you always say?" She tried taking another step away from him, but he blocked her path.

"This one time, I am making an exception." He offered her a quick smile before resting his hands on her shoulders. "Goodbye," he said, shoving her several feet backward.

Sarah and Mark peeked again. They watched in horror as the woman stumbled back, her feet gliding off the edge of the ledge.

With a scream, she vanished over the side, swallowed into nothingness.

CHAPTER FORTY-NINE

Joan had grown used to the room.

The elderly mother of two did not explore the small four-cornered space like she once had. When she'd first been put in there, she had paced along every inch, pressing weary fingers against the walls, searching for any means of escape that she never found. The door was locked from the outside, and no amount of pulling, pushing, or banging on the heavy metal would see her release. It'd only seen her nails get ragged and her hands get bruised.

The first time she'd been in the tunnel had been a blur. Heath had told her that was normal.

When she closed her eyes, she saw sterile, white walls that made her tremble. At the same time, she swore she could feel the comforting hand of her husband's fingers laced with her own.

It'd been days since she'd seen Ralph. His visits had stopped. She hoped it was because he was having so much fun on sushi night and waffle morning and tea club afternoon that he didn't have the time anymore. She hoped it was not because he'd been found out or because he'd forgotten about her.

She mused how different she'd become. She had nothing to do there but think. So she thought about herself and how she'd changed. Some days her mindfulness comforted her, but, mostly, it made her soul ache.

Her recent memory was sharper, like a blunted old pencil thrust hard into a spinning, high-powered sharpener to make it write well again. Everything had more clarity and definition to it. Every needle that had pierced her skin and every tear that had been shed was vivid in her mind. When she drank water, she could feel the individual little droplets coating her tongue. She could describe exactly what she ate three weeks ago and how much of it she'd eaten and how she'd put the oatmeal cookie aside because she knew it was Ralph's favorite and she'd wanted to give it to him when he came to see her again. He visited when he could, but creeping out of the facility and through the cemetery to the old man's tomb was hard on Ralph. His knees no longer supported him as easily. His hands had trouble clenching down. Joan had told him over and over again he didn't need to come to see her. She was fine as long as she knew he was safe. The deal had been just for her.

Joan hadn't known what to think the first time she'd woken up in the tunnels with Heath and the nurses leaning over her. She'd cried as they poked and prodded and bruised her. Time had been a blur. All she could recall now was the shock of discovering her own daughter had agreed for her to be taken in such an undignified manner. At first, she'd been angry at the betrayal, but that had been so long ago. The anger had faded away into nothing more than a dull ache in her heart. The beating organ inside her chest felt bruised.

In their own way, her children were both smart and independent. When she thought of them, she could still see them as infants, toddlers, and preteens, their eyes big and their hands small. She loved how Liv's hair had smelled like apples as she'd splashed among her rainbow-colored toys in the bath.

A soft, warm smile twitched on Joan's mouth.

Her memories were all she had in this rough, quiet, little dungeon. Though Heath had brought her books, he hadn't brought her the right kind. She didn't like the ones he gave her about child detectives and high school romance. The books were so worn she was sure he'd stolen them from a thrift shop. Of course, she doubted she would have liked much of anything with which he'd tried to bribe her into surrendering.

"Don't fight so much, Mrs. Hogarth," he'd told her, patting her shoulder as they tied her hands and legs down again last month to pepper her papery skin with needles.

Whether they injected her with something or stole something from her, she didn't know. She didn't care.

Joan would never stop fighting. She would keep struggling as long as she had to so she could return to her husband's side.

On one of the first days she'd been taken below, she'd asked when she could go back to Ralph. Celeste, the nurse, had giggled and given a wink. While she didn't answer with words, Joan had understood well enough.

Never, the nurse's eyes had gleamed.

Joan had cried again. She wasn't proud of how much she had sobbed in the beginning, at the thought of her husband being unaware of her condition or her whereabouts. The man in the cell beside her had reached through the bars and taken her hand in his.

"Don't worry," he'd smiled, copper-colored eyes gleaming, "I'll make sure Ralphie makes it to you again."

Joan had clung to that man's hand, burying her damp face into his palm. She knew they would never escape, but she appreciated the kindness.

Days later, she had been moved to a separate cell. Because she was special, Heath had explained, and she deserved some living space.

Joan wasn't sure what had become of the man in the cell beside her old one, but, a few months later, Ralph had knocked at her door. She didn't know how he'd found her or how he was able to open her door. She'd been so exhilarated at the time she hadn't thought to ask. She hadn't thought about anything but throwing her arms around her husband's neck and resting her cheek over his heart to listen to the gentle, familiar rhythm. It had been hurried and quick, and his hands had been clammy as he gripped her tightly, afraid to ever let her go again.

They'd rocked together, both teary-eyed and so joyous and so sorrowful. It had felt like they were back dancing in their kitchen like they'd used to do.

The musky scent of the tunnel laced with the heavy fragrance of sterile gauze and antibiotics did little to hamper their bittersweet reunion.

It'd been hard to convince Ralph to leave without her, but Ralph's knees were already aching so much from the journey underground, and Joan knew they wouldn't be able to travel fast or far. They'd be caught and she'd be put back in her prison and Ralph would be...she didn't want to think about what they would do to him if they found him.

Joan was content with the knowledge her family was safe. She would fight through the bruises on her arms, the shaved stripe on the side of her head, the chronic headaches, and the memories that were so clear they felt real.

So long as it was only her down here, with Ralph cozy and warm above and her children far away and happy, Joan would make it through another day.

Resting her head back on the flat pillow, Joan clasped her hands together over her heart and thought of sweet Ralph, his lopsided smile, and his warm, gentle embrace.

"Today is my best day because I am with you," she whispered aloud, as she and Ralph had said every night for forty-nine years as they slipped beneath her handmade quilt and then repeated it as they clung to one another in the dark depths of these dreadful tunnels. Stubborn tears formed and she resented them. She had gone so long without crying.

She could only hope wherever he was far, far away, he could hear her, and they would make their special saying true again. She hadn't forgotten for a single night to say it. His kind eyes were the last thing she imagined every time she closed her own.

"Today is my best day because I am with you." She repeated the mantra over and over again, slipping back into memories of Ralph at the lake, his gray eyes as bright as they once were and the smile on her face as real as it once was.

CHAPTER FIFTY

Sarah sat on the grass, her legs stretched out in front of her, her forearms resting on her thighs.

She'd made it all of twelve steps from the mausoleum before her hand went limp in Mark's fingers and her shaking knees collapsed beneath her, sending her sinking like a crumpled rag down to the ground.

The hem of her white coat was dingy from the damp earth of the tunnels, but she couldn't bring herself to care. Her blue eyes stared unfocused on her shoes as a soft, fresh breeze blew her hair into her face. She didn't react; she didn't even blink.

Mark bent down in front of her, reaching to take her hands in his. Her hands were icy against his fingers. He felt a tremor rolling through her.

"Sarah," he whispered, shifting so his gaze lined up with her though she didn't seem to see him, "you in there?"

Biting his lip, Mark glanced around. They stuck out like a bright red, throbbing thumb. After the incident with Graham, it was clear someone did not want them here. That someone was probably Heath. Mark wondered what would come crashing through the trees at them if they remained there too long.

"He killed her," Sarah breathed, her voice high-pitched and strained. "Heath killed Claire. He just...pushed her into the sinkhole and killed her!"

Mark bent closer, resisting the urge to press a hand to her mouth to quiet Sarah as her voice grew louder. He had no idea what he was supposed to say to her, nor what she was thinking. He didn't even know what he was thinking. His mind was such a blur.

Sarah blinked, though her eyes did not clear up at all. Her brow wrinkled as the wind again blew hair across her face.

Tucking her mussed brunette locks behind her ear for her, Mark settled down on the comfortable grass.

"He's a monster," Sarah continued, hands curling into tight fists. "We have to do something. We can't let him get away this. With any of this!"

She lurched to face Mark, then glanced over her shoulder at the tunnel as though she were considering storming down in there to punch Heath in the jaw. He certainly deserved a good beating, and Sarah wanted to be the one to do it, but they couldn't run down willy-nilly into the tunnels and hope for the best. Claire's murder had made that clear.

The shock still hadn't reached Mark. He could sense it buried down inside of him, clawing at his soul and shredding it with the frenetic adrenaline still pumping through his whole body.

While Mark and Sarah had hidden in the shadows, a long, silent scream had contorted Sarah's face. Heath had gazed over the rim of the pit into the silky blackness down below, allowed ten seconds to pass, clapped his hands together, and turned around to retreat into the tunnels. A cheery, whistled tune echoed around him. At the same time, Mark had grabbed Sarah and run to daylight. His entire body screamed at him to get out of there before they would have both joined Claire in the depths of that endless hole.

Mark was grateful his panic had subsided, though he wasn't sure he'd ever be able to sleep again. His body vibrated like he'd chugged a few hundred gallons of black coffee. He didn't want to sit still long enough to let his brain catch up with what they had witnessed. Heath wasn't afraid to deal with anyone in his way.

But why Claire? Wasn't she helping him? Mark felt as though nothing in this strange, twisted situation was adding up right.

Sarah gave a sound that sounded like a faint growl. Her eyes locked on her grandfather's grave once again.

"We know she was involved with whatever psycho experimentation is going on down there," Mark said, taking Sarah's face in his hands and pulling her close to him.

"But that doesn't make it okay!" Sarah cried, grabbing his hands and squeezing hold of them.

"It doesn't," Mark agreed, "but it means we have to be smart. Heath is dangerous, Sarah, and I think he's more dangerous than we can even comprehend."

Though fuming inside, Sarah fell quiet.

"You're right," she eventually sighed, though she wasn't happy about it. Mark could sense she was still entertaining the idea of good solid punch that would smash the nose on Heath's handsome face. "What should we do?" she asked.

Mark exhaled, listening to the wind that howled through the trees and sent fallen leaves skittering over the pavement like nails scratching over the concrete. His father had been so weak and frail down there in that terrible little cage, like an abandoned dog at the local pound. Leaving him down there even longer made Mark's heart want to explode right in his chest.

Did Dad feel forsaken and discarded like an old newspaper? Does he think I left him behind for good?

Closing his eyes, Mark breathed in the crisp air and counted to three before letting it slip out between his lips. He had to come up with a plan. He had to get his dad and the rest of those poor people out from where they were being held.

But what am I supposed to do? There's no way Officer Schumacher will entertain anything I have to say without more proof.

"For now, let's get the hell out of this place," he told her. "We can't sit here and wait for Heath to come and get us."

The nurse nodded, allowing Mark to pull her up to her feet. They walked toward the cemetery fence, keeping a vigilant eye out for Graham or anyone who might be watching for them.

"We can head back to the hotel. Maybe Stanley will be there and we can talk about what to...what to..."

Sarah stopped talking, her words slurring into silence as her jaw dropped. She blinked and rubbed her eyes as Mark frowned and turned to glance over his shoulder at the manor.

The dark tinted glass of the front doors had swung open as a young couple, probably there to inspect the grounds for a potential future resident, stepped outside.

A familiar red-headed woman sat behind the main desk of Springthorpe, her long hair braided. As the trio locked eyes, Claire Matthews leaped to her feet, palms slamming down hard on the wood desk as her eyes became wide as saucers.

Utter and complete shock was a two-way street.

CHAPTER FIFTY-ONE

It was impossible to keep track of time down below, Liv thought.

The darkness was a blanket, wrapped so tight around her she could barely breathe. She wiggled her toes and fingers and found that was all the movement she could muster. She couldn't tell if she was merely tired or still tied down. All she knew was she wanted to be back at home beside her dull husband. If she could squeeze her eyes shut and teleport back to him this instant, she'd even do her best to listen to one of his long-winded political speeches.

But she wasn't home, and she'd come to accept that she'd never see her children's faces again. She wished she had someone else to blame other than herself.

A door creaked and a thin sliver of light spilled into the room.

"Claire?" Liv asked, almost ashamed of her warbling, high pitched voice.

Fear dripped from every word like sticky sap from an evergreen.

"No, Mrs. Keller," the man responded in the deep, charming voice Liv knew well.

"Heath," she said, resting her head back on the hard table. She'd been waiting for him to come.

It was so dark she couldn't tell whether she was lying down or propped up.

There was a light whirr and a crackling pop as a bright overhead light turned on, blinding Liv. Her eyes had still been open. She yelped, squeezing her eyes shut. She tried to rub at them, but she wasn't able to convince her arms to move.

"I'm sorry for this inconvenience," Heath said in a jolly tone that was unapologetic. "If I had known you were joining us, I would have provided better accommodations."

Liv had never heard him sound so happy, aside from when she had signed those final forms last year.

"What's that supposed to mean?" Liv mumbled, blinking hard and squinting as black dots swirled and spun so fast in front of her vision she felt sick.

Heath didn't answer, grabbing a rolling chair and pushing it toward the woman. He settled down on it with relaxed ease, his ankle resting on his knee. He was so damn comfortable it irked Liv.

"Mrs. Keller, I discovered something while experimenting on Joan. Would you like to hear about it?"

"Experimenting?" Liv croaked, tears springing to her eyes. "You were supposed to help her. Not cage her up like a rat in a lab."

"I wouldn't say a rat. More like a guinea pig," Heath chuckled. "And what did you think I was paying you for, Mrs. Keller? What kind of medical system pays its clients instead of the other way around? Don't play the fool. It doesn't suit you."

"You made it...you made it sound like it was just some tests. You made it sound like it would help her. Like it would help other people."

"Don't pretend you signed her life away for any reason other than the money," Heath snapped, rolling his crystal eyes.

Liv gritted her teeth, wishing she could slap the smirk right off Heath's handsome face. "I wanted to help her. She and Dad only had each other. I wanted her to stay with him for a little while longer. I thought it would be like a miracle. I didn't know you would steal her in the middle of the night and pretend she'd died. I didn't know!"

"But you let me keep paying you. You let me keep Joan down in this place."

"I wanted her to remember Dad. When she forgot him that first time..." Liv trailed off, shoulders quivering, head falling back again, tears seeping out from the corners of her eyes.

A smile reappeared on Heath's face as he leaned over, resting his suited elbows on the edge of the table. "But you were correct in your assumption. It did help her, and it did help other people. And it will continue to."

He inspected manicured nails, giving another happy nod. "You know, Joan is quite intriguing. A unique brain structure, as well as a few interesting tidbits in her DNA. Just like Henrietta Lack's cells were so important to cancer research, Joan's are just as important for curing Alzheimer's."

Liv pursed her lips, giving a slight shake of her head. She didn't want to think of what her mother had gone through, what she had forced her mother to suffer through, how she had betrayed her family, and how she was going to pay for it now.

"We believe," Heath said, his fingers tapping a cheery rhythm on the hard plastic, "that perhaps some of her descendants may be equally interesting. Her samples alone have sent our research ahead by leaps and bounds. It's been fascinating."

Heath climbed to his feet, arms crossing over his chest as he gazed down at the gray-eyed woman. Terror made her gaunt eyes glisten. Liv had withered since the first time he saw her. Though her gaze had once been keener, she'd always been a bit frail. That weakness was why he'd chosen her. The weak ones, the desperate ones, they were easy to bribe, cajole, or threaten into submission. He'd had no idea how useful and valuable her mother would be. He'd assumed Mrs. Hogarth would be another boring, nearly useless subject. Oh, how wrong he'd been. That had been the ultimate lesson for him. Never underestimate anyone.

Since meeting her, Liv had turned into a shell, a hollow person, a rag doll. Intense guilt does that, he supposed.

"The preliminary tests are easy, Mrs. Keller. You don't have to be worried. Unless we find you are of no use to us. Then I'm afraid you'll have to be terminated. I'm sure you understand."

Liv inspected the opposite wall. Her head twisted to the side so she could turn away from the man beside her. She wanted to pretend he wasn't there. The white paint was clean and shiny, reminding her of fresh eggs at the store.

The Springthorpe director took a few steps toward the door. Liv was torn between begging him to leave on one light and refusing to do anything that would draw his attention back to her.

"You know you aren't the only one in your family line we are researching," he added with an artificial innocence that mocked Liv.

"Mark?" she gasped, lurching back toward him.

Her spine inched off the table. She wasn't tied down at all, but her muscles felt as though they were bags of sand.

Heath laughed and shook his head. "Oh, no. With your family, I don't believe the necessary genetic information we've discovered is passed down on the men's side, I'm afraid. He was useless from the start."

"Was?" Liv whispered, throat going tight. Her stomach twisted up inside of her like she was on that carousel ride again.

Heath smiled once more. "Your granddaughter, Liv, is quite a spunky little thing."

"I don't have a granddaughter." Liv shook her head. "Just three daughters."

"You do have a granddaughter. When was the last time you spoke to your eldest, Mrs. Keller? Perhaps your husband could fill you in on it sometime." He paused, laughed again, and shook his head. "No. I suppose that won't do, hmm? Anyways, the little one is playing in the other room right now. But don't worry, she won't feel a thing. Hopefully."

CHAPTER FIFTY-TWO

The head nurse was glad one of the other nurses had brought over a chair while Claire was at lunch because she'd sunk down so fast she was pretty sure her legs had slipped right out from beneath her like the floor had been waxed with Teflon.

"It couldn't be," she whispered to herself in an unusual stupor. "Could it?"

She'd seen them clear as day, even though Heath had assured her he would get rid of them. It was part of his plan, and when Heath had a plan, it was never derailed. Mark and Sarah were supposed to have been eliminated.

"Crotchety Claire, Crotchety Claire..." Graham hummed, popping up in front of her so fast it made her jump.

"Excuse me?" the head nurse snapped, shaking off the startled goosebumps prickling over her flesh and rising back to her feet, her hands clasped on her hips. "What did you call me, Graham?"

He giggled, bouncing up on the balls of his feet and glancing around to make sure no one was paying attention. One of the rules was to be discreet, and Graham had never sought out Claire before. It was always she who had found him. But Graham wanted his prize and he couldn't bear waiting any longer.

The woman glared at him with her green eyes sparkling, leaning side to side as she tried to stare out the glass windows of Springthorpe. Mark and Sarah were gone now and Claire shuddered. She hadn't imagined them. They'd been there. Like ghosts.

Bending over so he was at her petite level, Graham snapped his fingers in front of the woman's face.

"That is rude, Graham," Claire barked, hands falling off her hips to cross over her chest. "What are you hoping to achieve right now?"

She'd warned Heath it was a mistake to bring any of the patients from the tunnels back into the facility, but Heath had insisted. They'd told the less observant staff that Graham had temporarily gone home to a family that didn't actually exist. The progress with the old man's Alzheimer's that Heath had made was astounding. Though Claire had always believed Heath could change the world with his experiments, Graham was a true testament to the possibilities. The man had been almost catatonic when he'd gone down to be studied. The resulting Graham Jones talked too much, moved too much, and was very much a nuisance, but studying him was like peering into the future. It made her heart swell with pride at the thought of how much progress science and medicine could derive from this. It was all worth it to her. Heath was a mastermind.

While the experiments had undoubtedly changed the old man, he could be useful. Claire would've argued the extent of that usefulness, but Heath wasn't interested in listening. When Heath was invested in a project, he had tunnel vision. Nothing mattered but the outcome. Claire admired that focus and drive. She hoped to emulate it.

"Crotchety..." Graham pouted and gave his head a shake, stroking his white beard with a croaky clear of his throat. "I mean, Mrs. Claire. Ma'am. Nurse lady."

Claire resisted the urge to roll her eyes, fingernails digging into her arms as she tried to keep her professional composure.

"Yes?" she muttered in that dry, southern drawl.

"I want it back," Graham sighed, shoulders sagging. "I couldn't play with Mark and Sarah like you wanted. They're too good at hide-and-seek, but I still think I should get it back."

Bewildered, Claire shook her head. "What do you think you should get back?"

"The journal. Ralphie's. You took it from me and you said I could have it back if I did what you said. I tried to play with them, but they're really good at hide-and-seek-"

Claire held up one hand, silencing the older man so he would stop rambling on about playtime and stupid games.

"Graham, I don't have any journal. I don't know what you're asking me for." She was willing to write this off as delusional ramblings of a semi-coherent man-child, but Graham wasn't budging.

A storm passed his gray face, penny brown eyes narrowing on Claire as his lips tightened. It reminded the head nurse of a toddler getting ready to throw himself down on the floor to scream and kick until he was given ice cream.

"You took it from me," he repeated, more slowly this time, like it was Claire who had memory issues.

"I did no such thing," she retorted with a scowl.

"We're friends, Crotchety Claire, that's what you told me!" Graham's voice rose, booming on the walls.

Claire knew she had to settle this disruption before Heath found out about it.

"Play with Mark and Sarah and you'll get it back!" he shrieked in a high-pitched voice Claire assumed was a poor, earsplitting imitation of her own.

"We're friends, sure," she responded, trying to settle him before the wrong nurse came over and heard too much. "Of course, Graham."

"That's what you told me!" he repeated. "When we were together down below, you told me we were friends!"

Claire could see a meltdown coming full force in the immediate future. She swallowed, reaching over to take Graham's arm in hers. He relaxed, a silly smile forming on his cracked lips.

"Tell me about this journal," she forced a smile with fake sincerity. "When did you give it to me?"

"In the dark. When you came to me. After I played too rough with Ralphie's boy. I'm sorry about that. I told you I was sorry, didn't I?"

"You did, you did," Claire replied, her lips drawing into a tight line as she led Graham back toward his room, her mind spinning in complete confusion. They'd only made it partway down the hall when Claire stopped, her fingers clenching down hard on Graham's arm. The old man grunted in surprise.

"I'm sorry," she whispered. "Graham...Graham, you said we made friends while we were in the tunnels, didn't you?" Claire asked, wishing she'd been listening more closely to the words he'd been speaking.

Graham nodded, his droopy face still puckered.

"And you said I visited you here in the facility? You're sure it was me you saw?"

Again, the old man nodded, his arms wrapping around himself in a comforting hug. "Such pretty red hair."

"Oh, no," Claire whispered, eyes widening in horror.

"You'll give it back, won't you?" Graham whined, prodding her. "You'll give me Ralphie's journal, right?"

CHAPTER FIFTY-THREE

There has to be something in here..." Sarah mumbled after they darted around the side of the enormous building.

Though Mark wanted to keep running until he saw the border of Canada, Sarah sank down to her knees once more with a thoughtful click of her tongue.

Tugging the files free of her white jacket, the nurse spread the jumbled and crumpled papers out in front of them.

"I don't think it's a good idea for us to stay here," Mark said, brown eyes searching the lot around them, "with Heath and...Claire still out and about. They could be coming for us now."

"We saw Claire die," Sarah replied, dragging her eyes away from the papers long enough to frown up at Mark. "We saw her die and then we saw her sitting nice and pretty inside the facility. We need to figure out what happened."

"We can do this at the hotel-"

"Stanley said it himself. Nowhere is safe. We're no safer back there than we are here. At least here we're close enough to do something. Do you really want to leave your parents down there while we go eat cookies and sip coffee at the hotel?"

Mark compressed his lips, arms crossing over his chest. "I wasn't suggesting we go to the buffet."

With a sigh, Sarah gave a shake of her head and ran her hand through her long, dark hair. It'd long come loose from its ponytail, and the light blue band she'd been using to contain it had vanished.

"I'm sorry," she said, attempting the most feeble smile Mark had seen in a long time. The expression reminded him of Liv's forced, fake grins. "I'm so confused. I don't know what to think. My brain feels like it's running in a circle over and over, searching for the one bit of this that makes sense."

"I know," Mark acknowledged, kneeling down to help her sort through the papers. "Me too."

"You're sorry too, or you're confused too?" the woman asked with terse playfulness, pushing half of the stack toward him.

"Both," he chuckled.

Though they were hidden from view, Mark's spine went rigid every time they heard the hiss of the sliding front doors of the retirement home or the crunch of gravel beneath the tires of an approaching vehicle. It was odd how everyone was continuing with their everyday lives while Mark and Sarah were trying to piece together an attempted murder and a bunch of patients caged underground. It was surreal. Mark felt like he was dreaming.

"I keep replaying it over in my head," Sarah mumbled, though Mark wasn't sure if she was speaking to him or herself. "We saw her fall. It was her. Right? It was Claire. We heard her voice and she has all that red hair and she was so small…"

Mark didn't answer, his eyes locked on the sheet of paper in his hands. His stomach pitched, throat going dry as the guttural sound of surprise warbled deep in his throat.

"Mark?" Sarah asked, biting her lip as the man's face drained of color. "What'd you find?"

His face turned ghostly white. She was afraid to know what was printed on those typed sheets.

Without a word, a shudder rocked him. Mark thrust the paper over to Sarah as though he was glad to be free of it. He dusted his hands off, trying to push away the words burned in his brain.

After a lingering stare at Mark's pale face, Sarah inspected the paper. It was a spreadsheet, and a simple one at that, as there were only a few columns. Sarah recognized the names on the far-left side. Along with Ralph Hogarth, Joan Hogarth, and Larissa Stalwart were the names of some other people she had seen in the cages. Some sort of patient number was assigned to each of them. Beside each of their names was that of another and a date. While not every row was filled out, a few notable ones were.

"Oh, no. This is bad," Sarah whispered, dropping the paper and recoiling from it.

"The cremations…" Mark groaned through gritted teeth, arms coiled around his twisted stomach. "Heath was killing other people to fill the urns of those he took for research. He assigned them together like…like a seating assignment or bus buddies or some sick field trip partnering."

Mark grunted, one hand at his mouth. He recalled now how warm the urn had felt in his arms when he first received it. *It hadn't been Dad in there.*

Sarah grabbed the paper and shoved it back into a folder before pausing and opening the manila sleeve back up.

Mark had turned away, his mind reeling and his stomach retching. *Who had been the poor soul in Dad's urn? In Mom's?* He hadn't seen the name. He was glad he wouldn't know; it would've been burned into his memory forever.

"Look at this, Mark…" Sarah whispered, breaking through his thoughts. Mark shook his head. He couldn't take any more of the horrific secrets in those files.

Running a rapt finger down the paper she gazed down upon, Sarah held up a photo from inside the packet.

"It was clipped to this patient report," she said. "Look familiar?"

Mark swallowed the thick lump in his throat and took the picture between tentative fingers. It was too late to get cold feet. They'd long jumped headfirst into this horrific mess.

From the glossy surface of the Polaroid, Claire grimaced as unruly red hair curled around her shoulders.

"Why would Claire keep a photo of herself in there?" he asked, frowning.

"It isn't Claire," Sarah responded, reading from the report on her lap. "Cecilia Matthews...I think she was one of their research projects, Mark. Her only family is..."

"Claire Matthews," Mark filled in for her as she trailed off in shock. He stared down at the paper. "They were twins. Cecilia was diagnosed with early onset Alzheimer's when she was in her thirties!"

"Look, another of those fake death certificates..." Mark gasped, dragging it out from the file. "Fifteen years ago-"

"Signed by Henry Kramer..." Sarah whimpered, dragging it closer to her face as though she could change the words with her sharp stare. "Mark, my grandfather was the one who signed this!"

CHAPTER FIFTY-FOUR

With a jaunty nod of his head, the fifty-three-year-old director of Springthorpe Manor hopped over a crevice in the earth of the long, winding tunnel.

Heath Dole was on top of the world.

In the span of one generous twenty-four-hour day, he'd managed to smooth over all the unexpected wrinkles of his well-thought-out plan. For thirty-odd years, the place had run as it did with little in the way of trouble, aside from the rare complication caused by a family member who refused to accept the ill-timed passing of his relative at Springthorpe. Each of them had eventually come around.

Heath had never worried too much about that, though, just like he hadn't been too worried about his little predicament that afternoon. There was an easy way to deal with it. Claire was the one who worried all the time. She was lucky she was so helpful and that she had provided such a fascinating specimen for his research.

Cecilia Matthews, dangerous, clever and, unhinged, was– Heath paused to savor the past tense now associated with her deceased being–much less an ideal candidate for the research once Joan Hogarth was gifted to him. Where Cecilia had been intriguing, Joan was his scientific holy grail. It was with a serum crafted from her DNA that he'd treated Graham Jones, who had bounced back overnight from the useless state in which he'd previously existed. While in the minority with his opinion, Heath much preferred Graham with his newfound silly disposition. Plus, Graham helped with the child.

Heath had to admit he'd been shocked when little four-year-old Savannah Bennett showed up in the tunnel, playing ball with Cecilia. The woman had tossed that tangled web of hair over her shoulder and smirked. At first, Heath had been angry. He did not kidnap hapless children for his research. He used the elderly and aging, those who were well on their way to dying anyway.

Heath had no idea how Cecilia managed to get the little girl, but one scan of the child's brain told him this find was worth the mystery. Like her great-grandmother, Savannah was unique. He'd been less surprised when Liv was delivered to him.

Unfortunately for Cecilia, however, Heath hated surprises, no matter how useful they turned out to be. In his rigged strategy, there could be no wild cards.

Though he'd heard the sad tinge in her voice, Claire had seemed to be understanding when Heath had phoned her to explain his decision to end her sister's life. Her twin had been her only family left, after all. But all he'd had to do was remind head nurse Matthews of the significant progress they were about to make with Joan as their research project and no one to hinder them. With those loose cannons out of the way, their path would be clear, he'd explained.

That was why poor Nurse Kramer and Mark Hogarth had to die as well.

Heath was giddy at the thought of the pair of them rotting in some backwoods river in Canada, just where he wanted them. He'd already arranged for a letter written in Sarah's hand to be sent to one of her friends explaining how she needed to escape the stress of her depressing job in which she was surrounded by dying old people. By Monday, a similar letter elaborating his decision to stay in San Francisco would be on its way to Mark's place of employment. Liv, however, was more complicated. She was a wrench in his plan that Heath had not been expecting. Her husband would search for her. It wouldn't look good that the entire Hogarth clan had been wiped out on a single trip to his retirement home.

The blue-eyed man gave a shrug and a sigh. At least the troublesome three were gone and Liv was under his control. He would figure the rest out over a glass of scotch.

Heath's back pocket vibrated. He frowned in mild irritation, glancing over at his caged research subjects with the same distaste with which one would glare at a cockroach scrabbling over the kitchen tile. Had he a giant shoe, he would smack down every one of those people staring at him with those helpless, huge eyes. At least they weren't baying at him like trapped sheep or cattle. They'd learned long ago not to do that.

Turning away from the elderly patients, he fished out his cell phone and held it to his ear.

"Springthorpe Manor, this is director Heath Dole speaking. How may I help you this lovely evening?" he asked in his calm, practiced voice.

The woman on the other end gave a little giggle, "Mr. Dole, you sound so formal."

Cynthia James. Heath recognized her voice. Why was the psychologist calling him now?

Lord help me if another patient has bitten someone, Heath groaned to himself.

"What can I assist you with, Ms. James?" he asked politely.

"I wanted to give you an update on my appointment with Mark Hogarth, Ralph's son," she replied.

"I understand he went MIA sometime after our meeting together," Heath said, barely listening to the psychologist as he wandered back into the quiet space of his small office. "It's no worry at all you couldn't get him to come in. I meant to contact you earlier."

"Oh," she said, giving a thoughtful hum. "Well, as it turns out, I was able to drag him in for a quick appointment this afternoon."

Heath stopped walking, his fingers coiled around the cool metal knob of his office door.

His voice dropping low, he asked, "About when would that have been?"

She paused, popping her lips in thought and making Heath grimace at the sound. "Ah, I don't recall the exact time. Forty-five minutes ago? You might want to have a chat with your staff, however, because that nurse seems quite taken with Mark. I don't think she's gotten any work done at all today."

"Ms. James, if you'll excuse me, I seem to have some important items I need to take care of," Heath replied, making sure his even, smooth voice did not fluctuate one bit.

He couldn't let on that he was shocked that two of his troublemakers had resurfaced.

What the hell had happened?

CHAPTER FIFTY-FIVE

S arah cried out, shoving another paper into Mark's face.

He jerked back, shaking his head and grabbing the form so he could study it.

Another signature by Henry Kramer rested at the bottom of the paper, his scrawl neat and elegant. Mark's dad used to say you could determine much about a person through their signature. Mark wasn't sure what Henry's swirly letters were telling him now.

"Maybe it doesn't mean anything?" he shrugged. "Maybe Heath was duplicating your grandfather's signature? I wouldn't put that past him."

Sarah chewed an already brutalized lip and shook her head. "No. This is his handwriting. I'd recognize it anywhere."

She thought back to the numerous cards he'd given her and the countless times he'd filled out her school papers because her parents didn't care. He felt like a stranger to her now. A stranger she'd adored all her life.

"Maybe he didn't realize what he was signing off on?" Mark offered, though he had the distinct feeling he was being less than helpful.

The pretty nurse wasn't comforted by his attempts at soothing her. If anything, it made her more irritable. They both knew the truth. They swirled and circled around it like water rushing around a sink basin. They, too, felt they were going down that drain.

"I've found his signature on a few reports that are pretty explicit," she said. "They're researching brain chemistry and degenerative diseases in those tunnels. Grandpa knew what he was doing, Mark. He signed off on several terminations of the subjects."

"Terminations?" Mark asked, though he regretted it the second tears welled up in Sarah's sea-blue eyes.

"Terminations," she echoed, shuddering.

Mark went quiet, observing the scattered papers around them. Sarah had been flinging them this way and that, scouring them for more proof that her grandfather had played a part in the research when she already knew it to be true.

"And we don't even know where his body is," she continued. "I haven't found any information on whether he's become one of the research subjects or whether he's alive or whether he's dead…" she trailed off, her face contorting into a grimace.

"We need to go," Mark said, leaning toward her and snagging her wrists before she could flip through more of the sheets. "We can't stay here. They're going to come for us. Heath and Claire have already made it clear they're done with putting up with us."

No!" Sarah hissed, gritting her jaw. "I need to know more. I need to know *why*, Mark. I need to know why he would get involved in this!"

Her voice rose higher until it was shrill and strained. A single, stinging tear streaked down her cheek.

Mark swept toward her, wrapping his arms around her and squeezing her tightly, as though he could smother away her bewildered grief.

"I became a nurse because of him," she choked, her tears damp and warm on his shoulder, her fingers clutching his shirt so hard it tightened around his neck. He didn't relax his hold an inch. "I saw how much the patients loved him. I saw how much he loved them back. I wanted to emulate that. I wanted to help people like he did!"

"You are not your grandfather," Mark whispered in her ear. "You are not anyone but yourself, Sarah. You were helping people by following in his steps. You *are* helping people."

"By working here, I was killing my patients without even knowing it, Mark! How can I call myself a nurse? How can I ever return to my profession?"

He rocked her back and forth as the pair knelt atop crumpled grass in the shadow of the huge, ominous building. The air felt colder there. Haunted. Like the ghosts of all those murdered in cold blood between the walls were swirling in the endless fog and tearing at them with icy claws.

"I have to know why," she repeated, lifting her face to gaze up at him.

The tears had dried from her eyes but left streaks through the dust and dirt on her round cheeks.

With a firm nod, Mark cupped her chin with one hand.

"We're going to find out why. We're going to take that monster down," he promised her. "I swear we will, Sarah."

Her fingers trembling, she placed her hand over his. Her wide eyes stared so intensely into Mark's golden ones that he felt as though she gazed right into his very soul.

He whispered her name aloud, though it was stolen by the cold breeze. Even the simple word felt warm in his throat.

During this time of ice-cold fear and confusion, being next to Sarah kept his soul from freezing over. She kept him from giving up, from deciding this was all too much too handle.

Sarah turned her head so her lips pressed into his palm, her chin and cheeks still damp with her tears, though her eyes never left his.

He stared back at her, his throat going so tight he could barely breathe.

He sucked in a raspy breath, his mind screaming a hundred different thoughts at once. He wasn't sure what the feeling was exploding inside.

His heart thundered; his palms were clammy. Sarah's lips felt so delicate and soft against his fingers, and her eyes were such a deep sapphire blue he felt lost in them, adrift in an endless sea.

He didn't want to pull his hand away. He wanted to leave it on her smooth cheek forever. He wanted to hold her and never let go.

It was Sarah who moved first, leaning up onto her knees. The corner of Mark's palm where her lips had pressed in a faint kiss felt cold as she left it. Her other hand slid across his coarse, unshaven cheek as she leaned closer, the space between them melting away until the sweet lavender fragrance of her hair enveloped him like the warmest, comforting, exhilarating blanket he had ever touched.

Only when her honeyed breath breezed over his lips did he press one hand to her shoulder, stopping her before she could lean any closer.

Her eyes turned wounded as she jerked back from him, falling away as though he'd thrown her, though not a single muscle of his had twitched.

"I'm so sorry, Mark," she whispered, her face going pale and frantic. "I don't know what came over me."

Her trembling fingers swept up to her lips, pressing against them like Mark's lips had not.

"Sarah," he said, reaching toward her, though she recoiled, "listen to me. I want to. I want that. But now is not the time."

She gave a nod, her eyes dropping down to the paper-littered grass as Mark reached out and stole her hand, holding it between both of his in a tight and warm grasp.

"I mean it, Sarah. Soon. When we figure this thing out."

Sarah regarded him carefully, then mustered up the tiniest hint of a smile that sent butterflies bursting in Mark's gut.

"Let's end this," Sarah responded with quiet and firm resolve, her cheeks still flaming red but her eyes set on his.

CHAPTER FIFTY-SIX

So, it was you who broke into my office, Stanley?"

Claire Matthews gazed across the demolished room at the dark-haired man who sat doubled over in a stiff wooden chair. Some of the nurses had offered to pick up the mess for her, but she had preferred to leave it for the flair of drama it would add to her little interrogation. When Stanley gave a shaky sigh, she inspected her rose-painted nails as though she was bored of the conversation.

With the door closed, the office was dead silent except for the heavy breathing of the concierge and the loud tick of the clock behind him. His skin prickled, goosebumps crawling up and down his arms like ants at a picnic.

Without speaking, Stanley Stalwart gave a feeble jerk of his chin that Claire supposed was an attempt at a nod.

"Why?" she sank down into her chair, crossing one leg over the other and resting her folded hands in her lap.

Her mind was elsewhere, but she temporarily tried to focus on what was going on with Stanley.

Beside her, the phone was off its hook, the red-light blinking. Stanley couldn't keep himself from peeking at it now and then.

"I was angry," he said, lying.

He wasn't sure why his instinct was to protect Sarah and Mark. He didn't know them, and he certainly hadn't been their friend when he reported their every move, but he could barely face Claire without wanting to leap across her disordered desk and strangle her.

"Why?" she repeated, making Stanley's fingers curl up into fists.

He sucked in a ragged breath, his mismatched eyes narrowing on the petite redhead and asked, "Where's my mother?"

Claire smiled and Stanley's rage rose, swallowing him up. His heart felt like a black hole–empty, churning, and out of control.

"Something tells me you already know."

Stanley leaped to his feet, slamming his hands down on her desk. The potted plant that had been righted toppled over, spilling more loose dirt across the polished wood. Claire frowned at the fallen fern, giving a little sigh and clicking her tongue.

"Your mother seemed unable to control her anger as well, Stanley," she mused, cocking her head so she could gaze up at the man while his chest heaved. "That's why she had to be removed."

"You took her to be researched on and experimented on-"

Claire cleared her throat, cutting him off. "We are going to help your mother, Stanley," she rebuked with a smile so saccharinely tactful that Stanley's lips curled like he'd stuffed a spoonful of sugar between his gums. "You want that, don't you? Isn't that why you gave her to us in the first place and agreed to help Heath?"

"I thought I would be doing part-time hours here, not being your little spy. I didn't know you'd involve Mom's business in all of this-"

"Hush now, calm down. Do you want me to make you some tea?"

"I don't want any tea!" Stanley roared, still standing and tired of being interrupted. He slammed his palms on the desk again. Still, he got no reaction from the crimson-haired head nurse. "I want my mom out of there!"

"If you let us treat her, she could regain full functionality, Stanley. She could be her old self again. She could help you at the hotel. She could visualize you as a baby. She could tell stories about your childhood again. Wouldn't that be lovely?"

"Don't pretend your research is all gumdrops and rainbows, Claire. You and Heath, you're torturing people. You're killing them!"

"We're making fantastic progress. We may find a cure for all kinds of mental diseases through these trials. Don't you get that? This could revolutionize healthcare and people's lives. People wouldn't have to fade away as they get old. Instead, they'd stay sharp and smart and aware. They wouldn't have to live with the worry of waking up one day with confusion about where they are or who their family is."

"You won't convince me," Stanley seethed. "I want my mother. And I want her now."

The speaker of the phone made a faint crackling noise as the caller gave an impatient sigh. "Mr. Stalwart," Heath said from over the phone, "I can tell that we will not be able to convince you-"

"That's damn right," Stanley hissed. "There's nothing you can do about that."

Claire cracked a pearly toothed smile while Heath laughed and gave a long and low sigh that sounded like crackling popcorn over the phone line.

"My boy, I'm afraid that's where you're mistaken. You see, you don't seem to understand that I have your mother locked up right now, in my cages, in my facility, in my passage. She belongs to me. If I tire of her, or if you disappoint me, I will be rid of her. I'm sure you already understand how that process works."

"She'll go right into the urn of our next special subject," Claire added as Stanley's whole body sagged and he collapsed into the chair.

Claire's smile widened, her legs uncrossing then re-crossing the other way.

"What do you want?" Stanley asked.

"Mark Hogarth and Sarah Kramer. You know them?" Heath asked.

Stanley gave a nod though he knew Heath couldn't see it.

Heath continued anyway, "They were supposed to have been dealt with earlier, but apparently no one else can get anything done."

Claire's smile faded, tucking a lock of hair behind her ear and biting her tongue.

"It's your time to shine, Mr. Stalwart. Take them out and you can have your mother back. Fail and she's dead. We both know it wasn't you who broke into Ms. Matthew's office and stole her files. You're already a liar in my book. Don't make me see you as a failure as well."

"But-" Stanley whispered, but Heath was in no mood to converse anymore.

"This is not negotiable, Mr. Stalwart, and your mother's time is already counting down."

CHAPTER FIFTY-SEVEN

The smell of daises was so thick in the air that, for a little while, Ralph Hogarth imagined himself basking on the grass of Lake Jarvis while Joan sang at his side and picked tiny white flowers to put in the vase back at the cabin.

She loved to decorate that small wooden house with flowers of all kinds, but daisies were her favorite. Ralph had learned that, while Joan would graciously accept a bouquet of fresh cut roses or a box of chocolates or a beautiful necklace, it was those delicate little ivory blooms that brought a grateful tear to her eye.

Ralph's skin was cold and damp, not warm and tanned by long hours outside. Still, he kept his mind focused on the image of Joan's face and the sound of her laugh as she splashed into the lake's waters.

When she blinked in his memory, he found he could no longer recall what shade of caramel gold her eyes were. The loss made him tremble until he ached.

His body was so stiff he wasn't sure he'd be able to move again. He was afraid to open his eyes to see where he was. He'd much rather continue dreaming.

In his dreams, Ralph saw visions. He heard noises. Memories flooded back.

Graham had grinned and winked, thrusting a plastic ID card and some flowers into his hand as the copper-eyed man had led Ralph across the cemetery field. Ralph had been nervous. He didn't know Graham Jones well, and they weren't allowed to wander out of the facility, but Graham had been so utterly excited. He'd practically dragged Ralph out one of the many side doors of Springthorpe and led him to the giant mausoleum. Graham had refused to enter with him, just thrusting a finger and quick directions into the darkness.

"She's in there," he'd whispered, "Joan is in there, Ralphie! She's waiting."

Despite his better judgment, Ralph had entered and walked and walked and walked. For Joan, he would chance anything, even the risk of being trapped in some strange hide and seek crawl space by a madman. He'd passed horrible, unspeakable visions and people he recognized in cages, following nothing but his gut's intuition and Graham's sketchy instructions. He could hear Joan's thoughts, like he could feel her heart beating inside his, guiding him closer and closer.

Then, he'd seen a door and he'd known. He'd yanked at it and pulled, but it didn't open until Ralph had swiped the ID card.

She'd stood in front of him, her face hollow, her eyes watering, and she'd clutched him so tightly Ralph didn't ever want to let go. His Joan, his love, she was *alive*. She was standing right in front of him. He'd begged her to leave with him; he'd pleaded with her to let him stay. Neither option had satisfied her, however, and whatever Joan wanted, Ralph gave, no matter how difficult it was. So, he'd returned to where Graham was waiting and he'd given back the ID card. Graham had wrapped an arm around his shoulder and promised to let him use the card whenever Ralph wanted as long as Ralph told no one about what he saw. It was a secret, Graham instructed, one Ralph was afraid to reveal.

Every visit, Ralph and Graham would stop and collect a fistful of daisies to give to Joan.

With a shiver, Ralph tried to curl into a ball to warm himself, but he couldn't manage to move his stiff body. With a faint whimper, he hoped to retreat back to sleep.

Earlier, he'd dreamed he'd seen his son standing right next to him, reaching out as though to touch Ralph's face. His little Mark shared the same eye color as Joan and, at that time, he'd been able to recall the shade in all its gold-flecked glory. Though Joan had grown older, the creases in the corners of her eyes deepening like tiny canyons on her sweet face, those eyes had always remained the same. When he gazed deep into them, Joan was still the twenty-five-year-old she'd been when they met, spinning in wild circles with her skirt bunched in her hand. She'd stolen his heart that first minute he saw her. She'd held it in her palm ever since, doting on it.

When he breathed in again, Ralph smelled the daisies once more and thought he was near Lake Jarvis. He could feel the sun on his face and determined he'd just had a terrible dream. He would tell Joan, who would kiss him and make him forget. Then, once he caught one that was the right size, they would have salmon for dinner.

He cracked open one weary, crusty eye to survey the area around him.

It was bright and Ralph was relieved.

Sun? At first, he was sure of it. But the light was such a fake neon yellow that it hurt his head. *Not the sun.*

He was still down below. He was still trapped in that horrible, awful place.

At least, he was close to Joan. If he focused hard enough, he could see the little doorway that Heath kept her trapped behind, but, between Ralph's tumble and resting at such an odd angle on the dirt floor, he couldn't convince his old, swollen limbs to obey his commands.

Instead, he focused on opening his other eye, blinking to clear away the dust, grime, and exhaustion from his coal gray eyes.

For the briefest of moments, Ralph swore he saw Joan gazing at him.

That same kind smile, those same charming eyes, the daisies clutched in her long fingers. He could've sworn it was all there.

Then, one of the researchers gave an abrupt grunt of surprise, the door to the cell across from him clanging open with such a loud, mechanical squeal that Ralph flinched from his delirious state.

When he squinted again, Joan was gone and another woman was in her place.

This woman gazed at him with lifeless, frozen brown eyes from over a sea of scattered white petals.

"It's Larissa Stalwart," one researcher told another man behind him. "She's dead."

CHAPTER FIFTY-EIGHT

S o, we'll go back in there and just...just..." Mark trailed off, one hand falling to his hip as the other tapped his chin.

"Oh, don't worry. I've got a good plan," Sarah growled, pacing in a small circle.

She'd tromped through the daisies by her grandfather's tomb, which she was refusing even to acknowledge. Every time she did, she thought back to the hundreds of times in the last few years she'd bent down in front of his mausoleum, clasped her hands, closed her eyes, and talked to him. She'd told her Grandpa about her life, her troubles, her hopes. She'd cried to him when her patients had died. *How many of those patients had been murdered?* She couldn't help but feel as though somewhere out in the universe, he'd been laughing at her the whole time.

"You do?" Mark sighed in relief. "What is it?"

She gripped her fists up in front of her, scowling at Mark. "I've got my plan right here," she said, winding her arms back and forth like she'd seen the boxers do on a TV at the bar.

Mark laughed and laughed. He couldn't seem to stop. He sank back against the edge of the tomb, the ice-cold marble biting through his light jacket as his hands pressed against his aching ribs. He hadn't laughed like that in ages. It rocked his entire body, made his muscles ache, and made tears well in his eyes.

Sarah stared at him, bewilderment knotting her brunette brow, her arms extended in front of her like a ham-fisted impression of Mike Tyson.

"Are you laughing at me?" she asked, incredulous. "Rude!"

"I'm sorry," Mark gasped, trying to suck air down his throat, though he couldn't seem to stop giggling like a schoolgirl.

Mark's hysterical laughter was quelled when a branch snapped behind them. The pair whirled, memories of Graham and his weaponized wooden plank putting them on the automatic defense. Sarah once again fell into her clumsy fighting stance.

"There you are," Stanley's voice rippled through the trees as he stepped into the clearing.

Pale as a sheet, his dark hair clung down his damp forehead. He was shaking.

"Stanley?" Sarah said, darting over to him to place a hand on his shoulder. "You look terrible, what's going on?"

"They thought I broke into Claire's office. They found me in the hall," he replied, his eyes focused on his shoes.

He averted his eyes from Mark and Sarah. The way his whole body sagged made it seem like he was a puppet held up by invisible strings. Something in his expression worried Mark, who inched closer.

"Oh no, was it Claire? Stanley, we have to tell you about what we saw when we went down there-"

"I don't want to know," he interrupted, groaning like he was going to be sick.

A shiver rippled through his whole body as he ran both his clammy hands through his hair. He was feverish, trembling, and sticky with sweat.

It was nerves that haunted the concierge. Mark stared at the man in front of him. Stanley was panicking about something. Or afraid.

"Why are you here?" Mark asked.

Stanley gave another groan and shrugged away from Sarah's grasp.

Sarah glanced at Mark in confusion. He advanced to her side.

"Stanley, what's going on?" he demanded.

"They've got my mom," he moaned, voice shuddering as he swallowed a sob. "I'm sorry, but they have my mom..."

Sarah grabbed hold of Mark's arm, her eyes widening. Something was off about their meeting with the concierge.

"I know, Stanley, remember, we talked about that in the hall?"

"She can't die. She's all I have. I have to. I have to. I'm sorry." He breathed in another sharp, shuddering breath as his quaking fingers tugged a gun from his pocket. The metal gleamed black in the fading afternoon light.

"No!" Sarah cried. "No, Stanley, you do not have to-"

"They told me I did. Heath and Claire. If I don't, then my Mom dies. I have to kill..." he choked on the word like it made him sick. "I have to kill you."

"No, you don't!" Mark said, moving in front of Sarah.

He wasn't proud of how his knees were shaking. He'd never before seen a real gun. All he could think of was making sure Sarah was safe. If he could manage to distract Stanley, maybe Sarah could run. But the woman's long fingers coiled around the crook of his arm. He knew she'd never run and leave him. She'd protect him as fiercely as he would her.

Stanley lifted the gun, holding it between his damp fingers like he was afraid of it. When he pointed it toward the pair, the weapon shook so hard in his hands Mark couldn't even tell where the man was aiming.

"Calm down, Stanley," Mark pleaded. "Think this through before you-"

Before he could finish his sentence, the gun burst with a loud bang that made all three of them cry out in shock. They collapsed to the ground, hands over their ears.

"Sarah!" Mark yelled, whirling around to grab her.

She opened her eyes, scouring him for an injury before she thought to check herself.

"We're...we're fine," she whispered, quickly scanning their clothes for blood.

Behind Mark's and Sarah's heads, sawdust settled on the ground below the spot where a fresh bullet hole embedded in a tree.

They turned to Stanley, who was bent over the gun he'd dropped, his hands also on his ears, rocking back and forth and sobbing.

Mark flew forward, grabbing the gun and hurling it away from them. It fell into the grass, laying quiet and peaceful somewhere beyond them.

"That was loud," an irate voice growled as copper-eyed Graham peered through the trees.

Stalking through the grass, he'd been drawn by the noise. His hands clutched hard over his eyes, trying to forget what he'd seen. Visible anger simmered on his face.

His golden eyes gleaming like a cat's in the long shadows, he slunk closer.

Mark stiffened, still holding onto Sarah. *Was he here to finish the job from earlier?*

But the man didn't seem interested in harming them. He reached down into one of his overfilled pockets to grab hold of a daisy from within the fabric. He held it in his hands, shredding it and mumbling to himself.

Stanley patted the grass, seeking out the gun. "I have to save her. I have to get my mom out of there!" he cried, as the irritated old man dropped another shredded daisy in front of him.

"No use," Graham mumbled, squeezing his eyes closed again with a vicious shake of his head. "No use."

"I'm going to get her!" Stanley yelled back, jerking up to his knees and scowling at Graham. "I'm going to save her!"

"She's dead," Graham replied, rocking back and forth on his heels. "Had to be done. Had to be done. Bye, bye."

CHAPTER FIFTY-NINE

Claire smoothed her hands over the front of her scrubs, making sure they lay nice and straight against her body as she strode right past the art room, took a sharp turn down the hall, and descended the stairs. At the dead end, she grabbed hold of her ID card and swiped it against the unblemished wall in a single, practiced gesture. Her tapping foot echoed as Claire surveyed her surroundings. Her eyes searched through the shadows as the hair on the back of her neck stood on edge.

She felt as though she were being watched, which was a ridiculous worry since she knew full well her every movement was being recorded.

The wall parted in front of her, revealing a small elevator into which she stepped.

Ever since she was young, Claire had been a woman of routine. Even as a child, she'd considered herself a grown-up. While her little fingers braided her hair the way her mother had before she'd forgotten how to, Claire would run down in her mind her list of responsibilities for that day.

Even back then, her days were always the same: make lunches for Cecilia and herself, go to her elementary school classes, come home and do homework, tend to Mama. Mama hadn't moved much, lying limply on the couch and talking to herself while Claire would tuck a scratchy but warm blanket under her chin. Mama would gaze at her, seeing without seeing.

While young Claire was cooking, cleaning, tidying, and caring, her sister Cecilia was dreaming. Where Claire was stern and dedicated, Cecilia had been born with her head in the clouds. Cecilia wanted to be anywhere but their dingy little two-bedroom apartment. She'd write stories where she was a butterfly. Claire found that absurd. But her twin sister was insistent.

"They're beautiful creatures," Cecilia would say, "and they can fly. They'd fly right up and out of here."

Claire had asked Cecilia why she wanted to leave so badly. Her twin sister had grinned with more glee than Claire had ever felt in her life.

"To be free," Cecilia had whispered, emerald eyes gleaming, "to be able to do whatever I want."

At that, Claire had ripped up all of her sister's stories and put them in the trash while Mama babbled.

Early-onset Alzheimer's ran in their family, passing from generation to generation. Claire had grown up in fear of its shadow. It lurked everywhere, in every distracted thought she had and every time she forgot where she'd put her keys. Claire had begged her mother for answers. *Why had she had children? Why had she cursed them like this?* But Mama had merely smiled and stroked her pretty hair.

Claire had grown in fear. Cecilia had grown running from that fear.

In middle school, when Child Protective Services caught wind of the twins' living conditions, the girls were taken and shipped west into foster care. Cecilia had loved it while Claire despised it. Despite sharing all their DNA, the two girls had never been close or all that friendly to each other. Still, they made it through foster care together and found themselves fresh on the street on their eighteenth birthday.

It'd been October, near Halloween, and the houses were decorated with scary pumpkins and fake spiders in their sprawling webs.

Sometimes, when she was sleeping, Claire would dream she was still standing there on the street, without any idea of where to go or how to get there. She'd reach for her sister but find her gone.

Claire went to college while Cecilia pretended to be a painter and then a writer and then a sculptor. Although Cecilia was as logical and drawn to science as Claire was, she refused to accept that similarity between them. She thought their identical looks and bright red hair was enough! So, she pretended to be the creative type while Claire applied herself in her coursework.

It was an eagle-eyed professor who took notice of Claire.

Dr. Henry Kramer had called her into his office one day after Claire had set the curve on one of his most difficult exams. She'd missed only one question, and she was able to argue with him so eloquently that, by the end of the conversation, he even doubted his own answer.

He told her about his other job which was at Springthorpe. He told her about his handsome, young colleague with eyes like glass. He told her he thought she would be perfect for the team.

She'd shown up at the manor that afternoon. Only twenty years old, she'd been wide-eyed, ready, and eager. For two years, she worked in the facility without any notion of what was going on below. It was Dr. Kramer who'd implored Heath to show Claire their intensive research. She'd overheard them arguing about it once in Dr. Kramer's office. The next day, Heath had guided her to the elevator behind the art room and down the short flight of stairs. He told her if she breathed a word about what she was about to see, he would kill her.

He hadn't been lying or dramatizing that afternoon; Claire had seen it written in those dazzling eyes. But Claire was too excited to care. She'd nodded and stepped beside him into the cramped space.

What she saw was amazing, a veritable wonderland of scientific progress. Not entirely legal, but fantastic. She'd marveled at Heath's accomplishments. He and Dr. Kramer were at the pinnacle of something great. Brain disease would be a thing of the past with the two of them guiding the way.

Claire hoped for the day she would no longer have to fear her every looming birthday.

At age thirty, when Cecilia had deteriorated before her eyes, Claire had donated her sister to Heath.

Dr. Kramer had been gone by then, and Claire was glad. He would've disapproved of Claire's bringing family into this. He was against that.

Heath was fascinated with Cecilia, so much so that Claire had stopped going into the tunnels except for once a week when she'd check the patients and guide in the new herd they had assembled in the art room near the elevator, leading them down two by two as if onto Noah's ark. Claire wasn't sure whether she was jealous of the attention her sister received or if she was disturbed by the needle-pocked arms, vacant eyes, and vengeful whispers. In the early years, Cecilia's head had been shaved a few times, her scarlet hair growing in raggedy over multiple jagged scars lining her skull like tiny ravines.

For the most part, Claire organized the research from above while Heath directed it from below. Claire avoided Cecilia, whose mind bloomed over time with more clarity but an equal portion of newfound bitterness. Claire knew she was hated by her twin, but Claire was also sure it'd be worth it. If it didn't help Cecilia, perhaps it would help Claire in the future; if not, maybe it would still help others.

She had tried to explain that to Cecilia once, but Cecilia only screamed and thrashed and begged to be made into a butterfly.

The doors of the elevator swung open, yanking the head nurse from her memories, memories she was quite grateful to have. Every time she entered the elevator, she went over her story, trying to figure out if there was any part she'd forgotten, if there was any hint of her own mind fading. Claire was a woman of routine, after all.

Claire stepped out and blinked away the light, her eyes sweeping the hall. She knew her sister was no longer there. She hadn't decided whether or not she was relieved that Heath had dealt with Cecilia. Claire hadn't yet fully processed the loss. She still sensed her sister inside her like she always had. Despite the hatred that grew between them, they were still twins, two halves of the same person. Claire felt as though Cecilia's blood ran through her.

"There you are," Heath sighed as Claire approached him. "Have you heard anything from Stanley yet?"

Claire shook her head. She'd received no updates. She was sure Stanley would finish his job before finding out about the little mishap they'd had regarding his mother's death.

"I'm sorry about your sister," Heath offered.

He wasn't apologizing, just going through the motions. Claire would have preferred he skip the niceties altogether. She shrugged.

"You know I'd do anything for you," she replied, voice full of the same earnestness that had been there since the first time she'd spoken those words to him in the elevator all those years ago.

"Good." He stepped back and pointed to a familiar door.

Claire's stomach twisted. Cecilia's old room. Heath arched an eye, watching her, and Claire kept her face perfectly arranged.

"Anything," she repeated.

The meaning hung in the air. Claire had given him her twin, the other half of her soul, and she'd let him destroy Cecilia like a bug crushed beneath a boot. She'd remain loyal to Heath's cause.

Again, he nodded, a satisfied smile on his mouth. "That's good to hear. Because it's time for the child's procedure."

CHAPTER SIXTY

No!" Stanley howled while Mark patted his shoulder and tried to ignore the fact that the dark-haired concierge had tried to shoot them. "No, no!"

Sarah shot an uneasy glance at Mark before turning back to Graham, who was seated at the base of a weathered old tree. He wove daisies together, still grumbling to himself.

Were they really about to console two men who had tried to kill them within the last twenty-four hours? It was a strange, strange day indeed.

"Graham," Sarah said, using her most patient and gentle nurse voice she reserved for her most troubled patients, "are you sure Ms. Larissa is dead? You're not thinking of when she was taken into the tunnel?"

Graham glared at Sarah in response, cross with either her tone or her question.

"I saw it," he huffed with a shudder and a shake of his head. "I didn't want to go back down there. I hate going down there. But I had to. One more time, one more time." He spoke like he was quoting someone or reading a story. "I didn't even get the journal," he added, staring at Sarah like it was her fault. "Liars. All of them."

"You were the one on the phone, weren't you?" Stanley croaked, leaning over so he was on his hands and knees in front of Graham. "It was you who I had to call all those times! That voice…"

A slow smile twitched on the tiny corners of the old man's mouth as he stretched out a daisy toward Stanley. "Smart boy. Good boy. Want to play?"

Stanley grabbed hold of the daisy with a rough hand and threw it away. It fluttered through the air, losing its petals while Graham's expression melted into horror.

"Not a good boy!" he screeched.

"Why was I talking to you?" Stanley demanded. "You're one of the crazy patients here. Why did he make me talk to you?"

"He?" Graham echoed, blinking, then shaking his head. "No. Crotchety Claire. Crotchety Claire told me to talk to you. Listen. Be quiet. Those were the rules. She told me I'd get it back. Liar."

Stanley collapsed again, weary with grief and irritation. "Mom, I'm so sorry. I'm so sorry, Mom."

"Do you know who killed her?" Mark asked the old man while resuming his awkward patting of Stanley's shaking shoulder.

Graham nodded but offered no further information, his lips pursed. He glanced at the flower Stanley had tossed away, lamenting it.

"Who was it, Graham?" Sarah asked, kneeling down next to him. She paused, smoothing the faded old scrubs the old man wore. "You know we have to fill out paperwork on this, right? Do you want to be the one to fill it out?"

"Why me?" he scoffed, weaving another daisy into the tiny crown in his hand. Sarah didn't believe the small little blooming halo was going to fit on his head.

"Well, you're one of us, right? You work here? Isn't that what you always say?"

He nodded but regarded her with a suspicious eye.

"So, will you help me fill out the paperwork on Larissa? We'll have to write the cause of death and who did it."

"I tried to play with you," he sighed with wounded eyes, gaze shifting back to his crown as he jerked away from Sarah. "I tried to play with you and you ran away to hide. You hurt my feelings. I don't want to play now."

Sarah started to argue, but Mark cleared his throat, shaking his head. He wasn't about to have Graham go all psycho on them again. Avoiding death twice was enough for one day.

"I'm going to the police," Stanley cried out, straightening up onto his knees. His eyes were so red and swollen, he couldn't even see straight. "I'm ending this now. I can't...I can't sit here knowing they killed her. I can't!"

"Wait, Stanley-" Mark said, but the man threw Mark's hand off of him and stumbled to his feet.

The remaining trio could only watch as he vanished down and around the hill.

"Do you think they'll believe him?" Sarah asked, settling down so she was sitting on the grass. She was exhausted, her legs aching from all the running, her heart so heavy it felt slow and swollen inside of her.

Graham frowned at her before handing her one of his flowers.

"If he makes it there, maybe," Mark replied.

Sarah shook her head, turning back to Mark. She tucked the flower behind her ear. Graham smiled.

"If they've already killed Larissa," she whispered, "Mark, who knows who's next on that list? They could go for your mom or your dad."

Mark's mouth twisted but he gave a nod. That same thought had been running on a loop in his head since Graham had told them about Larissa's death.

What am I going to do if I go down there and find Dad already dead? What if I've lost my chance to stop Heath?

"Mark," Sarah said like she could tell where his mind was going, "the only place we're getting answers is down there. Sitting up here and stewing isn't going to do anyone any good."

"Yesterday up here, today down below," Graham hummed, "that's how Springthorpe goes."

"They could be killing everyone down there, going systematically down the list," Mark mumbled, shaking his head at the thought.

Graham's eyes shot up, his hands stiffening on the miniature crown. He didn't speak but his eyes darted between the two of them as though he were watching a tennis match.

"Let's go," Sarah replied, climbing to her feet. "We have to go make sure they're okay."

Mark nodded as the nurse leaned over and helped him stand. Dusting off her pants, Sarah turned back to Graham, whose face was contorted.

"You go inside, Graham, okay? Can you do that?"

He gave a faint nod, peering at the facility then back at them.

"Don't tell anyone you saw us either. It'll be a secret." She smiled though her face was pale and hard.

Graham liked secrets, but he was too distracted to promise the pretty nurse that he'd be quiet. Without saying anything to them, Graham stood and sprinted through the cemetery and back to the manor, not bothering to go around to a side door. Instead, he flung himself right in through the front, his daisies floating free from his pockets in a floral trail behind him.

Swallowing the thick lump in her throat, Sarah turned back to Mark.

"If we go down there..." she said, choking on the words, "if we go, we may never..."

With a firm shake of his head, Mark stepped forward as her words faded on her tongue, wrapping his arms tightly around her waist and pulling her into him.

They clung to one another, pressed chest to chest, their hearts beating in rapid time.

"We're going to come back out," Mark whispered. "We're not going to be trapped down there. We won't. I promise, Sarah."

Sarah squeezed her eyes shut, breathing in one last gulp of fresh air before Mark stepped away, took her hand firmly in his, and pushed open the mausoleum door.

CHAPTER SIXTY-ONE

Four doughnuts sat uneaten in the box as a tiny black fly buzzed from pastry to pastry, munching pink icing from its minuscule front legs.

Chuck typed, his gaze darting to the various screens, not lingering on one for more than a second or two at a time. His eyes ached, strained from the bright screen in his dark room, but he barely blinked until the corded black telephone at his side rang, making him jump. He hadn't even had any time to stand up and turn on a light.

"What?" he barked, keeping the landline's earpiece cupped to his cheek with a round shoulder as his fingers drummed on the arm of the chair. "Yes, like I said, it was that man who broke into the head nurse's office. Yes. Dark hair. Weird eyes. Right." With a roll of his eyes and a shake of his head, Chuck slammed the phone back down and groaned.

They believed everything he said. They always had. He could've told them an elf had broken into the office and they'd gasp and ask if he was serious.

Hell in a handbasket. That was the saying. That was sure happening today. It'd started like any other day of work—so easy, so typical. He hadn't known today was going to be the day that everything changed. He wished he'd had more warning, more time to prepare. When Heath had called him earlier and told him to "take care of" that nurse and the special patient's son, he'd known. It had clicked with Chuck right in that instant.

Springthorpe Manor was about to change forever. Chuck realized that, but he didn't know how it would be different nor how much it would change. No one did. No one could. It hurt to think about the possibilities.

His fingers danced over the sleek black cell phone on the other side of his crumb-covered keyboard then returned to typing. He switched his cameras to one of many within the tunnel, rewinding his footage. He didn't have to study for long.

He watched the cage open, saw Larissa Stalwart gaze up in bleary-eyed confusion. It was over moments later. She had felt nothing, he hoped. Swallowing, Chuck clicked the red erase button and watched the images vanish, like they'd never existed, like the cameras had simply been blinded for those few minutes in time.

He could kiss his job goodbye with that one simple action, but it'd give him some much-needed time.

Pausing, he stretched his aching arms out in front of him, cracking his fingers. He'd only just leaned back over his sticky computer when his corded phone rang yet again. With an irate growl, he grabbed the receiver and accidentally slammed it against his ear so hard stars burst in front of his eyes.

"What?" he snapped again, rubbing his hand over his throbbing forehead and wishing the facility could run more than three seconds without someone calling him. He listened briefly then said, "That old man who just came through? Graham Jones. That's his name. He's fine. He likes to pick flowers in the cemetery. Leave him alone. He's cranky. Might be a biter too. Leave him be."

Flicking through his video streams, he slammed down the phone before the nurse at the front desk could question him anymore. The old man in question ran by, heading down the hall of the art room, but Chuck didn't stop to watch him.

The security officer didn't stop clicking until he was gazing out over the cemetery, the picture so clear he might've been standing right there in the cool breeze. On the video, the pair was out there, still very much alive, though he caught them only just before they vanished into the tunnel entrance. Chuck viewed Stanley Stalwart darting past the camera at the end of the drive, and he didn't have to think twice about where Stanley might be heading.

"It's too late," he whispered to the empty walls of his office, to the fly eating his doughnuts.

He slumped down in his chair, blinking his dazed eyes, his shoulders going lax. When the phone rang again, Chuck didn't move to answer it. Instead, he let it ring into the dark.

Once it stopped ringing, he leaned over to the other phone, the small black cell that had so rarely been used. Swallowing hard, he speed-dialed the only number saved to the device.

The moment the phone clicked, he began speaking before the person on the other end could say a word.

"It's going down," he whispered, staring at his monitors with glazed eyes. "Get the hell out. Do you hear me? Get. Out. Now."

CHAPTER SIXTY-TWO

The young girl leaned over her coloring book. Her face was pressed close to the page as a yellow marker scribbled.

Claire smiled, leaning against the one-way glass of the room. She almost pressed her hand against the glass but stopped before touching it.

The little one had no idea she was being observed. All of her daily activities were being monitored and recorded with such precise accuracy that not a minute of her time went undetailed.

Claire found herself envious of the innocence and ignorance. She'd never had any sort of naivety, not with her childhood. She'd grown from three to thirty seemingly overnight. She'd had to babysit both her mother and her sister. Through all those years, no one else had taken care of Claire– except Heath. In his own way, the Springthorpe director did look after her. He made sure she had a purpose, a home, and a job. It was more than anyone else had ever given her.

"Her name is Savannah Bennett," Heath said, handing Claire a sheet of paper clipped to a heavy board. "Four years old. Intelligent. Definitely related to Joan. Her DNA has the same fascinating benchmarks. It's quite marvelous. Two perfect specimens for our research."

"Two?" Claire asked. "What about Mrs. Keller? Isn't she here as well?"

Heath blinked, realizing he hadn't had the time to brief his head nurse on the situation. He didn't have the time right then either. There was too much going on, and there were too many other preparations that needed completing. They had limited time to secure their progress and the future of their research.

He nodded. "Mrs. Keller is here, but it turns out she wasn't a match. Taking care of her is already on my to-do list," he quipped with a faint laugh.

"Ah," Claire murmured, regretful that Liv would not be able to advance their studies. "Shame."

Heath nodded again. "Truly. She showed such potential."

"When did you have time to acquire Mrs. Keller?" Claire asked, staring up at him. The past twenty-four hours had been a nonstop flurry. "You're so busy all the time, when did you have time to track down both this little girl and Liv?" She paused, her brow wrinkling. "When did this become part of the plan?"

While Heath by no means shared every detail of what went on in the tunnels with Claire, he typically kept her much more in the loop with regular updates.

Heath cleared his throat, an action Claire recognized. She wouldn't be getting any more answers. She was content with that. She'd risen to where she was by being careful with her curiosity. She only knew what Heath wanted her to, and that was fine. She had her work and she was able to admire Heath's scientific progress. She loved it all, every single bit.

Claire turned back to the paper, running a trimmed nail down the page.

"Sedation and surgery?" she read, continuing on, "...hemispherectomy?"

Heath gave a sharp jerk of his chin. "We have to study her brain, Claire. Don't you agree? It'll be much easier to do once we have some of it under a microscope."

Claire gave a hasty nod, not willing to risk Heath's thinking she doubted him even for a second. She'd given him her sister to study, and she'd let him end Cecilia's life. It would tarnish Cecilia's sacrifice–as well as the sacrifice of the little girl in the other room–if Claire didn't believe in him. Claire hoped Savannah would survive the procedure with no lasting damage. The longer the girl lasted, the longer they'd be able to study and use her. They wouldn't need much from her, just a small biopsy.

"Savannah," Heath repeated. "Be friendly. Use her name. Make her feel relaxed." He smiled at Claire, arching one of his dark eyebrows, and added, "You tend to be a little stiff, Ms. Matthews."

Claire mustered up her best non-condescending smile and nodded, handing the clipboard back to the Springthorpe director. She liked to think of herself as pleasant to converse with, but she wasn't about to argue with Heath.

He stepped away from the window, watching as Claire cleared her throat, gave a small nod of encouragement to herself, swiped her ID through the reader, and pushed open the door.

"Hello, Savannah," the head nurse said as she entered, hands clasping in front of her. The pneumatics hissing, the heavy door slid shut.

She was nervous. Usually, it was Heath who made her nervous. Funny that a little girl also incited that uncomfortable feeling. Claire didn't do well with kids. She didn't like them.

Savannah glanced up once, then did a quick double take, throwing her arms in the air with a shrill cry Claire wasn't sure emanated from excitement or fear. She would've guessed fear, being trapped in this little room with Cecilia's fingernail marks all over the door.

"Cecilia!" the little blonde girl stumbled over the long name, pronouncing it so wrong that it made Claire's ears hurt.

"What?" Claire shot back, startled, grimacing as Savannah leaped to her feet and ran over, throwing tiny arms around Claire's legs and squeezing tight.

Claire sidled away, pushing the child back with a single finger prodding into the center of Savannah's forehead.

She could see both Liv and Joan in the little girl, though Savannah's eyes were brighter, her face was rounder, and her hair was blonder. She was cute, as far as grubby-handed little monsters went. Claire's green eyes drifted toward the small tray of medical supplies left on the counter for her. The sooner Savannah was sedated, the better.

"I made you a picture. I wasn't sure when I'd see you again," Savannah said, hopping over to the little table where she'd been coloring.

She picked it up, holding it out toward Claire. "See, there's you and me and Graham and the flowers."

"Graham?"

"He's so nice. Is he coming to play, too?" Savannah asked. "Are we going up there again?"

Claire gave a numb shake of her head, running her fingertip over the red-headed likeness of herself in the messily drawn picture, a daisy crown atop her head.

Cecilia, what had you gotten yourself into? First Graham and now the child?

CHAPTER SIXTY-THREE

She dug her fingers hard into the crumbly earth of the tunnel, pushing and pulling herself inch by inch further down the long and rutted path.

IV tubes trailed along the ground after Liv, scraping along the damp dirt floor like little red snakes coiled with her blood. Ahead of her, Ralph sat propped up in his cage, his body angled in an unnatural slouch, his chin tucked into his chest. From where she crawled along the floor, Liv couldn't tell whether he was still breathing or not.

The tunnels were so twisted and winding that Liv hadn't been at all sure where she was going. It had taken her what felt like years to push herself off that table and slide like a worm across the floor toward the crack of light where the door was still open. She could hear Heath and Claire talking somewhere further in the darkness, and she crawled with desperate, sloth-like movements in the other direction toward the big bright lights lining the wide breadth of the tunnel.

Liv's thoughts were muddled. She didn't think she'd been led down this way when the dark-haired concierge had kidnapped her and delivered her back to the manor. She'd been brought in through the front of the main Springthorpe building, past the front desk and down the halls. Claire had emerged from the shadows of a back corridor past the art room like she was a part of the darkness, her braid unraveling and her smile strangely huge.

Earlier, after Heath had left her, when she tried to move again and found it impossible, like her muscles weren't attached to her body at all, she'd almost lay back on that table and waited for her inevitable fate. Liv knew they were going to kill her. Heath had said as much. But she couldn't die without apologizing to her parents. She'd never meant for this to happen. She'd thought it would help her mom, that she could come back and they could all have Christmas together again without her mom's panicked confusion ending the festivities when the lights on the tree blinked. Liv had been wrong.

"Mark, it's your sister!"

Liv collapsed onto her side at the sound of the familiar name, her weary arms limp and her legs covered in crimson earth. She looked up and found Mark standing two feet in front of her. His jaw was slack in shock and his eyes huge. His features were so much like their mother's, Liv wanted to cry.

"Mark," she whispered. She expected tears to fall from her eyes, but she was too fatigued, and they didn't come, so she said his name again and again.

Am I dreaming? Liv wondered.

Her little brother rushed forward, taking her up into his arms and holding her. She was so tiny and frail, he was worried he'd break her.

"What are you doing down here, Liv?" he asked. "Did they take you, too?"

She swallowed, sucking in a dry breath. "I'm sorry. I am so sorry."

"You have nothing to be sorry about, Liv. Heath is the one-"

"No," she said with surprising firmness in her tone, grabbing his face in her muddy hands and forcing him to make eye contact. "I put Mom and Dad in here, Mark. I did this to them."

Mark fell silent. Though he wouldn't admit it, his initial instinct was to throw Liv back on the ground where she'd been crawling. But Mark had learned enough about the conniving Heath Dole to know there was more to Liv's story. Even as anger rose around his heart, Mark pushed it away.

"Later," Mark said, giving her one more squeeze. "We can settle this later. We have to get Dad out and find Mom."

Liv bit her lip but nodded, letting Mark steady her on her feet as they turned toward their father.

Next to them, trying her best to figure out what eight random numbers would be the key, Sarah had been punching numbers into the code lock on the cell's door.

"Is that…is that my girl?" Ralph wheezed, his lungs full of dust, dry earth, and who knew what else.

Liv bent down at the side of the cage, reaching in and taking his hand.

"Hi, Dad," she whispered, as Mark knelt beside her, his hand resting on his sister's shoulder.

Mark's eyes wandered to the cell behind his father, where a woman lay curled and so still it took Mark a long, terrible minute to figure out it was the dead body of Larissa Stalwart. They'd left her in the cage, an unceremonious burial ground, like her gray, stiff body was forgotten. It made Mark nauseous.

Ralph reached out, touching his son's hand next. His eyes were glassy and confused. Mark doubted he had any idea where he was.

"Daisies," he whispered and smiled. "I want to get your mother some daisies. Won't she like that?"

Mark nodded and grabbed his father's hand, clutching it tightly. Ralph's fingers were so cold it hurt to touch them, like the man himself was carved from ice.

"We have to get him out," Liv whispered. "Mark, he's going to-"

"He's not," Mark shot back, though he sounded much less convinced aloud than he had in his head. "He's not going to die here, Liv. No one is. Not anymore," he continued with a grimace.

Not like poor Larissa. This place had claimed enough lives. It was ending now.

"He's going to come back. Heath is going to come back." Liv shuddered, turning toward the blue-eyed nurse focused on the keypad. "Please hurry."

Sarah's long fingers moved like lightning, tapping over the touchscreen while the two siblings watched.

The doors hissed, the locks popping as the metal grate moved. Ralph gazed up in shock, shielding his eyes with a weary hand like he was expecting the thunderous noise to bring rain.

Mark's eyebrows shot up in shock.

"I can't believe it," Sarah whispered, stepping away from the cage as the door slid open. She stared at the keypad like it was a beast or an ugly contorted face that haunted her nightmares. "It doesn't make sense."

CHAPTER SIXTY-FOUR

Clapping resounded down the hall as Mark and Sarah whirled toward the surprising noise with the grim knowledge that their time to escape had run out.

There would be no easy way of leaving now.

Though she was still struggling to convince her lethargic body to move, Liv scrambled into the cage. She wrapped her arms around her father's neck and held him gently. He patted her hand.

"Oh, Liv, you haven't hugged me like this since you were a child! What is it you want? Ice cream? A dollar?"

Liv didn't answer, squeezing her eyes shut and cradling him against her. For a man who was once so hearty and robust, he felt shriveled. She hated seeing him this way. The time he'd spent down here had not been good for him, not that it would have benefited anyone's disposition. The stress had most likely taken him further into his disease.

Heath strode down the tunnel, his smooth palms still clapping together. He beamed at the group before him, a long and satisfied laugh booming against the walls. The poor people in their cells turned toward him. Soft cries begin to whine out from their dry throats.

The sound was a horrific symphony of agony and terror.

Mark clenched his hands, wishing he'd taken that gun of Stanley's. This could've all been over in seconds. Sarah moved to stand beside the brown-eyed man, her chest heaving, eyes narrowed like daggers on the smug Springthorpe director who stood before them.

"What is it that you want, Mr. Hogarth?" he asked Mark. "Would you like a tour of the lower level of our facility? I don't typically permit this, you know, but I would love the chance to brag for once."

"I don't want a damn tour," Mark hissed back. "I want you to stop pretending what you're doing here is the same as a clinical trial for new cough drops."

Heath laughed. "There is no clinical trial for new cough drops, my boy. And sometimes to make progress, you have to…skirt the rules."

"Skirt the rules?" Sarah cried. "This is torture, you bastard!"

The director hummed, tapping his chin. "Believe me, in ten years, when we're discussing a viable cure for brain diseases of all sorts, no one will be concerned with what we've had to do to get there." He paused, glancing back at Mark and tilting his head to the side. "You know your mother has been instrumental in our success. Thank you for that, Mrs. Keller," he added with a smile at Liv, who refused to acknowledge him.

"Where is she?" Mark whispered. "Where is my mom?"

"Joan?" Ralph said, perking up and peering around. "Is Joan coming now? Where did I put those flowers?" The old man patted the dirt floor next to him, a frown marring his face. "I always bring her flowers."

"I have them, Dad," Liv whispered in his ear, squeezing him tightly and hoping to ease him. "Don't worry."

Beaming, Ralph relaxed. "That's my girl. Always prepared."

"I suppose Mrs. Hogarth could join us." Heath's brow knitted. "Only for a minute though. Stress affects our research, you see. This little reunion could put us back days. I suppose we can manage though."

He turned and walked down a side tunnel. He tapped a code on the keypad, stepping back as the door opened.

Had Mom really been so close? Mark hadn't had the faintest idea.

"Mrs. Hogarth, your family has arrived for a visit," he smiled, reaching in and taking her arm.

Joan Hogarth stepped out of the room into the bright lights, blinking round golden-brown eyes and holding up a hand to keep the fluorescent lights off her face.

"Mom..." Mark choked, taking a staggering step forward and nearly falling to his knees.

Even after all of this, he'd doubted he would ever see his mother again. He'd never thought he would see her kind face or hear her loving voice. But here she was right in front of him.

"Joan!" Ralph cried, straightening up with sudden strength. He gazed at her, his eyes round and huge. "My Joan!"

Heath released his hold on the woman's wrist, letting her run forward.

Though she still appeared the same age, there was a youthful vigor about the seventy-six-year-old woman. She ran with more ease than Mark had recalled, darting as quickly as a twenty-year-old again. Joan ran past her children, her eyes only on her ailing husband. Liv scooted to the side and Joan bent easily, no popping in her knees or her hips, as she took Ralph in her arms. They clung to one another. Ralph peppered his wife's face with delicate kisses.

"My Joan," he said, pulling back to gaze into her lovely eyes. "I brought you daisies," he said, before blinking and shaking his head, "but I don't recall where I left them."

She quieted him, pressing her forehead against his and reveling in the sensation of his soft skin on hers. He smiled, running his hands up over her shoulders to tangle in her hair. She kissed him and nuzzled her nose to his.

"Today is my best day," she whispered as he gave a low and rumbling chuckle.

"Because I am with you," Ralph finished for her, squeezing her to his chest as tears streamed down his face.

His Joan was in his arms once more, right where she belonged, and it truly was his best day. How he had missed her and longed to hold her those days they'd been apart.

"Why are you here?" Joan whispered. "Why are you in this place?"

Ralph laughed softly. "I came for you, darling. We all did."

Liv buried her face in her hands, guilty tears seeping through her fingers at last.

Sarah regarded the reunion, her hands clasped over her heart.

"See what I can do?" Heath boasted, walking toward them again.

Mark turned to face the approaching man. Mark was so angry and heartbroken and overjoyed to see his mother that he couldn't speak.

"Do you recall Joan's condition when you brought her here, young Mr. Hogarth? Do you remember how she struggled to recognize you? Your sister? Even your father? But look at her now." Heath waved his arm at Joan as though he were showcasing a sports car and not Mark's mother, bowing toward the ground and then straightening. "It's a shame I can't allow you to marvel at my work for any longer."

CHAPTER SIXTY-FIVE

Wanna color with me?" Savannah asked, watching Claire with curious eyes. "I have a purple crayon for you!"

The little girl tugged at one of her lopsided pigtails, curling the blonde locks around one of her tiny fingers. The woman moved back and forth along the counter, rustling medical instruments that clanked together and made goosebumps prickle up on Savannah's arms.

She hated that sound. She knew needles were coming.

Cecilia was acting so strangely today. She was ordinarily so funny and silly. She always had a new story to tell her. They would sit in the middle of the carpet and giggle for what felt like hours.

Today, though, Cecilia was stiff and nervous. It made Savannah worry.

"What do you want me to do?" Savannah asked as the medical utensils clinked together. "Do you want me to count to a hundred again?" She stroked one of her arms where a fresh bruise from drawn blood sat like a black and blue puddle.

"You can count to a hundred?" Claire asked, shooting an interested glance toward the girl.

As she turned, she held in her hands a long, sharp needle. A clear, frightening liquid dripped from the tip.

"No..." Savannah shook her head, her jaw beginning to quiver at the sight of the shot.

Clearing her throat, Claire set it back down on the counter and held up her empty hands.

"Just checking some things," she lied.

Thick, hot tears dripped down the child's face. "I'm tired of this game," Savannah whispered. "I want to go home. I want Mommy. I want Oliver."

"Oliver? Is that a stuffed animal or something?"

Savannah shook her head, ignoring the fact she'd drawn several portraits of Oliver for her red-headed friend over the course of the time she'd been there. "We have a puppy. He has brown fur and his tongue is so big." Savannah laughed, but it didn't stop the tears from spilling down the apples of her cheeks. "Do you have a doggie?" she questioned.

Claire shook her head. Animals were a waste of time. She thought better than to say that aloud though.

"I want to go home," Savannah repeated. Though the girl's voice was quieter now, Claire could hear something like panic rising on the edges of it. "I don't know why you brought me here. You said we would play, but it's like being at the doctor."

"I brought you here?" Claire echoed. "Are you sure?"

Apparently, Cecilia had figured out how to have free reign not only within Springthorpe, but of the outside world as well. Claire shook her head in disbelief. She was glad her sister was gone. Left untethered, Cecilia could've ruined everything if she'd had more time.

Savannah didn't answer, grabbing the drawing she'd done of herself and Graham and Cecilia and crumpling it between her hands before hurling it at Claire.

"I want to go home!" she shrieked.

Claire stiffened, narrowing her green eyes. She reached behind her and grabbed the sedative injection. She'd had enough of the mouthy kid. She wasn't sure why anyone reproduced.

"You're not going home," Claire said. "No one goes home once they come here."

"No!" Savannah yelled, her voice so shrill and piercing that Claire came close to dropping the needle.

"Shut up and behave!" Claire screamed back, startled at how loud her voice was. She'd never screamed in her life.

Even Savannah seemed surprised for a brief moment, her eyes wide, but then her entire face reddened and scrunched up until she became a puckered lobster.

Claire rushed forward, determined to stab the sedative into the child's body before the girl burst like an earsplitting volcano.

As the woman rushed across the room, however, the door flew open behind her.

Graham stood there, panting, his cheeks reddened from his sprint.

"You will not kill her!" he shouted. "Crotchety Claire, you will not touch my friend!"

Savannah gave a slight squeal and ran to the old man, tangling herself around his legs.

"I'm not going to kill her," Claire explained, holding up her hands and trying to force a smile onto her thin lips.

Both Graham's and Savannah's eyes went straight to the large needle still in the head nurse's hand.

"You're a liar!" Graham shot back. "You're a mean liar who took Ralphie's book from me and won't give it back!"

"Liar!" Savannah screeched along.

Claire's head throbbed from the noise, fury welling up inside of her at the insubordination of the pair before her.

"I did not take that journal, Graham! It wasn't me!"

"You took me from the park!" Savannah cried out. "You said we would play!"

"I didn't take you!" Claire stomped. "It wasn't me!"

Claire scowled, eyes darting between the childish old man and the actual child, trying to figure out how she could contain the situation.

She quickly concluded that Graham would have to be taken down first. He was too strong and too stubborn to work around, and there was no way he would let Claire pick up the kid and give her an injection. She'd known he was going to be trouble. She just knew it.

The head nurse lurched forward, jabbing the sedative at Graham's neck as he dodged her with more skill than would have been expected of a ninety-year-old. He grabbed Claire's wrist, twisting it behind her back. As he did, the plastic key card tumbled from his pocket.

"Take it, Savannah!" he yelled. "Take it and run to the elevator. The one you take to go to the garden. Don't stop running until they bring you to your mommy! Scream and scream and scream!"

Savannah didn't have to be told twice. Snagging the key card, she turned and darted from the room while Claire wrenched herself away from Graham.

"We can't let her go!" Claire cried out in haggard desperation. "I have to get her!"

She couldn't let the most promising subject they had escape. She couldn't disappoint Heath. She could not let Savannah get up to the main hall where guests and unaware nurses would crowd around her.

Everything would be ruined. Even dead, Cecilia had found out a way to ruin Claire's day.

"No!" Graham shouted, shoving Claire away from him. "Let her go home! She has to go to her mommy!"

Claire struggled with Graham as he grabbed her again, capturing her slender wrists in his hands. She was much smaller than Graham, standing three heads below him, but she was quick and had more determination in this one moment than Graham had ever had in his life.

With a shrill cry, she slammed the needle into Graham's neck with the entire force of her lithe body, his secure hold on her going lax, his eyes rolling backward.

"Crotchety Claire," he gasped collapsing to his knees. "Liar!"

CHAPTER SIXTY-SIX

My birthday..." Sarah said through gritted teeth as Heath approached with a hearty whistle.

The man stood a few yards away from them now, his icy eyes taking them in with disturbing pride.

"Why was my birthday the code to open the cage?" Sarah demanded in a tense and quiet voice, nostrils flaring.

Heath laughed, hands resting in his pockets. "Do I really need to answer that? I have a feeling you've already pieced that together, if you're as smart as your grandfather believed you were, anyway."

Her jaw twitching and her shoulders trembling, Sarah gave a firm shake of her head. "He wasn't involved in this. He couldn't have been. I know him-"

"Not as well as I did, my dear nurse Kramer," he responded. "Dr. Kramer was a talented, inquisitive, genius of a man. Without his funding, this research never would've taken off. I owe him for all of this." Heath lifted his hands, gesturing to the tunnels. "I am permanently in his debt."

"He funded it?" Sarah echoed, sagging to the side. "He made all of this happen?"

Heath nodded. "He helped me select the first candidates for our research thirty years ago. I was only twenty-something then. So young, so curious. It was his research that gave me this grand idea. When I told him, he was fascinated. He was determined to have a hand in it."

Sarah straightened, shoving her hair out of her fiery eyes. "There's no way he would've agreed to cage these people, to lock them away for the rest of their lives and treat them like lab rats. It's not true!"

Heath paused and shrugged. "Plans have…definitely been modified since his sacrifice. Progress is change, after all."

Mark stiffened, one of his hands pressing against Sarah's side. She, too, had gone rigid, staring at Heath with unblinking, bewildered eyes.

"Sacrifice?" she repeated.

"He understood the meaning of what we were doing down here. He understood what was needed for progress. Your grandfather was a kind man, Sarah. I'll give you that. He only chose patients who were on their deathbeds. But he knew we would need a healthy, strong brain to study, to gain a true foothold in our research."

"You killed him," Sarah's voice was no longer a whisper; it was a strong, sharp hiss. "You killed my grandfather!"

"Oh, my dear, it was hardly murder. He volunteered!"

"Why would he do that?" Sarah cried. "He was all I had. He would never choose to end his own life!"

"Well, my dear, he did it on one condition." Heath smiled. "Isn't that how it always is? There's always some sort of catch to a selfless act?"

"Forcing someone to agree to be killed is hardly selfless," Mark growled. "Is that how you operate? You kill off anyone who bores you? Anyone you don't need anymore?" He pointed at limp Larissa in the cage, whose body had grown as stony and cold as a fallen dead tree in winter.

Heath laughed and nodded. "Yes, my boy, that is exactly how I operate. But that wasn't me." With a disinterested flick of his wrist at the body of the woman, he added, "I probably would have, though. Useless woman-"

"Why did you kill him?" Sarah interrupted. "Why did you take my grandpa away from me?"

"His conditions to our agreement were simple," Heath shrugged. "First, you'd always have a job here. Second, and most importantly, you would never find out about any of this."

With a mocking smile, Heath tilted his head back and tapped the sign of the cross. "Sorry, Dr. Kramer. At least you'll have your granddaughter with you soon."

CHAPTER SIXTY-SEVEN

Heath gazed down at the stunned, disheveled, and injured wrenches who had tried so hard to hurl themselves in the midst of his ever-meticulous plans.

It made his gleeful smile stretch wider over his flawless white teeth as he considered how much they had overestimated themselves and their abilities. Heath Dole had never met a rival who didn't crumble in his shadow. He had never been bested. He'd never been beaten. He had no intention of starting a nasty habit like that now.

Every one of them stared back at him, all slack-jawed and glassy-eyed, contemplating their fates and his glorious intelligence. There would be no magic wand waved to save them. There would be no superhero in a cape swooping down to pluck them free like a bound damsel lifted off a set of train tracks in an old western movie.

Heath pitied them, as much as one could pity insects in a trap, anyway.

They were a silly little bunch who had wandered too far from the common areas of Springthorpe. There was nothing that could be done now. They'd seen too much and knew too much. Sarah, Mark, and Liv had caused too much trouble for the facility director to pardon their mindlessness.

It'd been a long, long day and Heath was aching to head back to his home, sink into a bubble bath, and let the warm water soothe away the soreness in his tired feet. He was worn out from chasing his troublemakers back and forth across the acreage of the retirement home. At least now he had them cornered and subdued.

Heath anticipated this would all be over with delightful swiftness.

Ebony metal gleamed under the beaming bright lights overhead as Heath shifted, exposing the gun at his waist. He soaked in the distress that flashed over their faces. His fingers swept over the holster, then tugged the pistol free. As a means for killing, he disliked guns because they were so artless and crude. But they were efficient, and there had been a stark lack of efficiency at Springthorpe lately.

He lifted the weapon, holding it with calm grace in his steady hand as he pointed it first at Sarah Kramer, then Mark, and then Ralph. He lined up each of their faces down the end of the handgun's barrel, pretending to shoot it each time, even adding in the thrilling little sound effect of the gun blasting that made him feel like a child playing cops and robbers. Funny, how back then he had always played a robber. Now, he felt more like the cop, doling out justice to those who dared stand in the way of immense scientific progress.

Sarah winced as the gun passed over her. Mark blanched and Ralph coughed and closed his dull eyes.

Joan glared, moving in front of her ailing husband.

"He won't last long," Heath shrugged. "Look at him, already pale as death." The blue-eyed man clicked his tongue in feigned sympathy.

Refusing to acknowledge the man's bitter words, Joan turned back to her husband, pressing her forehead against his and wrapping her arms around his body. She held him tightly, sharing her body's warmth with his own to ease his rigid limbs. Liv joined her, and the three held onto one another.

Heath rolled his eyes, disinterested in their pitiful familial bonding, turning back to Mark and Sarah who had managed to hold his attention for longer than most others had. He wished he could lock the exasperating pair up in one of his cages and watch them scramble in an attempt to escape, but he had learned he had to be rid of the interesting ones. In the long run, they weren't worth the trouble.

"I suppose I should get this over with," Heath sighed, flicking the safety off his sidearm with an unhappy twitch of his lips.

Blood was going to get everywhere. It would take hours to have it all mopped up and cleaned. Heath hated messes. He liked everything neat and orderly and not sticky with warm crimson gore.

He paced closer to them, the barrel of his gun still lifted and pointed at Mark and Sarah, shifting between their heads. Unlike Stanley, Heath knew how to carry his firearm, and he knew how to aim with precision. His father had been a hunter, training Heath at an early age the proper way to manage his weapons. Heath detested the sport. He found it senseless, though the skill had proved useful.

Sarah lurched forward. Mark tried to grab her by the wrist to pull her back but missed as she moved. "You're a real piece of work, Heath," she seethed. "Tarnishing my grandfather's name with this disgusting place, ruining lives. You make me sick."

Heath laughed and shook his head. "Astute observation, nurse Kramer. You have always been a perceptive wonder," he jeered with another roll of his eyes. "No wonder your grandfather was so proud of you."

In the bright light, his clear blue irises seemed so pale they blended in with the whites of his eyes, making him seem more creature than man.

Sarah stepped again to the side, Heath's eyes and gun trailing her. She stared straight at Heath.

Mark felt something inside of him buzzing, like there was something important he didn't understand, that he hadn't caught onto.

Sarah inched further away.

Heath wasn't paying any attention to Mark, who was still as a statue. His only focus was on Sarah as she edged toward the entrance of the cave.

"Now, now, nurse," Heath sighed. "Are you really going to try to run and make this harder?"

With a grunt, Mark threw himself forward, knocking Heath's loaded arm up toward the ceiling.

"We're not going down that easy, you monster!" Sarah snarled. She jumped, winding up one lean arm and a curled fist and hurling it as hard as she could against Heath's jaw.

CHAPTER SIXTY-EIGHT

The first shot left everyone's ears ringing loud like metal church bells in their heads as Heath let out a furious roar and lowered the gun to aim again.

Sarah stumbled to the side. Her hands were clamped hard over her ears and her eyes were squeezed shut. Mark saw her lips moving. She was screaming something so intensely that her face turned a horrified red, though Mark could hear nothing at all but the shrill scream of his torn eardrums.

Everything seemed to move in slow motion. It took only seconds, but it seemed like minutes. Mark had blinked his stunned eyes as though a thick blindfold had been removed.

Mark's gaze flickered from face to face, taking in the terror on his parents' faces and the tears surging like a waterfall down Liv's stark cheeks. As Sarah fell to her knees, still gripping her ears, sprays of dust swept up around her like a little dark cloud, tiny particles clinging to her scrubs like she'd had a snowball of dirt tossed at her chest.

It was when Mark forced his stiff neck to turn back toward the irate director that sound returned and time zoomed forward so fast Mark could feel the velocity knocking in his bones, forcing him down to his hands and knees on the gravel floor below his exhausted body.

"No!" Mark yelled as Heath lowered the barrel to point down at the top of Sarah's head.

Mark had made a promise and he was going to keep it. There would be no more death in these tunnels. Not now. Not unless the death was his own.

Digging his feet into the ground, Mark lunged himself as hard as he could at Heath, barreling him over with such a force that the gun went off twice more, though the bullets found no human home, one rocketing off into the distance. One of the fluorescent lights overhead burst and went dark, leaving half the tunnel in shadows as shattered glass showered down on their heads like sharp, crystal snow.

The two men rolled across the tunnel floor, kicking up dirt and grabbing at limbs. Heath dragged sharp nails across Mark's cheek, scratching the younger man as he tried to target Mark with the gun.

Mark's chest heaved. His brain was numb with panic and determination. He had to protect his family. He had to protect Sarah.

He didn't care what happened to him as long as they were safe, as long as they could feel the sun on their faces and breathe in clean air again. With a mighty roar of his own, Mark grabbed at Heath's hand, slamming his wrist on the ground. Heath refused to drop the gun no matter how hard Mark crushed at the director's wrist.

Instead, Heath shoved upward again, forcing Mark to scramble backward across the tunnel. As he stumbled back, slamming into the bars of the cage, one of the old patients inside let out a low, terrified wail, covering his eyes with his hands as the cluster of caged people gathered together.

Mark thrust himself off the bars, using the momentum to grab hold of Heath and whirl him hard around, slamming Heath back against the cell where, only seconds prior, Mark had been. Mark pinned Heath down, unable to resist smacking the man's head once, then twice, against the cold metal.

"What do you think you're doing?" Heath growled at him, clear blue eyes transparent and severe. "You think if you roughen me up a little, I'm going to let you waltz out of here with your family?" He gritted his teeth, still holding the gun, which was pointed upward.

The bone-thin people in the cell wandered forward, staring at Heath as his body was pressed against the metal.

"No. You're going to let me take all of these people!" Mark seethed, disgusted and angry. He was so full of adrenaline his eyes wouldn't focus. "You tortured my family. You tortured countless innocent people for your own sick joy!"

"It was all in the name of science, Mr. Hogarth. Look at your mother! Look at how healthy she is. This changes everything, don't you see? Don't you understand how we can change the world with this?" Heath's eyes shone with a passion that revolted Mark.

"I don't care! You can't imprison people, making them your personal guinea pigs to be experimented on!"

Heath's weakened prisoners clawed at him from where they were trapped inside the cage, grabbing hold of his arms and yanking his body like they were trying to drag him into the cage where he had kept them imprisoned for so long. Their brittle nails scraped and scratched at him, ruining his fine clothes as he yelped and tried to rip away.

Desperate to be free, desperate to be let out, they clawed harder. Though Mark still had him pinned, Heath twisted, the gun exploding again in his squeezing grip.

"I won't let you!" Mark cried, loosening one hand to try to snag hold of the pistol before the Springthorpe director could aim it at anyone.

Heath took that one moment of Mark's distraction to lower the weapon, the cold metal brushing right across Mark's forehead. As Heath's finger squeezed the trigger, Sarah bound forward, wrapping her arms around Heath's to yank his aim away.

A shot rang out as white, hot pain exploded in Mark's shoulder. He tumbled backward with a sharp cry, his hand covering the red blood gushing from his wounded flesh. Then, he saw Heath turn toward Sarah, and Mark instantly forgot his pain.

Both Mark and Sarah threw themselves at Heath once more as he let loose the rest of the bullets, missing every time as he shot in a blind panic, only the ceiling left wounded from that round when his gun clicked empty.

Panting, Heath tried again and again to shoot the gun. The chamber remained empty and, like a cat without claws, Heath was left staring at Mark and Sarah.

"It's over," Mark growled. "Accept it, Heath. You've lost."

A dark scowl formed over Heath's irate face as a long, shrill hiss whined over their heads, drawing everyone's eyes upward.

CHAPTER SIXTY-NINE

The doors of the empty tunnel elevator had just slid apart for Claire when the first tremor struck. With a startled grunt, Claire stumbled, pressing one hand against the elevator doors to keep them open while her distressed green eyes swept up and down the hall.

For the briefest of moments, the head nurse thought she'd imagined the roll of the earth. Between Graham's attack and the little girl's escape, this entire day was going to hell.

When Claire raised her eyes again at the flickering lights in the tunnel, a large, damp piece of sod slapped her in the face, leaving dirt trailing down her cheek and the taste of grass on her tongue.

She had not imagined the vibrations.

She swiped away the clump of earth, holding a hand over her face to shield the small speckles of dirt falling like raindrops from between the metallic streaks of pipes coiled above.

Her ears started ringing. Something was wrong.

She whirled on her heel, shooting a desperate glance around her as the dirt fell heavier and faster. Pieces of concrete supports that had been drilled into the tunnel walls wobbled loose and sent heavy stones pummeling downward.

Sucking in a breath, Claire knew there wasn't time to hesitate. The tunnel echoed as she darted forward, her footsteps punctuated by the whistling of rock and sand.

"Heath!" she shrieked when she rounded the next tunnel and gaped at where Heath was grouped with Mark, Sarah, and the rest of Mark's family in the main belly of the tunnel where the cells were located.

Mark was bent on the ground, his jacket covered in a bright scarlet blossom of blood while Sarah crouched over him.

Heath towered above them all, a gun held in his hand, his head tilted up toward the ceiling. She paid no attention to the others, focusing only on Heath, the one who mattered more than anyone—more than everyone.

"Heath, it's the gas pipes!" she screeched, cupping her hands around her lips. She yelled over the sound of the grumbling tunnel. Her eyes strained, making a vein throb on her forehead.

Claire hadn't finished that short sentence before the shrill hiss overhead turned into a scream as though the pipes were rushing fire through their metal cores. Many of steel tubes contained dangerous gasses that Heath used in his experiments. Other pipes were used to keep oxygen circulating in the tunnel.

The director of Springthorpe Manor turned toward her, his face pale with realization. He took one step forward before lifting one of his hands to point past her.

Claire knew exactly what he meant. She'd already planned for this.

"I'll get it!" she promised, giving a sharp nod. "I will."

Swallowing the thick lump in her throat, she whirled on her heel and ran through the corridor as the swollen metal coils burst into thunderous flame. The entire tunnel shook as fireballs shot huge, scorching fireworks that left the earthen walls a charred black.

CHAPTER SEVENTY

That's right!" Sarah yelled after Heath Dole as he ducked around a falling lump of clay and ran toward the front of the tunnel where it met with Henry Kramer's grave. "You run away like the coward you are!"

Foaming at the mouth with pure rage, Sarah bent down and scooped her arm under Mark's, helping him to his feet. She'd wanted to chase down Heath and hurl him into that pit he'd thrown Cecilia into, but she couldn't leave Mark behind. She couldn't leave any of these people behind.

"I'm fine," Mark assured her, though he couldn't move his arm and his vision was blurring. He shook his head slowly, using the ripped piece of fabric Sarah had torn from her scrubs to press against his bloody wound. "You need to open the rest of these cells, Sarah, hurry! We need to free these people."

Overhead, the pipes were spitting flames like the devil himself was hacking up a hairball. Burning dirt, ash, and ember rained down on them, the roll of exploding pipes thundering further and further down the tunnel. They didn't have time. They were either going to be consumed by flame or swallowed by the bucking earth if they didn't move immediately.

The woman's brow knotted as she glanced at the blood seeping from between Mark's fingers but she gave a firm nod, darting toward the nearest cage and typing in the code before swinging it open and rushing inside. Sweat was already pooling on the back of her neck, the metal burns as hot as coals.

"Come on, let's move!" Mark said, clapping his hands together with a wince as he ushered the herd ahead of him. "Get these people out, Sarah, do you hear me?"

She nodded from where she stood ahead of him, separated by at least thirty-five hobbling, aged bodies. Some limped along while some barely managed to put one foot in front of the other, but they clung to one another, moving as a solid, bumbling pack after the blue-eyed nurse. Sarah wove between them, keeping them moving, making sure all cells were emptied, and helping the weakest of the prisoners to walk. She reminded Mark of an eager sheepdog, keeping her brood safe and plodding toward a greener pasture, but he didn't have the time to waste watching her quick feet.

Mark rushed back into his father's cage, helping Liv to her feet as Joan pulled Ralph to his, the once-burly man leaning on his wife's shoulder, though she didn't seem to struggle under the weight.

"Mom," Mark said as the woman's caramel eyes met his own, realizing he hadn't yet had a chance to speak to her.

He couldn't believe he was gazing into that face again, a face he had believed to be deceased for so long, a face he was so sure he would never again see. He wasn't sure whether to laugh or cry.

She winked, brushing her fingers against his forehead. "Now is not the time, dear," she said, as the flames overhead reflected in her eyes. "The ground is quite literally caving in around us."

Mark laughed, giving a nod as he held Liv around the waist. She wobbled in his arms, not meeting his eyes.

Joan swept an arm around Ralph, guiding him forward as the ground shook once more, almost sending them both blundering sideways against the molten rails of their cell as fire surged down over them.

"Fitting," Mark murmured to himself as he thought the entire cemetery might first cave in on them and then evaporate into the depths of hell.

As Mark led Liv out of the cell and glanced over his shoulder to make sure everyone had escaped, his eyes landed on the only one remaining.

Larissa Stalwart's dead body remained limp and pale on the dusty ground as it shook. Her eyes were half open, hollow and glazed as a doll's. Mark swallowed and pushed his sister forward.

"Can you walk?" he asked Liv.

She bit her lip, clinging to his arm. "Mark, I can't leave you. This whole place is going to blow-"

Mark could barely hear her over the sound of metal shattering like fragile glass, spewing more fire with every second they waited.

"Go," he admonished her. "I'll be right behind you."

Hesitating again, Liv turned and stumbled after her mother, who reached out to take her daughter's hand.

As the ground roared once more, Mark ducked into the cage. With a grunt and a grimace, ignoring the screaming pain in his shoulder as best he could, he scooped up Larissa's body.

Cradling the woman against him, he climbed back to his feet as the floor cracked and moaned, the metal cages of the bars ripping apart with the strain like they were made of twigs.

He hadn't made it two steps before the ground behind him split wide open, gulping in the fireballs falling like hail.

CHAPTER SEVENTY-ONE

Claire was proud of her steady hands.

Even as the pebbles falling around her became golfball-sized and then larger, she didn't tremble. The dirt was streaming down in such dense sheets it reminded her of a hurricane.

Her scrubs were damp with sweat caused by the intense heat in the tunnels. She found it harder and harder to breathe as smoke ebbed in through the doorway. But she remained as focused as she would any other day in the office.

She pretended it was just another Tuesday and that she was finishing up her paperwork at the end of the day, that she could wrap up here and soon make another cup of coffee.

With a calm manner, Claire packed.

The small back room once had sterile white walls that were kept so clean she'd practically had to wear sunglasses to enter it. Those same walls were now cracked and streaked with mud. Still, Claire didn't panic.

She couldn't. She wouldn't let herself.

Sorting through critical medical files and invaluable research notes, she put them in a waterproof, fireproof pouch. Those records alone would be enough to restart their research once they escaped this mess. She was convinced they would still be able to change science forever.

Claire cleared her throat, shooting a glance at the open door a yard or so away. She could see the crumbling tunnel, the fallen cells, the empty rooms. The heavy metal door swung back and forth, not from a strong draft but from the rate at which the tunnel was vibrating.

She was going to get out of here. She had to. Heath needed her. The world needed her.

Moving faster now, Claire rushed to the refrigerated shelves on the other side of the room, flipping open glass containers and pushing a variety of assorted bottles and serums into the pouch while keeping it hugged to her chest.

It was as she moved over to the last shelf that she paused and did a double take, doing a quick blitz of mental math.

How many vials had they made from Joan Hogarth's samples?

They'd used a few for testing and one for Graham. They should have had at least a dozen vials left in the cold cabinet where the most valuable of their scientific creations were stored. Instead, there were two lone vessels resting in the refrigerated case.

Claire scooped them up and added them to her bag, still keeping it clutched tight in one hand while she flung open the rest of the cabinets and knocked aside the other glass bottles and instruments within them.

Joan's serums had to be there somewhere. Claire couldn't leave without them.

How was she going to tell Heath she'd lost them and that she'd allowed them to get taken?

They would need everything they had collected if they were going to start their testing again. They'd need a good foothold after they lost everything else.

Had it been careless Celeste who put the bottles back in the incorrect place?

Claire allowed herself one sharp cry of frustration as the room gave a monstrous shake, hurling a large row of glass bottles over Claire's head to shatter against the opposite wall. Claire grabbed at the counter, struggling to stay on her feet.

There was no time.

She would have to hope the vials and information she'd managed to save would be enough. With her and Heath's minds put together, they could start again. They could still change the world.

As Claire turned toward the open door, a massive slab of concrete crashed from somewhere overhead, landing in front of the head nurse's feet and cutting the tiny room in half.

She stared at the wall in front of her. Pressing one hand against the massive, thick barrier, she could sense the heat of the fire beyond. Claire turned in a dazed circle as though she expected to find another door, another escape, but there were only trembling, crumbling walls.

She wasn't going anywhere. She was trapped.

Claire sucked in a breath laced with spilled chemicals, dust, and cinder, still hugging the pouch to her chest.

The walls were screaming again, the tunnel overhead so hot it glowed a beautiful shade of blue, bursting detonations sounding like the entire planet was being ripped apart at the seam.

Letting her eyes fall shut and the ashes and grit spill over her cheeks and clot in her hair, she tipped her head back.

Claire had no regrets. She had given Heath her all.

CHAPTER SEVENTY-TWO

Dark gray clouds scattered across the gray sky as the elderly patients dispersed across the cemetery graveyard like wandering, wailing ghosts.

Some collapsed into arms of the officers who had gathered after a nurse called in a found child when Savannah had shown up. Others were led to benches that lined the manor's long driveway.

Officer Schumacher gazed out over the sea of people, his jaw hanging open, his arms crossed over his chest. When Stanley Stalwart had burst into his office with the same deranged eyes Mark Hogarth had displayed earlier, Schumacher had shown up here thinking he was going to be able to bust a drug ring.

He'd never expected anything as horrific as this. His brain hadn't entirely processed the scene yet. Before this, he'd never witnessed anything worse than a skipped traffic light.

Throngs of nurses rushed outside toward the elderly, aiding the officers and the fallen. Those who had been imprisoned down there for months or years were so bone pale they matched the stony marble of the mausoleum.

Leaning on Joan, his arm around her shoulders, his head pressed against her own, Ralph surveyed the swaying mass around them. While the rest pooled forward to escape the cemetery, the elderly lovers stayed in place, like a steady rock in the middle of a flowing river even as steam rose up from the cracked and mottled earth beyond the tomb.

"Joan, darling," he mused, pressing a kiss to the side of her head. His whole body hurt and ached like he'd tried jogging again, though he didn't recall having gone for a run. "Have we come to the fair?" he asked.

"Yes, dear," Joan replied, turning a sunny smile up to him as she brushed clods of dirt from his long, pale lashes. "Isn't it lovely?"

Ralph wrapped his arms around his wife. Too stiff to sway with her like he wanted, he held her closely instead.

Liv stumbled past them, still trailing IVs like a criminal dragging chains. Her eyes were hazy and clouded, full of dirt and guilt and remorse.

It was only when her gaze found the little blonde girl standing beside an officer that she felt a strength, an urge she had never felt before. Liv had failed her family to a horrendous extent. She would spend the rest of her life trying to make up for it, haunted by nightmares of her father's limp body and her mother's gaunt face. Liv had made many, many mistakes. Irreconcilable ones. But she was going to change.

She was going to love. She was going to treasure and cherish. She was going to force herself to do it. She never wanted to hurt her family again.

"Savannah Bennett," Liv said as she rushed toward the police officer. "That's her name. Her mother is Samantha. Savannah is my granddaughter," she choked, staring at the little girl who gazed up at her with curious eyes.

"Do you like to color?" Savannah asked, her face streaked with dirt and tears and set with two gray eyes that shone like moonstone.

Liv couldn't answer, her throat too tight. She only gave a small nod.

"Wait, ma'am, come back!" another officer nearby called, pushing back Liv and the child to chase after Sarah as she took off running through the crowd of people. "Tell me again what happened here!" he shouted.

He slowed to a stop, watching her brunette locks vanish among the assorted gray heads of the patients and rainbow scrubs of the nurses. With an impatient sigh, he glanced at his nearby partner and shook his head in disbelief.

Sarah whirled in a circle as she halted near the tomb. Officers were cordoning off that area where the ground was vibrating. Sarah's eyes flashed from face to unfamiliar face as her feet darted back and forth in sheer desperation.

As she rushed toward the tomb to go back inside, the entire back half of the cemetery collapsed inward with a colossal eruption as fire shot up toward the sky. Blistering steam and smoke surged out of the mouth of the toppled mausoleum. Sarah and the officers lunged backward, barely managing to escape the blazing sinkhole.

"Mark!" she cried out, arms held up in the face of the heat even as her skin scalded and reddened. "Mark!" She yelled his name as though she could convince him to come crawling out from within the fallen tunnel, as though she could drag him out with her words alone.

"Sarah..." his breathless but calm voice spoke from behind her.

She whirled around, her blue eyes meeting his golden brown eyes as Mark eased Larissa's body to rest on the ground.

He'd barely straightened when Sarah threw herself into his embrace, her arms tangling tightly around his neck. Though the movement made his shoulder sear, he couldn't have cared less. He was so thrilled to have made it back to the surface, to have his parents with him, to have Sarah in his arms.

"We did it," she gushed, warm tears prickling the corners of her eyes. "We actually did it. Mark can you believe it-"

He cut her off, hands sweeping up to her cheeks as he pulled her closer, his mouth capturing hers. They swayed together, holding one another close, memorizing the sensation of their lips pressed against one another.

Mark pulled back when his lungs ached as much as his wound, pressing his forehead against the beautiful nurse's as she gazed at him with electric, captivating eyes.

"I believe it completely," he smiled.

A soft cry behind them caught their attention as Stanley stumbled forward, a blanket draped over his shoulders.

"It's true, then," the dark-haired man whispered, falling to his knees beside his mother. "She's dead..."

Mark and Sarah nodded. The nurse moved closer to rest a hand on his shoulder. "At least it's over now."

Stanley swallowed and nodded, stroking Larissa's hair.

"Thank you," he said, his gaze shifting to Mark. "Thank you for bringing her back to me."

"No one was getting left behind," Mark responded. "No one."

Sarah sank back against Mark's welcoming side, pressing her face into his neck and holding him tightly as his good arm swept around her, his lips pressing against her forehead. His eyes surveyed the people around them, shuffling back and forth between the cops, nurses, and patients.

It would have been a perfect scene had two people not been missing.

CHAPTER SEVENTY-THREE

The bright lights of the cop station shone overhead, reminding Mark of the illuminated tunnel.

When he closed his eyes and sank down against the rough plastic of the waiting room's chair, he imagined himself back down below. The soft whispers between the cops and those still giving statements became the muted whines of the caged patients.

Sucking in a breath, he forced his eyes back open to remind himself he was no longer breathing in the dank air and falling dirt.

A cup of coffee appeared in front of his face from Sarah's extended hand. He took it, trying to inhale the rich scent of the warm liquid like it was pure gold. He'd be blowing black chunks out of his nose for days.

"Still nothing?" he asked, clearing his throat and hoping the leftover grime and dust would clear out soon enough.

Sarah shook her head, crossing one leg over her other knee and jiggling her foot.

"There's no sign of either of them."

Mark crossed his arms over his chest, staring forward at the room where his parents were talking to the detective.

So far, Heath and Claire were nowhere to be seen.

When Mark had first broken free of the tunnel and gazed out at the cops, he'd been hoping they would've already captured Heath and loaded him into a police car to be put behind bars, as he had so loved doing to others. Unfortunately, the man seemed to have vanished into thin air.

Liv sank down on the other side of Mark, heaving a sigh and turning her face toward him. Though still pale gray, her eyes had a shine to them Mark could recall from their youth.

"I know I don't deserve your forgiveness," she said before Mark could say anything. "And I know I don't deserve Mom and Dad's..." she trailed off, throat going tight as she lost her nerve. Her eyes averted back to her folded hands, the entirety of the English vocabulary failing her.

Mark watched her, taking in her thin arms polka-dotted with angry red marks and scars from the needles Heath and his researchers had jabbed into her. He knew the outside wounds had nothing on the ones in her heart.

If he was honest with himself, he still felt that simmering resentment, anger, and betrayal for what she had done. But she was his sister, and they were all lucky to be alive. There was no point in holding onto those wretched feelings, especially when his mother had already made it clear that all was forgiven. Without a word, he leaned over, laying his hand on hers and giving her pale fingers a delicate squeeze.

Her startled eyes returned to meet his, tears blooming in their watery gray depths. His seeming acceptance of her apology humbled her deeply.

There was no amount of disappointment or anger Mark could feel for Liv that would rival that within herself.

Sensing curious eyes on them, Mark turned his head, meeting a familiar gray-eyed stare from across the room where a little girl sat propped up on an officer's desk. Her legs swung back and forth, dirt sprinkling the carpet beneath her every time her shoes bumped the heavy wood of the desk.

"That's the girl?" Sarah asked with a faint whistle of surprise. "She's beautiful, Liv."

"I still can't believe it," Liv responded. "I kept thinking Heath was lying to torture me, but then I look at her and it's as clear as day. She looks just like Mom, except the eye color, I suppose."

"She looks just like you," Sarah offered with a faint smile and a wink.

Liv blushed and gave a small wave to the child, who was all too happy to return the gesture.

"Savannah!" A woman's voice rang out from the front door of the cop station. "Savannah, my baby girl!"

Both the little girl and the band of people on the waiting bench turned toward the voice, watching as a blonde woman darted through the station. With a squeal, Savannah leaped straight up to her feet on the desk, plodding dirty footprints over the papers and knocking over the keyboard as she sprung off the glossy surface and into the woman's arms.

Liv gasped, shooting to her own feet at the same time. The woman's eyes darted toward the movement from over the girl's head as they clung to one another.

Liv and her daughter gazed at each other for the first time in six years.

Liv took a small step in her daughter's direction, but the woman turned her back instead, allowing the cop to guide her into a nearby room.

Mark took his sister's hand again, noticing her shaking.

"Can you imagine Samantha's shock right now? Give her some time to breathe, to relax, to accept that Savannah is safe," he suggested.

Biting her cracked lips, Liv mumbled a subdued agreement. Her eyes were wide with pain. Sarah moved in closer, wrapping an arm around the woman's thin shoulders, as the door right across the hall opened once more.

"Thank you for your time, Mr. and Mrs. Hogarth," the detective said, his face as haunted as Mark was sure his own was–as everyone's was.

This case was going to stay with many people for a long, long time. The detective waved in the next person on his lengthy list of those waiting to have their statements taken, the door swinging shut and leaving the group in the hall in silence.

"Mom…" Liv choked as she wrung her hands and gazed at Joan, fumbling for something, anything she could say. "I am so sorry-"

Joan stepped forward, wrapping her daughter in her arms. "You can say you're sorry as much as you want, dear, but it won't erase what happened. Let's move on, shall we?" The woman lifted her head and pressed a hand to Liv's cheek. "Life is too short to live in the past. I think we've all learned that lesson."

Liv nodded, though she was dying to grovel, dying to beg and plead and prostrate herself, to offer whatever she could to repair the damage she had done. There was no way to replace the lost year, though, and Liv would have to live forever with what she'd done.

"Let's get out of here," Ralph sighed, placing his hands on his hips and shaking his head. "I am dying for a slice of pizza. I feel like I haven't eaten all day!"

Joan beamed while Liv shook her head, glancing back at Mark as they headed for the door.

Mark and Sarah took a slow step after them, their arms wound around the other's shoulders, Sarah's head resting against his good shoulder.

"Do you think it's over?" she asked. "Really over?"

Mark turned his head and kissed her hair that still smelled of earth and embers.

"I think so," he said. "I think the final explosion wiped out everything Heath had."

CHAPTER SEVENTY-FOUR

"Mr. Vida, as I've told you, there is nothing left in that account. We were faxed the papers several weeks ago, and we implemented the desired changes immediately. Yelling at me isn't going to change that."

Robert Vida stared out the window of his Salem, Oregon, home as the person on the phone continued ranting in his ear. As his chest heaved with short-breathed fury, he watched the rain drip down the foggy glass in slow, crooked streams.

"I don't understand how that's possible." Robert shot back, gnashing his teeth. "I did not sign anything regarding the insurance claims!"

"You did, sir. You recently had to refile the annual claims, and it was then that you asked us to donate the remaining funds, as well as any future credits in your account, to DanausSci."

"I've never even heard of such a thing," Robert exclaimed. "Why would I have transferred all that money to some unknown science organization?"

"I'm afraid I have no answer for you. Are there any other questions?"

"This is fraud…I will sue you. This is blatant theft!"

"Can you really sue us, Mr. Vida?" the person on the other end of the line wondered aloud. "Most people don't use our financial guidance unless they are trying to stay out of the legal scope. I can fax you a duplicate of the papers you signed."

The door swung open behind Robert Vida as he shifted from one foot to the other, squinting at the reflection of the visitor in the glass.

With a faint gasp, he slammed the phone down and whirled to take in the sight of the petite, red-headed woman before him.

"Claire!" he gasped, sinking down into his chair with a shake of his head. "It's been weeks. Where have you been?"

She was a little worse for wear–a few scars on her face and burnt fingertips–but, other than that, she appeared as prim and poised as ever.

"Is this where you're going to reopen the facility, Heath?" she asked, inspecting the heavy wood of the office floor and scuffing her shoe against the grain. She paused, eyes darting back to him. "Or should I say Robert Vida now?"

"No, no," the blue-eyed man sighed. "The police would track down this residence soon enough. I didn't want to leave until I was sure that you...I thought you'd perished, Claire. I'd thought it was all lost."

The woman didn't answer, staring at him. When he inspected her, he could see she held a zipped pouch between her arms that he knew was crammed with more medical knowledge than had been produced by any other organization in the last twenty years.

"Did you manage to get anything?" he implored, gesturing at the bag. "Did you get to the room with the vials?"

When she nodded, he gave a relieved sigh, clapping a hand over his heart as though it'd begun beating again for the first time since that day when the tunnel had collapsed. Thanks to a robust insurance policy to be dispersed to an already lucrative offshore account, Heath hadn't been at all concerned as he fled through one of the numerous hidden exits of the tunnel. However, now he had to deal with some bureaucratic mix-up before he could access his mammoth stores of cash.

At least they had something to start with now. This was a small setback. In a few months, he could set up in a new location with a new staff that idolized him and, as Robert Vida, he would return to his place at the pinnacle of scientific progress.

"Good. Very good," he said with a shake of his head. The phone rang again, making him seethe, like every trill it sang out was an insult. "Ms. Matthews, why don't you go take a rest for now? I'll fix this mess and prepare our next move."

"Of course," she responded, turning as he picked up the phone and barked a greeting to his perturbed accountant.

"Oh, Ms. Matthews!" he called, stopping her in the doorway. "Leave the pouch. I want to inspect it."

With a wink, he turned back to the window as his accountant rambled in his ear.

When he turned back again as the door closed, he ran a finger over the stuffed pouch Claire had left on his desk beside a glass of his favorite whiskey.

He reached for the delicate crystal glass, grateful for anything that would make the phone call a little more bearable, and downed the entire thing before tugging the pouch toward him.

He'd been expecting the pouch to be heavy with paperwork, medicines, and glass bottles. It moved with such ease across the table, it startled him. Frowning, the man unzipped the bag and then tugged at the bottom of the bag, spilling its contents out across the polished surface of his desk.

Wrinkled old napkins fluttered over the wood, falling over the sides and littering his carpet.

Bewildered, he dropped the phone on the ground as he grabbed the bag and inspected the inside as though he expected his numerous serums and medical miracles to appear before him.

"Claire!" he called, coughing and shaking his head.

The first step across the room was a long, powerful one–his eyes narrowed, his mouth a hard line of fury–but the second was shorter. On his third step, his foot dragged sloth-like across the hardwood. His momentum sent him staggering forward. He fell, landing so hard on his chest that the wind was knocked hard from his lungs. Black and blue stars dazzled before his eyes.

Heath Dole rolled onto his back, clutching at his neck as he panted, struggling to drag in air. The empty whiskey glass glinted gray like the clouds outside the window.

CHAPTER SEVENTY-FIVE

Six months ago," the pastor read from his large black book, gazing out at the people dressed in cheery shades of pink, purple, and blue. "Joan and Ralph received a second chance at sharing the joy of their lives together after it had been robbed from them. Though it might have seemed at the time like they would never get another chapter to their love story, you should never underestimate true love, undying love, unyielding love. There was no distance that could keep their hearts from finding one another again."

He shifted, eyes turning toward the photo of Ralph and Joan that had been blown up to poster size and rested over a large white vase filled with fragrant lilies and lots of daisies.

The picture was a reshoot of their original fiftieth-anniversary photo, which had been ripped up and tossed into a bonfire by Joan. For the reshoot, the pair had stood on the dock of Lake Jarvis, beaming at the camera, holding one another, and laughing. Though it wasn't visible within the blurred edges of the picture, their family had clustered near them, cheering as the photo was taken.

Thomas and Liv had stood with their children, the blonde woman's arms around the shoulders of her eldest daughter while Savannah stuck an inquisitive toe in the lake. Mark stood behind the camera, making sure the shot was perfect while Sarah peered over his shoulder to inspect the image.

Even Stanley had joined them, having sold his hotel and inherited a small fortune from his mother's will. He lazed in the grass in a patch of daisies, gazing up overhead at the clouds.

There was no talk of Heath Dole or Claire Matthews on that glorious, lakeside day. They wouldn't tarnish their newfound happiness by bringing up the immoral and vicious pair who had nearly ruined each of their lives.

The day after the photo had been taken, as the others were on the fishing boat and Liv, Mark, and Joan relaxed on the sunny shore, Joan had wrapped her arms around her children and held them tightly.

She gazed into their eyes, memorizing the colors and flecks of the pretty irises and the way the sun was reflected on their pink cheeks. Even pale Liv was getting some color, though her shoulders would turn lobster red by evening if she wasn't careful. Joan tried mapping out their faces in her mind in the hope that she would be able to take those memories with her.

When Mark became concerned about the single tear that snaked down Joan's cheek, the woman had sighed and pressed a kiss to his cheek and then to her daughter's. Then she'd told them.

Joan Hogarth had little time left.

Though the experimentation had been a success, it was a temporary one. Without constant doses of the serum crafted from her body, Joan would soon shrivel in body and mind. She could already sense her memories fading, the clarity dulling.

When tears welled in Liv's eyes, Joan had laughed.

"Don't you see what a miracle this has been?" Joan asked, tipping her daughter's face up to gaze into her eyes. "Don't you see I've had more time with my husband and my family? I was given a gift, dear, and it has truly given me my best days."

The boat had been pulling to shore then, waves crashing against the hull, and Joan made them both promise to keep her secret quiet.

Mark and Liv stood together now, a breeze blowing over the lake as the pastor continued to speak about the kind and precious love Joan and Ralph had shared during their long years on this earth.

To no one's surprise, the pair had passed together, asleep in their bed with smiles on their faces not a month after that day everyone had gathered together. It'd been Mark who found them in the guest room of his new San Francisco apartment which he shared with Sarah.

The lovers' ashes would be spread over the lake they cherished so much, so they could spend eternity in the warm, crystal clear tide.

Mark closed his eyes and breathed in the clean, fresh air, grateful for peace at last.

CHAPTER SEVENTY-SIX

Sometimes she felt as though she were still falling.

The red-headed woman jerked awake, hair sticking to her damp skin as her chest rose and fell in a startled panic that would soon fade. She had only been dreaming.

She pressed a hand to her heart, listening to the rapid rhythm as it thrummed against her palm. Shaking her head, she slid out of the unmade bed, tiny feet padding across the carpet of the boutique hotel.

Reaching the window, Cecilia Matthews gripped the drapes and pulled them back enough to press her forehead against the glass.

Vancouver was breathtaking. She'd heard it would snow there. Cecilia had never seen snow. She'd never seen so many sights. She'd spent so much of her life trapped and tormented.

Across the room on the couch, a yawn drifted through the small hotel room. Cecilia glanced over to where Graham slept, his long lashes dusting the tops of his high cheekbones.

She chuckled. Graham had been angry at her when he'd woken up where she, with help, had dragged him up onto the grassy knoll at the other end of the cemetery to watch the fireworks below. They'd both been bruised, battered, and burnt, but when she'd handed him the journal, he'd quieted.

Sometimes, he still called her Claire, but she didn't mind. She'd found it fun to be Claire at times.

There, sitting in the grass, she'd felt it among the faint quakes and shudders–the last beats of her twin sister's heart. It had made Cecilia sad, but it'd been a price she was more than willing to pay.

Cecilia had bided her time the past fifteen years, being somewhat useful and somewhat troublesome to those who had kept her locked away. Once she discovered how to, it was hard for her to sneak free of the facility while knowing she would have to return. If she wandered too far, she would lose access to the serums that gave her clarity, that kept her from forgetting.

And so, Cecilia had planned and brooded and wished. She would get out. She would eventually get away.

She'd been waiting for Joan, not the old woman specifically but for the final key to Heath's research, and ultimately, her own plan. Cecilia had been tangibly closer to her freedom, to leaving the tunnel behind her forever. It made it easier that she hadn't been alone. Graham was easy to manipulate, and it was easy to manipulate others through Graham.

The only one she was sorry for leaving behind was the little girl. What a valuable little treasure she'd been. Spunky too. Savannah reminded Cecilia of herself when she was little. She also regretted having to kill the old Stalwart woman, but at least Graham had left her some beautiful flowers.

If Stanley Stalwart had killed Ralph's son and the nurse outside the mausoleum, Cecilia would never have had a chance to get what she'd needed. That was funny to her now, seeing as how she'd tried to have Graham kill them in the same exact place hours before that. After they had lived through the failed attempts on their lives, they'd actually come in handy. The pair had been a welcome distraction, keeping Heath away from the pit where Cecilia had remained hidden until the cell phone in her pocket had vibrated.

Cecilia hadn't been sure her plan would work. She hadn't been sure until Ralph Hogarth had accidentally stumbled into it without falling to his death. It was then that she knew it was ready.

With meticulous care, she had chiseled and built a small platform down in the pit using some handmade tools and some she'd stolen from the facility. She hadn't been sure it was large enough or close enough to the surface to be able to climb out. Inadvertently, Ralph had become a test subject and had demonstrated her plan could work.

All she had to do was make trouble and wait. Reliable Heath had proven he was inclined to murder her.

The fall was harder than Cecilia had thought it would be, and she really did think she was going to die, but her hands had found the ledge, and she'd grabbed it while biting her tongue so as not to make any noise after that initial, shocked cry. Though it was only minutes, she'd hung there for what felt like hours.

"It's time," a tired voice came from the mussed hotel bed as Cecilia shifted and gazed at the man lying there. Chuck smiled. "It's time for another dose."

Cecilia caressed his face, grateful for those eyes that had seen and heard it all. All the times he had warned her, all the times he'd used his electronic gaze of security cameras to keep her safe and hidden as she wandered the halls of Springthorpe.

She turned and headed to the small refrigerator, sinking to her knees as she opened it and gazed inside.

Ten bottles of serum tucked into a container labeled with DanausSci stickers gleamed under the dim light as she ran a finger over each one, counting them, even though she knew how many were there. She picked up a vial and handed it to Chuck.

With the serum, she and Graham would be sane for years. She would be able to continue what Heath had started, but she would do it properly and legally. DanausSci would be legitimate and wouldn't cage humans like laboratory rats. Because the serum had worked for her, Graham, and Joan, Cecilia was certain it would work for others, too.

At the sound of soft, flapping, little wings behind her, the woman turned and gazed across the room at two large jars. On the bottoms of the jars, ripped newspaper lay under sticks and vibrant flowers. One news headline was barely visible.

Criminal scientist suffers stroke, is confined to facility he once ran.

She smiled, then moved to sit where she could peer into the jars while Chuck gently injected her with the serum.

Butterflies in each jar flexed their wings so beautifully and elegantly that a hopeful, joyful tear ran down Cecilia's cheek.

With another bright smile, Cecilia opened the lids. She watched with delight as the colorful butterflies took flight, dancing and fluttering around her face.

A Note from the Author

Did you enjoy this book?

Thank you for purchasing and reading my book! If you enjoyed it, I'd really appreciate it if you would leave a review on Amazon. I love getting feedback from my readers, and Amazon reviews really do make a difference. I'd love to hear your thoughts. Thanks again.

Also, please check out my website at www.daleripley.com for more information and news.

Sincerely,
Dale Ripley

Acknowledgments

The Springthorpe Agenda has been in the making for about twenty years now. Over the years, I had dozens of ideas and plotlines and visions. At various points along the way, I wondered whether a novel would ever become a reality for me. Finally, it's here and I get to thank those who inspired me, helped me, and believed in me.

Thanks to Stephen King, Dan Brown, and David Benioff for inspiring me with your great works of fiction. I can only hope to be a small fraction as good at storytelling as the three of you are.

Thanks to author Holly Tierney-Bedord for being an inspiration and fueling my fire. Whether you knew it or not, you amazed and impressed me and helped me realize it could be done.

Thanks to Kathy for always believing in me. I just wish I would have finished this project before I lost you. I hope they have books in Heaven and you check this one out.

Most of all, tremendous gratitude and thanks to my wife, Katie. This was not possible without you. You believed in me when I didn't believe in myself. You helped me through the tough parts and kept the dream alive. You allowed me to be frustrated when I needed to be, and you cheered me on when I achieved all the small victories along the way. Thanks for being a tough, insightful, and phenomenal editor. You made this novel so much better than I ever could have alone. You are always my Princess.

Discussion Questions

SPOILER ALERT – To protect your reading enjoyment, **DO NOT** read these discussion questions until after you've finished the novel.

1. How did the story make you feel as you read it? Could you empathize with Mark and Sarah?

2. While reading, could you picture the book as a movie? Which actors and actresses should play the various roles?

3. An underlying theme in *The Springthorpe Agenda* is the undying love between Ralph and Joan. Have you ever known an older couple who portray such fondness and tenderness toward one another?

4. Ralph loved Joan from the moment he saw her. Do you believe in love at first sight?

5. Why do you think Liv had been so uncaring? Was she depressed? Do you know anyone like Liv?

6. Liv vowed to change after her experiences in the Springthorpe Manor. Can a traumatic event change a person's values and behaviors?

7. Why do you think the author incorporated butterflies throughout the novel?

8. Lake Jarvis plays a significant role in the story. Do you have a retreat, sanctuary, or favorite place to which you frequently return?

9. If you switch the first letters of Heath Dole's name, you get "death hole." Did you catch that trick with the antagonist's name when you read the phrase in chapter 45? Do you think the author used that name on purpose?

10. In chapter 64, Heath claims, "In ten years, when we're discussing a viable cure for brain diseases of all sorts, no one will be concerned with what we've had to do to get there." Does the end ever justify the means?

11. In chapter 71, when Claire is trapped, did you find yourself hopeful that she'd somehow escape or glad that she was trapped and might die there?

12. As you began reading chapter 75, as the pastor read from his large black book, "Six months ago, Joan and Ralph received a second chance…" did you think they were renewing their vows after their 50th wedding anniversary? Did you feel let down when you learned the event was their funeral, or did you feel it was their time to pass (the circle of life)?

13. Do you think the author left the ending open for a sequel?

14. If you could give the novel a new title, what would you name it?

15. If you could talk with the author, what would you want to know?

89709722R00214

Made in the USA
San Bernardino, CA
29 September 2018